Love is Mortal

A Valerie Dearborn Novel

Caroline Hanson

ACKNOWLEDGMENTS

As usual, it takes a lot of people to help me complete a book. Not just my family who have to put up with my charming personality (it's even worse when I'm writing) but my friends too.

To Carrie-- it really is a big deal. Congratulations! And I always have to thank Melissa, who is still gullible enough to believe that we will one day have a set workout schedule. Lauren Stewart-- you know what you did and I guess I have to thank you for it. And finally, to Yajaira Diaz and Mandy Norrell for their general awesomeness.

PROLOGUE

London, 1530

The air stank. The smell of unwashed flesh and burning candles. The smell of perfume and worn clothing. Marion loved a good party, but usually she just came for the food. She ran her finger down the Fey queen's arm and watched as goose bumps rose on the woman's flesh.

Pretty.

Marion loved women, but was anything more delicious than a woman dressed for a party? Maybe it was the dancing—that it made them blush and pushed all that warm blood close to the surface of their skin. Maybe it was the sweat—the slight sheen and taste of salt, the way her lips felt as they slid over flesh damp from a night of dancing.

Or maybe it was just because they were usually so happy that it made them beautiful to drink from. They were human presents she got to unwrap. She licked her lips and saw her lover track the movement. Annika's breath hitched, breasts straining against her low-necked dress. Marion was sure she could see a hint of nipple.

The fashion *did* seem to include showing a rather large amount of breast, but the Feyqueen was particularly daring.

Heaven forbid she leave something to the imagination. Perhaps it was because she was a fertility goddess at heart. She smiled. It could be downright difficult to get that woman to keep her clothes on. Marion felt very lucky that her goal of retrieving the Sard, a mythical object of Fey power, allowed her to mix work with pleasure.

"Annika," Marion murmured and stepped closer, wanting to take a bite out of her right there. She was about to do it, but then she saw *him*.

Lucas. His arctic blue eyes fastened on her. His arms were crossed, and he looked irritated. *As always*. He was watching her, waiting for Marion to do what she was supposed to do. *I hate doing what I'm supposed to do*. Marion sighed. "Business. It's always business."

Annika blinked up at her, her long, light brown lashes reminding Marion of a doe. "Did you get the book? And I very much hope the answer is yes," Marion said.

Annika swallowed nervously, and Marion tried not to frown. *Damn the woman.*

"No, Cerdewellyn is watching me. He is suspicious."

This was not good news. "What did you tell him?"

"Nothing. He does not know a thing," she said sincerely.

Lucas was leaning against the wall, the fingers of one hand drumming against his lips, a sign of his impatience. She hated the drumming. The man needed sex or an empath. He'd been dry for a while now. 10 years? Maybe 20? It made him an unpleasant bastard.

Annika touched her arm, hand slightly damp from nerves. Or fear. Both were a turn-on. "I would need a promise, Marion."

"My heart," Marion said, knowing she was the picture of desire and concern. "I will promise you *anything* in the world. You know that."

Annika frowned. "No, from Lucas. I need a promise from him that he will let me live, and stay with you if I steal the book from Cer."

Marion shrugged. "You are at a vampire ball, and you are safe. And of course that will last as long as we are together." The Fey were such sticklers when it came to promises.

"Cerdewelleyn...he knows the vampires seek the book. He does not trust me and I...Oh Marion," she swallowed hard, clearly overcome with emotion. She was whining.

Marion could not stop herself from pouting. She *did* stop herself from screaming. "The book, my heart. Lucas will not save you without the book." Her voice was rising, and she took a calming breath, planted a smile on her narrow lips. "How difficult can it be? The Book of Life and Death must be close to him, yes? Lucas is not—" Marion floundered for the right description of Lucas that wasn't a lie, finally settling on, "totally unreasonable. We can travel, see the world. You will be safe for all time...*After* you get the book."

Annika began to shake her head back and forth, almost a little frantically. "What does it matter? The Sard is gone! It has been missing for centuries."

The woman was an idiot. Of course the Sard was not missing. Why would she want the book if it was missing? It was a wonder the Fey were not all imbeciles if this was the woman they were bred from. Or had bred from. It had been a while since a Fey entered the world. Hadn't it? Marion wondered if she should take an interest in her lover's life. Annika might like that. Marion vowed that the next time she saw Annika, she would ask her about her day.

She put her hand on the queen's waist. "The book can do other things. Spells and things…it is not solely for the Sard." But Annika was right of course. The Sard was a jewel of pure, untapped power and could only be used in combination with the book. Marion had the jewel, but it had taken centuries to get this close to Annika, the one person close enough to Cerdewellyn to have access to the book he kept so well-hidden in the land of Fey. Marion knew a battle was coming. The Fey were weak, almost gone; their only chance of survival was to find the Sard and unleash its power, restoring Cerdewellyn to greatness.

Annika laughed unhappily, her voice high. Tears filled her eyes. "Spells! You want the book for spells? How can you perform a spell if you can not find a *witch*? Do you know how we live now? How bad things are? Lucas will not come to a truce with Cer. He will not stop until we are all dead! Cer wants to—" she stopped herself.

From across the room Marion saw Lucas incline his head. Was he listening? Was his hearing that good? She wished he would go away. If Annika saw him, she would get all upset. There would be a lot less sex and a lot more crying.

"Cer wants to do what?" Marion asked quietly.

Annika shook her head, lips clamped shut.

Oh, please. As if the woman could keep a secret. "It is too late now, my heart. Cer is the walking dead. He simply needs to lie down," Marion cooed, "Your loyalty must be with me if you want to survive. Get the book, and you will be protected. Lucas will guarantee it."

Annika said quietly, "But Lucas wants to kill us all."

Marion was beyond exasperated. "So? I want puppies for breakfast, but that does not mean it is going to happen! Do you know how hard it is to get puppies in winter? Anyway, he will leave you alone *if* you play your part. Go back to Cerdewellyn. Reconcile with him. Use those sweet wiles of yours, and get him to trust you again. Then get the book and come back to me."

After a painful moment where Annika seemed to think about her options, she nodded.

Marion hoped the night was salvageable. She would not sit around listening to the woman complain about how everyone she knew and had ever loved was dead. If Annika was not going to play, then she needed to go home and get started on finding the book. They had all lost people. Everyone in the world would change their grief if they could. They could not.

But I will. If Marion could get the book, she would be able to end her own grief. She would have enough power to get back what she had lost…

Marion looked back towards Lucas, but he was not paying any attention to her. He was turned, candlelight flickering off his black silk jacket. His hands were behind his back, and he looked very casual—if one ignored the fact that his fists were clenched, and his expression was too blank. As if he were working very hard to give nothing away. He set his feet, as though he wanted to back up but was determined not to.

She felt the change in the air, as if it were charged before a storm, Fey power slithering through the room.

Cerdewellyn.

Marion felt a tug at her dress, like a small hand grabbing at her waist. Her body froze. *Do not look down. Do not.* Another gentle pull at her waist…just like her Margaret used to do. Heart pounding, mouth suddenly dry, she looked down, hoping to see Margaret one last time. It was an illusion; of course she knew that it was an illusion. But that was what made the Fey so powerful. They knew one's darkest heart, one's most secret desires, and even though it wasn't reality, one would sacrifice all just for the chance to believe. It made one's mind a traitor, a willing accomplice to living a lie and inviting death.

Marion knew there was no child at her side, no little girl with beautiful big eyes looking up at her with adoration. But dear God she wanted it.

Then Marion heard a giggle behind her. So familiar, devastating, and beloved that Marion cried out, her hand flying to her mouth as she turned, desperately searching. It did not matter if it were real or a trick, so long as she could see her again.

There! Marion dashed forward, following a small flash of red. Little Margaret in her red dress. Tears filled her eyes as she remembered that day. The red dress Margaret had been buried in. Costly silk and a beautiful bow at the back, little pearls dangling from the bow's ends.

"Margaret!" she yelled and did not know which way to turn, how to find the only person that had ever mattered to her. Couples danced all around her, blocking her view like a giant storm toying with a tiny ship. Margaret bobbed into view again, past a brunette in a pink dress. Margaret peeked at Marion over her shoulder and vanished behind two women drinking champagne.

Marion stumbled after her, lost to everything and everyone around her as she pursued Margaret around the giant ballroom. She was always one step behind, could never get close enough to see her. Cerdewellyn could kill her right now, come up to her and cut off her head, and she would not even notice, so consumed and obsessed with her little girl, lost to the past and her own grief. The past brought back to life. If only she could hold her one more time.

Annika touched Marion on the forehead, and the glamour dissipated, a dream shredded before her eyes. "It is not real, my beauty. None of it. It is all Cerdewellyn. Come back to me. Pay attention, Marion."

Marion blinked at Annika, feeling confused and alone. "Margaret," she said in a whisper, throat scratchy as if she had screamed for hours.

"It is only glamour," Annika smiled sweetly, as if she were the mother and Marion a child who had woken from a nightmare.

Her heart still pounded, tears threatened. "No. It is more. It must be. I felt her...I heard her. She is here. She—" Her words cut off as she looked behind Annika and around the room. Every vampire and human alike were frozen and still, eyes wide open and staring at nothing. "No," she whispered, and fear choked her. "All of them? Cerdewellyn couldn't have captured all of them."

It was impossible. To control a room of hundreds. Others and humans alike, leaving them vulnerable to destruction. "How? Cerdewellyn has never been so powerful." She looked over the heads of the still people and saw Cerdewellyn, his tall, dark form and black hair moving through the crowd of statues. He touched the vampires as he passed, and with that touch, they turned pale, skin fading chalk-white, patches of ash appearing on their skin as if they had not fed in months. She could see their vitality being leeched from them. As if with each touch, he drank their essence, consumed their strength.

Annika smiled at Marion condescendingly. "Everything came from the Fey, Marion. Vampires, witches, the wolves, even the cursed empath. It is all born from Fey magic. We have no choice now. This is the Fey's last gamble. Cerdewellyn will take his power back, from one and all, reabsorbing everything to bring us back to what we were."

"No." She could not take her eyes off Cerdewellyn, saw him moving closer and closer to Lucas, who was still, unmoving and unblinking, caught in Cerdewellyn's trap. Lucas blinked slowly. Then his chin jerked as though he did not like what he saw.

Out of the corner of her eye, she saw a puff of gray ash as one of the vampires crumbled, all the energy sucked from him until he was utterly destroyed. "He has never had that much power," Marion said. She felt dumb, rooted to the spot in confusion.

Annika looked at her sadly. "No, Marion. He did. It has just been a very long time, and it comes at great cost."

Cerdewellyn closed the distance between himself and Lucas.

"He thinks he can walk up to my king and kill him with a touch?" She took a step forward, propelled into action in order to save Lucas, but Annika restrained her, fingers biting deep. For a moment, she was surprised. Annika was so gentle; let herself be pushed around so much that Marion had forgotten the woman was strong, a fierce Other in her own right.

"Stay by my side or I cannot protect you," Annika warned.

"I have to—"

She shook her head sadly. "Our home is gone, Marion. He destroyed it, pulled it up at the roots and consumed it for this. An attempt to make himself as strong as he once was."

The bitter truth was suddenly revealed, and Marion wanted to claw out Annika's eyes in retribution. "You brought him here! You betrayed me. Do you think he will take you back? Faithless. Wanton. The world knows Cerdewellyn would rid himself of you if he could."

Annika's pale cheeks turned red with fury, her lips mashed together, as though biting back words. "Just sit down. Do not help your king. Stay out of the way, and then we will be together. Yes, I care for myself. But, I care for you too. I am a survivor first. If you want to survive the night, you will not help your king."

The faithless creature. She was a coward. A traitor to one and all. Marion didn't know what to do. "It seems more likely that Lucas will slay Cerdewellyn." Annika rolled her eyes. "These men. Let them slaughter each other."

More vampires disintegrated, Cerdewellyn leaving a trail of ash in his wake, as he closed the distance between himself and Lucas. Fifteen feet, then 10 and Lucas didn't do so much as flinch let alone defend himself. Cerdewellyn stopped before Lucas, extending one hand slowly, settling it on his shoulder. Smoke rose from him, his skin turned pale, and suddenly Lucas stumbled backward, breaking free from Cer's hold.

There was a glint of silver, the flash of a knife, and an unholy snarl of rage as Lucas threw himself forward, attacking Cerdewellyn in an uncoordinated way. As though he were wading through something sticky and heavy as he tried to get to Cer.

Cer stayed out of reach, appearing calm and composed, as though Lucas in a rage was nothing to worry about. His tone was soft, at odds to the murderous tension between the two of them. "I always wondered what nightmare gripped you. I'm surprised, Lucas."

"Are we going to talk now, Cerdewellyn? You don't wish to have this be our final fight? You've come this far, surely you won't leave now."

"I've come for Annika."

Lucas was breathing harshly, body trembling as though he were weak. "Woman trouble. I sympathize. Why don't you stay and let us finish this as gentlemen? There will come a time, Cerdewellyn, where you will be on your knees before me, and everything that was ever yours shall be slaughtered around you." He smiled at Cerdewellyn, the smile cold and emotionless.

Pitiless.

Lucas clasped his hands behind his back, inclining his head as if they were giving a friendly greeting to each other, exchanging pleasantries. He smiled as he said, "And you will remember this moment as your greatest failure. You do not commit. You will not risk your people. You are so busy trying to protect what you have left, trying to retreat from my advances and save everyone around you that you do not attack."

"You seek the end of the world, Lucaius."

Lucas laughed. "No, I seek to win. I am willing to gamble everything to achieve my goals. My people know this and live in fear of me. Your people do not fear you. Even your queen has no fear of you. You are not ruthless, Cerdewellyn and *that* is why I will win. Because I will find the moment, and I will take it, be damned to the innocents around me."

Marion shivered at the promise in his words.

Cerdewellyn and Annika vanished, chaos erupting around them as the humans and vampires awoke, coming back to themselves. Marion stumbled through the crowd to Lucas, not heeding the fury in his gaze. "It is done. Give up on the book, Marion. I want Cerdewellyn dead, and an end to this. I will wait no longer."

Terror pierced her through the heart at his words, and she grabbed his hand, vanishing with him, leaving the chaos of the ballroom behind, and reappearing in an English graveyard. Taking him with her had cost her, and she was panting.

"I saw her! She was there, and it was real, Lucas." Her voice broke. "You promised me you would not kill Cer before I have the book! I swear on her grave if you break this promise to me, I will—"

Lucas laughed, running his hand through his long, blond hair. "You know better than to believe a promise from me." He looked around them, kicking a nearby headstone absently. The anger seemed to leave him; shoulders relaxed, and he tugged on the cuffs of his shirt and adjusted his jacket. She could see him composing himself, letting the anger fall away from him, replacing it with icy boredom. On a sigh, he said, "I hate England. Never put your hand upon me again, Marion. A dead little girl cannot buy you forever."

CHAPTER

1

Valerie knew the water was consuming her. Cerdewellyn had pushed her from the cliff, and as she'd hit the water, every bone in her body broke. Every muscle tore open. Valerie had heard that people didn't die from falls. They didn't die from landing, or even from every bone shattering. No, what killed them was the *bounce*. The tiny bounce off the ground and back down again that pushed all the broken shards of bone out of place and deep into one's internal organs.

What a shitty way to die.

The water was cold and dark; it sucked at her and she sank deeper, the ocean floor rising up to meet her. *This is your fault, Valerie. You were the one who couldn't say no to Lucas.* Hadn't he told her what he was? Over and over again. A moth to a flame, and she'd always known that she was the moth, and he was the fire that would consume her.

But maybe that wasn't quite right.

Maybe that was the easy half-truth.

Lucas had been drawn to her too. Maybe *she* was the flame. He'd stoked the fire, but she was the one who burned. Let the blaze get out of control.

She opened her mouth to scream, and the water was thick as it spilled into her mouth. Absorbed into her pores. If she just stopped fighting, this would all go away. No more pain, no more unhappiness.

No.

She heard *his* voice. Not God, who never seemed to speak to her—but Lucas.

Her lover.

Her betrayer.

Was it his voice deep inside of her that was telling her to fight? She had given him her body, her heart, her blood. And what was more generous than that? It wasn't like borrowing a car or a twenty—it was blood. She needed that! And she'd given it to him.

The water was frigid, and the pain in her body was indescribable. She was a sack of meat, her body a weeping and broken pustule of flesh. This was fatal. This small moment in time before she died for good, and she was *still* thinking about that as shole.

Lucas.

Fuck him. He didn't deserve her thoughts. Didn't deserve to be the last thing she thought of before she died. Her lungs burned, her body thrashed, and even though she knew it was certain death—her mouth opened, desperate for air. Water poured inside her mouth, but it wasn't just water. It felt like...*magic*. This was the magic of Fey stealing inside of her, and replacing the air in her lungs with its power. She would take it into her like oxygen, and it would filter through her, be carried along her bloodstream until she was something else. Cerdewellyn had told her he would make her his queen—one way or another—but she could breathe, and it would be easy for she could say no, and it would be painful. This was fucking painful.

Do not give in.

Behind her eyes, like a fading mirage, she could see Lucas. Saw his eyes snap open wherever he was. He spoke her name in a whisper, and demanded again that she not give in. How did she fight this? Fight dying, drowning, and being taken over by magic.

Valerie felt Lucas give her his strength. His own power coursing into her through the connection they had. His power was dark, had a hint of death, and if it had a color it wouldn't have been black—but red. A red so dark, it looked like murder. A color so deep, it swallowed everything around it. And yet he was offering it to her. Something she could take to make her strong.

But she didn't want to take anything from him. As if Lucas were there with her, she felt him after her—close. His lips pressed against hers in a phantom echo of reality. She wanted his breath in her lungs, his hands on her, holding her close and keeping death at bay. Valerie was too weak to fight Cerdewellyn's magic on her own. If she didn't have Lucas's help, she'd give in. She couldn't fight everything. Fight Cer, fight dying, fight the pain, fight to say no, and fight Lucas too. Something was going to fail.

She had to say 'yes' to something...to someone.

I'm sorry, she heard Lucas say in her mind, as if he were trying to persuade her to let him help her. She felt his hands on her face, the large palms, his cool flesh as he pulled her closer to his soft lips.

No.

No apology would be enough. Pain ripped through her as she thought of Lucas. It was both physical and mental. She could never forgive him. She never wanted to see him again.

Is Cerdewellyn a better option?

Valerie didn't know if that were her thought or his. She was light-headed, the importance of struggling and the reason for fighting was slipping away from her. Fighting was hard, hating worse.

Please. Do not let me be the death of you.

As if it were a dare, or something scary—she agreed. Making the decision and acting before she could have a chance to think it through. She reached for the phantom ghost of Lucas, kissed him, forced her way inside of him, taking him by surprise. There was a moment of struggle where he wasn't kissing her back, wasn't giving her what she needed to survive.

She crystalized her intention, focused her will. Suddenly, he gave way, let her wash over him, drink him down and take his strength, plunder his mouth and his body as she pulled the darkness from him. His energy and his soul, everything he might give to her—she took.

More.

Valerie felt his power surge through her veins and begin to fix her. Her bones knit back together as she drifted.

Floating.

Waiting.

Resisting Cerdewellyn's magic. She'd be damned if she'd be his queen.

CHAPTER

Rachel awoke to Cerdewellyn throwing her shirt in her face. She sputtered and sat up. He stood before her, hands on his hips, his expression cold. His black hair was disheveled, his clothes a mess, his black jacket torn at the pocket, his breeches covered with mud. A streak of dirt was on his cheek, and it was so unsuited to his uptight and stuffy perfection, that it would have been funny under different circumstances. She had no idea what those circumstances might be, but considering he'd just woken her up from a marathon night of sex, blood, and more sex with Jack; this wasn't it.

"Come along then," Cerdewellyn said, and left the room, the sound of his shoes echoing faintly as he walked off without her. Expecting Rachel to follow him. And be quick about it, apparently. "Shit," she muttered and pulled the shirt over her head. She dragged on her jeans and shoved her feet in her shoes as fast as she could.

"Jack!" she said, through gritted teeth. No response. "Jack! Wake up, damn you!" Still no response. How long would he be out? Rachel left him there and stumbled after Cerdewellyn, trying to get her thoughts in order. He'd expected her to follow him, wasn't waiting for her to show up or slowing down in any way to accommodate her.

The pure arrogance of him wasn't that surprising. He'd always been a king. Even if he had no subjects, he still expected people to fall in line and do his bidding. He started speaking, not even turning to make eye contact.

"I have Lucas. He is gone, do you understand? *Mine.* And if I have it my way, he will be dead soon. If you try to rescue him— your wolf dies. You were Lucas' creature. Now you are mine. I do not hold your vampirism against you. Not in such desperate times."

"You mean cause I'm the only witch around?" she said, sarcasm dripping from her tone.

"Indeed," he said seriously. His creature, huh? Lucas wouldn't think Cerdewellyn was getting much of a bargain. She had been the worst, most treasonous creature he had. One of the many things she didn't have time to dwell upon.

"Is Lucas…hurt?"

"Not really." He sighed in exasperation. "The empath fed him; he is insensible, and locked away securely."

Rachel frowned. "Like in a dungeon?" Lucas was going to be fucking pissed.

"Do not concern yourself with him. Your energy must go to pleasing me." He entered the dining room, and all the torches flared to life, a lick of power making her shiver. The flames hissed, illuminating every spider web, all the dust, as well as the decaying tapestries.

And then there were the bodies sitting at the dining room table. Desiccated and still. Their hair faded and thin. It was the sort of tableau Marion might find amusing. Drag up a whole bunch of bodies for a tea party. Rachel's attention kept coming back to one woman in particular. Her hair was long, stringy and white, matted with cobwebs, her eye sockets huge, skin ill-fitting like a rotting apple. Her hand was open, a goblet no more than half an inch away from her outstretched hand. Had she just taken a drink or set it down? She wore white as though it had been her wedding day.

Creepy ass shit.

Cerdewellyn gestured towards them with an open hand. "These were my people. They betrayed me, and this is the price. They could not survive without me. I am the Fey King. All magic comes from me. The witches, the wolves, the vampires, even the empaths. All of it came from me."

"Then why did they betray you if they needed you?" Rachel asked, wondering just what he wanted her to do and hoping to delay it.

Cerdewellyn stopped near a chair, his hands resting on the back, a contrast of his healthy olive skin to the mummy before him. "I suspect they did not believe it. Most of them had heard of my power, but never experienced it. Not when it was terrifying. But it makes no difference why they did it. They were all my children. I blame Annika. And I blame myself for being blind."

He gestured to the middle of the table where a bundle of wet rags lay before her. Rachel stepped closer to see what the hell it was. Curtains fished out of the deep? Did he think she knew a good dry cleaning spell? It was covered with moss, stringy and dark. Oh fuck. It was a body, a woman, and clearly, she'd been dead for a long time.

"You are a witch. You are to put her soul back into her body."

"She's...dead." Now that she knew what she was looking at, it was obvious that the thing before her was a woman. The rags were actually a dress; the moss was really her hair. The strange lumps were her shoulders and knees.

Cer ignored her statement of the obvious. "I can do nothing with the remains as they are. Her spirit is here. She is Fey. You will combine your power with mine, and we will draw her spirit forward, so it may re-anchor to her flesh," he said.

What the hell? "Why? She's gone. Even if this chick's soul was lurking around, sticking it back into a dead body is...morbid. Torturous even depending upon what you believe. Sticking her soul back in her body will not bring her back to life."

He looked up from the body slowly and met her eyes for an instant. "I need Virginia's spirit to be anchored to her own flesh. Come," he commanded and extended a hand, broad palm turned upwards. She didn't want to touch him. Although Rachel had never met a live Fey before this shitty trip, she'd heard stories, and was smart enough to know that touching one was probably a bad idea. Sensing her hesitation, he said, "I will take your wolf, and I will make him mine if you do not do it."

Of course he would. "Blood. I cannot do anything without blood," Rachel said.

"I have that too." He shoved the table hard with one hand; the table so heavy it would have been immovable for a human, and yet he shoved it away with ease. Lying at the feet of one of the dried-out Fey women was a were wolf. Bloody, harmed and near death, the animal made no move to run away.

"He comes back here. To his love. He is hurt and near death, and he comes to her. That is the power of devotion and love," Cer said, voice hollow. "He should have come to *me*. To his king and maker."

The wolf looked at her with human eyes. His muzzle was coated with blood, his breathing labored. Blindly, she reached out and Cer clasped her hand. "I will say it first, and you repeat it. Here is the blade. Finish him when you need to." He held a knife out to her, and she took it, the hilt warm from his hand. "He does not deserve to die by your gentle touch."

The Wolf whined, its tail thumping on the floor anxiously. "I would not save you, even if I could," he said to the wolf.

Here it was. Another death for her magic. If she didn't do it, he would take Jack. He could. He was Cerdewellyn. Even diminished, he could shred her bond with Jack and make Jack his pet. What choice was there? This was what happened when one was vulnerable. When one had a weakness. It was exploited. *I know better.*

Cer began to speak. She took a deep breath and tried to center herself. Tried to follow what he was saying. She repeated the words, her voice stronger than she expected. She felt the power build up inside of her. And then Cerdewellyn's power lit along her nerves, combining with her own. His power was warm; if it had a texture, it would have been like soft moss, verdant and soothing.

She felt the dark, cold stickiness of her own black magic, the way they mixed together, becoming something new and greater. Cer released her hand, but their connection held. He drew the rags and body towards the edge of the table, then lifted it and set them gently down on the ground. The wolf watched them, still wheezing, occasionally whining. But it didn't try to run.

She drew the blade across her forearm. Her blood welled and dripped down onto the bundle of bones. Cer dragged the wolf to his feet by the scruff of its neck. Power built within her, cresting close, ready to detonate.

The light flickered. As though all the oxygen in the room had been consumed.

She had the bizarre urge to apologize to the wolf, which was disturbing and ridiculous. Why would she apologize? She'd never done so before. All the deaths. All the murders. No reason to start now. She shut down the sympathetic pang, felt her lips pull back in a smear, and without flinching, she stabbed downwards. Through the rib cage and into the animal's heart in one clean stroke. Only it wasn't just an animal, but a person too.

Damn it.

Cerdewellyn scooped up the bundle of rags and bones, carrying it in his arms easily. He led them out of the castle, Rachel trailing along behind him. She supposed the other option was to turn and run away, but...it wasn't a real option, was it? If she turned and ran she lost Jack. Her feet crunched on the gravel. She was finally here, at a crossroads. Metaphorically, of course. She had stuck with Marion for decades, followed along, not caused a lot of problems. And look at her now.

Bound to Jack. So that she had an obvious weakness. One that would haunt her and make her vulnerable. But she couldn't leave him. So she had to own it. Jack was her responsibility. Even when it was that time of the month, and he was howling at the moon, he was still going to be her problem.

The feeling of vulnerability was odd and unsettling. As if she might come under attack at any moment. Cerdewellyn led them to a rocky beach. He set the bundle down on the ground and waded into the water. Waves surrounded his feet, his ankles and then his knees and thighs as he walked into the water. She squinted, wondering what he was doing. And then she saw another body.

Valerie's.

Dead and floating, face down, her hair fanning out around her in a morbidly pretty way. Like Ophelia, perhaps. She was dressed and peaceful;she even had her sneakers on. The scene was so horribly wrong, so off on a fundamental level that Rachel had to steel herself to stay still, not to go forward and grab her, flip her over and try to save her, even though it was obviously too late. Valerie was dead.

Jack would be devastated.

Cer reached Valerie's body and pushed it away from him, back towards the breaking waves and away from shore. Her body floated out towards the deep, never sinking under the water, but staying on top. Like the tide had reversed and was going to take her out to sea rather than spit her out on dry land.

Cer turned back, shaking water off his hands and pushing his dark hair off his face. He looked grim and harsh, his face pale and unhappy in the dim light. From several feet away he met her gaze, and she felt sick to her stomach. "She keeps coming back. She returns to the shore again and again. She is trying to save herself."

"I'm not sure your definition of saving herself would be the same as mine," Rachel said, looking at Valerie's corpse. Had her voice wobbled? *Nah.*

"She is not dead, but undergoing a transformation. She should be at the bottom of the ocean, weighted down with my magic, filled with it to the gills. She should wake and come to me. Instead, she is here." He carefully wiped his hands against each other, as though gathering his thoughts. "What was his connection to her?" Cer asked, crossing his arms. He was still in the water, waves breaking against his calves as he waited for her answer. His handsome features were hard, his black eyes absorbing all the light around them, perfect in this washed-out world.

"Who?" Rachel asked dumbly.

"Lucas. She is fighting, and I want to know how. Is it just her innate ability? How close is their bond?"

She shrugged. "I don't know. I wouldn't have said it was anything...special. He's had an interest in her for a long time, but I assumed that was because of what she is."

"But it is physical. There has been blood exchanged. They have that bond." Valerie was hard to see now, floating further and further away. The waves were pallbearers carrying her away.

She still had that god damned urge to grab hold of Valerie and haul her back to shore. "Valerie is drawn to him. She desired him. He slept with her. Nothing more than that. And the blood... that was my fault. He was lying to her, and she wanted to know the truth. I told her she could make him drink her blood. He was keeping his distance, so he couldn't have wanted her *that* much." Was that the right thing to say? She still had some loyalty to Lucas, especially if it didn't cost her anything.

Cer stalked towards her, large steps bringing him close. She had to look up, and the smile on his face was almost a sneer, his words a growl. "But he succumbed. Why? Because of his natural gluttony? Because she was there and he was hungry, or because he feels something for her?"

"Why can't it be all of that?" she asked. Her gaze slid back to the ocean. Valerie was gone. The ocean dark and lifeless. It was dusk now, and she thought there was a storm coming too. *She's alone out there in the cold*, Rachel thought, and then wanted to smack herself. Valerie was not her fucking problem.

"She is fighting, and I want to know if it is him. If he is helping her, somehow."

She felt herself frown. "You think Lucas would sacrifice himself to help her? That is not his style. Plus, I don't think she would accept his help, even if he offered it. Not now. After what he's done. He was a bit of a jerk."

Cerdewellyn exhaled hard and turned around, crossing his arms and staring out to sea. "Good. She is down again. Give me your hand, I want to reconstruct my Virginia's body."

"Yeah, that's a great idea," Rachel said flatly. Why the hell would he want to make the dead body look pretty? Did he have some kind of necrophilia fetish?

She took his hand in hers. Warm, dry and firm. He gripped her tight, and she felt his magic coming towards her, spilling upwards from the water, invisible but tingling, like prickling electricity. He led their joined hands to the bundle. She felt sweat break out on her forehead despite the cold. The rags were slimy, and Rachel really wanted to let go. He closed her hands on the bundle of rags.

Rachel thought she was holding a thigh bone, but wasn't sure. And dear God—the smell. Cer put a hand next to hers, and she realized he was bleeding. He'd cut himself for the magic. He bid her to cut herself too, and she hesitated, just needing to double-check that there were no other options.

Nope.

Rachel raised her wrist to her mouth, biting deep. Blood dripped on to Cer's hand, and he wiped it across the rags. The rags moved. Shifted. And she tried to pull her hands away. But Cer's grip was like iron. No escape.

He held her hand, squeezing her fingers tightly, his Fey strength grinding her bones together as she tried to pull away from him. The sky turned darker, not like night, but like the apocalypse. She could feel him pulling the energy from all around them as they chanted the spell: the air, the sky the ground, even the rocks, the power and life force that kept this world going was being stripped from the land, funneled through her to him and then out again into the corpse laid out before them.

The ground started to shake, an earthquake that started off as sound, the faintest vibration, growing into a low rumbling, then an all-out shudder and rupture, as if the very world was crying out for him to stop. Then the world stood still. If this realm had been a person, she'd say they died. All at once, Cerdewellyn released Rachel's hand.

The rags fell open, and the bones were revealed. Flesh crawled out of the chest cavity, covering her like pouring plastic into a mold. Then her auburn hair grew back, becoming lustrous and healthy. She looked perfect.

Perfect—but still dead.

She wouldn't have been surprised if the girl opened her eyes and spoke. She was so close to being alive. A body. A spirit and a body...but it still wasn't right. Some element to life was missing. Long ago, he would have been able to bring her back to life.

Cerdewellyn rose slowly, tears on his cheeks as he brushed a finger across the dead girl's alabaster face. He hoisted the body in his arms and stumbled towards the water. He was exhausted; she could see the magic had taken a toll. She watched him go into the water and instead of letting Virginia go, he just stood there holding her body as if she weighed nothing. As if he could hold her all day, and wanted nothing else but to be near her. He didn't say anything, and lord knew Rachel was anything but empathetic, and yet she could see by the way he stood and gripped her tightly that he didn't want to release her.

He straightened his shoulders and took another step into the water. He murmured something and let her go. Virginia sank instantly. After all, the dead didn't fight. Gray clouds rolled in from the east, darker than any storm she'd ever seen. "What is that?" she asked.

Cer shook his head slowly. "It is the end. The end of the world if I fail."

She had the oddest sense that she should console him. But Rachel didn't give in to soft emotions. If her heart urged her to do something, it was undoubtedly wrong. She made her voice hard. "You throw away your magic on a corpse."

"No. It is my final gamble." He seemed to gather himself, shoulders straightening as he stood.

The end of the world he said, and she knew he was right. She had felt the fortifications of this world collapsing. And feel a gaping hole out to the west. "The spell is gone; you're free," Rachel said.

Cerdewellyn said nothing. His chest expanded as he took a deep breath in, jaw clenched tight. He looked at the ocean for a long moment, and then he turned back to her, gaze bottomless, his soul dead. "The enchantment that kept us here...it was not self-sufficient. It required a certain amount of power and energy to maintain itself. It failed, yes?"

Her throat was scratchy. It was never good to deliver bad news. "It's broken. You're free."

He gave her a look, slightly sardonic despite his grief. "I can leave. My people...they could have left too," he laughed, harshly. "After all this time trapped here, they finally could have left. Except that they are all dead."

His attention drifted, locking onto the open wound in the sky that was where his world had shattered and was bleeding into... where? The human world? The ether? A magical graveyard? She didn't know.

Cerdewellyn didn't turn to look at her, but said, "I have never been much of a torturer. I have spent most of my existence creating and protecting life, but that does not mean I do not know the best way to harm. The Fey are superior to vampires in every way, not just because we are life, but because we nurture and make things grow."

Rachel thought that was a bit much. "You make your kind sound like saints. How many people disappeared into your world? How many did you force to your will?"

"Force to my will?" he said, as if she were speaking another language. "The Others are mine. Parasites to my power. The humans are meant to be ruled. It is in their nature to submit. My father walked into the mortal world, and all bowed before him. They will do the same for me. We are gods. And we need to be worshipped. One cannot rule with kindness."Now he looked at her. "I need a witch. I have no need of a wolf. He is disposable. You are not. Do you understand?"

"Yes," she said, mouth dry and heart thudding with fear.

"Where is the Sard?" he asked, voice calm and reasonable like all the best interrogators used. The tone of voice that said 'tell me what I want to know and I can make all of this better.'

"What *is* the Sard? I don't know anything about that," Rachel said, voice laced with confusion.

"It is Fey magic. All the power my people once had, lies within the gem. I am the one who can harness it. It has been missing for centuries. You find it for me, and your wolf lives. You have four days. If you do not find it in that time, I will kill your wolf."

"But I don't know where it is!" she cried.

"Then you had better find it," he said. Then he turned and walked away, heading towards the storm.

CHAPTER

An eternity later, Valerie saw a shaft of light appear above her.

The sort of light people see on the last bus out of Lifes ville.

She kicked towards it; her limbs uncoordinated. She broke the surface with a desperate gasp. A wave pushed her, propelling her into a rocky ledge. She reached up and clung tightly, scraping her legs as she pulled herself out of the water, flopping onto hard stone.

It wasn't land, nothing more than a rocky outcrop in the middle of the sea, but there also weren't any monster-eels, plus she could breathe. It was like paradise in comparison. Valerie coughed, blood pouring out of her mouth. Her chest spasmed, muscles convulsing as she tried to breathe. She felt like metal wires were spearing through her veins, wrapping around her ribs and twisting tight. And then the pain began to ease. Enough that other pains became noticeable. Her hands were bloody and raw, her arms and legs covered with bruises she could barely see in the faint light.

Her wounds healed as she watched, the pain in her chest disappeared, and she wondered how it was possible to be healing so quickly. Had Cerdewellyn done something to her? She'd imagined seeing Lucas, having him hold her, taking strength from him, but that wasn't real, right? Those were just her delusions before she'd almost died.

Probably.

The ocean was loud, waves breaking against the rocks as if they were reaching for her, wanting to drive her back into the deep and keep her there. Across the water, she could see Cerdewellyn's castle. Both the castle and the cliff Cerdewellyn had chucked her off looked miles away.

She wondered what was real. The cliff was painfully real. Wasn't it? Did someone really get thrown off a cliff and live? And if that wasn't real, where the hell was she? What about the big, black creatures from the deep, and Lucas with his blood and sympathy. That seemed unlikely.

"Welcome to the Land of Fey," a soft voice said, and Val yipped, scrabbling to her feet and whirling around to see who was talking to her. A young woman sat on a rock to the side of her, a few feet away from the ledge and the lapping waves. She smiled at Valerie shyly. Her hair was curly and fell to her waist. She wore a simple shift made of linen, and her feet were bare, toes tapping lightly against the rock she sat upon.

Valerie coughed again, and the girl slipped off the rock, coming closer. A goblet appeared in the girl's hand, and she held it out for Valerie, her face a picture of concern. Valerie was inclined to take it. Except she couldn't. What if this were just another trick? A mirage Cerdewellyn created in order to get her to accept his magic by eating or drinking something? Val cleared her throat. "Thanks. But no." She coughed again.

"Welcome to the Land of Fey," she said again. As if she were giving Valerie another chance to get the social niceties right.

Val managed a weak smile as she tried to figure out what the hell was going on. Middle of the ocean, almost dead but miraculously healing, creepy girl who was undoubtedly from the past staring at her like she was a meal. *Bad, bad news.* She decided the best thing to do was stall.

"Thanks, but...uh...I'm not sure it's been a very good welcome."

The girl's head tilted to the side in question, and she looked genuinely upset. What, was she on the tourist board?

Val, always the victim of verbal diarrhea, explained, "Between the bad food, violent people, and massive amount of blood that has been spilled—mine, in particular—I can tell you, the Land of Fey has been less than welcoming."

The girl's smile faded, and she studied Valerie's jean-clad legs in a way that made Val double-check to make sure she was still dressed.

"As much as I would love to sit around and talk corsets with you, I can't. I gotta go. How do we get back to shore? Do you have a boat or a unicorn, even a magic carpet nearby?"

The young woman's expression deepened, verging on a pout. "What do you want with my Cerdewellyn?"

"Nothing. I'd be happy if I never saw him again." Val paused, chewing her lip while she tried to work out the dynamics here. "*Your* Cerdewellyn? What, is he your cradle-robbing boyfriend?" Val wished she could take the words back. She'd only been not choking for ten whole seconds, and she'd managed to say something offensive. *Nice.*

"Cerdewellyn is my destiny," the girl said, gaze drifting down to Valerie's tennis shoes.

"Hmm. I don't go in for destiny. Got enough problems with the unplanned. So where is Cerdewellyn? I'm ready to go home."

"I do not think you will be leaving," Virginia murmured, still looking at Valerie's shoes curiously. "No boat. No unicorn. No carpet to save you. Tell me what hold you have over my Cerdwellyn," she said in a flat, drawled tone. Her words made Valerie's stomach cramp. The chick was whacked, there was no other way to describe her.

Val shrugged. "Nothing. The last thing I want is to hold him. And he certainly doesn't want to hold me. Kill me, yes. He told me he'd let me go." She remembered his words, that he wanted a favor, would make her his queen and a full-blooded empath. Although he'd taken his favor by force. Kind of like the difference between a car-jacking and offering someone a ride. "I thought the Fey were bound by promises?" Val shuddered, "I want out of this *fucking* place," Valerie finished.

"Out what?" Her eyes snapped to Valerie.

"I want out of the Land of Fey," Val said, enunciating each word clearly.

"You are not the first, nor are you the last to desire such a thing." The girl stepped forward, closing the distance between her and Valerie to a few feet.

Val looked around, seeing nothing but rock and water. How the hell was she supposed to get out of here? "Look, you seem very nice, but I really have to go...shit, I guess I need to go back to the castle. So, if you could just show me—"

"What do you intend to do at my castle?" Anger laced her voice.

What was it with this chick? Val tried to explain, even though she knew it was useless. Her mind kept drifting to other things, still trying to work out what was real, what was fake, and what was dangerous. "I think my *friend* is engaging in the hookup from hell. Like worse than just getting an STD and I've got to..." *What? What are you going to do, Val? Throw them a condom? Throw water on them?* At what point was Jack responsible for his own actions? Maybe she shouldn't interfere. Leave them here and take care of herself.

You can't do that. Jack wouldn't leave you. The girl took a step closer, and Val backed up automatically. She didn't want the girl to get too close to her. She wasn't sure why, but the odds of this girl being a friend seemed low. Maybe that was just her luck lately. How come she couldn't have a nice supernatural life like the girls on Charmed or even Buffy? They all had friends. Even on Supernatural, the boys had each other. What did she have? Nothing, but one damned traitor after another.

"Cer made it seem like there was no one else here," Val said, still stalling. Should she jump back into the water and hope she survived?

The girl smiled, but it didn't reach her eyes. "My name is Virginia."

"Well, Virginia, I'm Valerie." She frowned. The name Virginia sounded familiar.

"I know who you are, Valerie Dearborn. I saw you come into our world. I saw you meet my Cerdewellyn. I saw you with the vampire."

Val just knew she meant Lucas. "Yeah, I have really bad taste in men. But I'm turning over a new leaf when I get out of here." She looked around again. Maybe the water really was the only way out of here. *Dammit.* Her gut told her she had to get out of here, even if it meant a swim that would have made an Alcatraz escapee shudder in fear.

"You brought our greatest enemy into our world."

Valerie swallowed hard. *Not much I can say about that.*

"You bring him here, and yet I cannot get to him. My Cerdewellyn has returned, and yet he does not know me, nor see me. I was slain centuries ago, and yet here I am. *Waiting.*" Virginia's throat worked as if she were swallowing tears. "He believes me gone. How can he not *feel* me here? You must help me return to him." Her hands were clutched to her chest as though it was the only way to keep from breaking apart.

Val's instinct was to say yes she would help Virginia, but—her instincts sucked. And there was something more than a little bit off about her. "I'm sorry, but no. I'm turning over a new leaf, and it doesn't involve helping people. I'm all helped out. I helped my ex, I helped Lucas, Rachel and Cer, and no offense, but the whole lot of them screwed me over big time. So I'm done. But I will *definitely* tell Cer that I've seen you. And if, by some miracle, I don't run into him, I will leave a note." Val nodded. "Big note in a super obvious place."

"You do not understand me, Valerie Dearborn. I have been here for longer than you can fathom. I made a mistake. I trusted when I should not have, and it led me here. It endangered the people that were to be mine, and led to centuries of ruin."

"When you put it like that, it doesn't sound good; you're right. And that's why I will tell Cerdewellyn to come and help you out." Valerie was still backing up slowly, as Virginia took a few steps closer.

"I was murdered," Virginia said, as Val's foot reached the edge of the rock. And oh crap, was that a wobble at the end of that statement? Valerie didn't want to see this chick cry. *Don't do it. Don't listen. You know you're a chump for a sob story.*

Walking away. Or swimming away. Either way, she was abandoning a person in need. This was her new leaf, right? She felt terrible. Like she'd turned the leaf over and found dog shit on the other side.

"Please!" The girl cried as Val shifted, ready to jump back into the water.

Lightning flashed in the sky, and thunder boomed, but she still heard Virginia's next words over the storm. "He is my love. I have known him, been *for* him, my entire life. My purpose was to be his, to save *our* people from the destruction Lucas caused. You do not know what Lucas is capable of."

"I know what Lucas is capable of," she said unhappily. *All too well.*

"If you know what he has done, how could you consort with him?" she said, looking horrified.

"Cause he's hot and a good liar," Val snapped, not wanting to get into a conversation with anyone about Lucas.

"What is the purpose of *your* existence, Valerie Dearborn?"

"Well…I wouldn't say I have a destiny or a purpose, per se. More of a general outline. You know, the normal stuff. Go to school, meet nice boy, get married, have kids, worry about my lack of pension."

Virginia looked confused. "Do you think it is fair that I had so much potential, so much to do, and a man who loved me, and yet that is gone?"

"Do I think it's *fair*?" Val repeated. "I know that answer. Life isn't fair. I'm sorry for what happened to you, but...I can't do anything about that." Virginia narrowed her eyes and lunged forward, grabbing for Valerie. Valerie screamed and jumped, hitting the water with a clumsy splash as she tried to escape.

CHAPTER

"Time to go, lover boy."

Somebody shook him. Jack's eyes flew open, heart suddenly pounding, locking onto Rachel, who was standing next to the bed and looking down at him. He shifted his legs, and discovered that he was naked. The events from last night were the faintest blur—almost dying, pain, and then Val's voice begging him for something...what had it been? He had a suspicion that something really, *really* bad had happened the night before.

There has got to be a good reason why I'm naked.

Rachel crouched down next to him, shoving the dream or memory away, replacing it with her, and only her.

"What happened?" he asked, voice just above a growl.

"I can safely say that last night was the biggest night of your life," she said flatly. And she didn't smile at him, which, for some reason, was vaguely terrifying. She was sincere. Rachel didn't do sincere.

"What was the biggest night of my life? And why am I naked?" he asked, peeking under the sheet just to make sure. Rachel rolled her eyes and stalked away from him, doing a circuit of the bedroom like an animal in the zoo; trapped and pissed.

Jack felt off...different from head to foot. And the smell. It was like his nose was on overdrive. It almost hurt to breathe, as if the air were freezing cold. The room smelled like old stone, stale air and sex.

Had they? No. He *wouldn't* have. Rachel's gaze skated over him and he felt it like a touch, as if it were her finger trailing down his neck and chest to where the sheet lay, covering the lower half of his body. She pouted when her gaze reached the sheet.

He took in her choppy dark hair, the pouty lips and stunning beauty. Her neck was dark, bruised, as if an animal had given her a hickey.

What the fuck happened last night? "We didn't..." he said, demanding confirmation.

"We did. In fact, I did—more than once." She threw him a glance over her shoulder, and he tried to ignore the effect it had on his libido. "You did too. I'm impressed. What you lacked in finesse, you made up for in enthusiasm." She smiled at him, and denials came to him, begged to be spoken. But he just couldn't say them.

They were in Cerdewellyn's creepy castle, and he was tucked up in a huge canopy bed, the sheets musty and rumpled. He scrubbed his face with his hands. He needed to shave. Shower. *Get the fuck out of here.* "Why are we here?"

Rachel cracked her knuckles, and he could feel how agitated she was. "Hmm. Okay. I will give you the recap, because I think you're going to be ornery otherwise. We stormed the castle, you got swiped by a werewolf and almost died. I saved you, you're welcome, and then you had to be bound to someone. Yada, yada,

yada, and you chose me. After that, it got physical. And now it's time to go."

Parts of that made sense. "Explain more," he said, and began looking for his clothes. He threw the sheet aside and picked up his boxer briefs, aware that Rachel was watching him dress. He scowled at her. "You can look away, you know."

She put her hands up in the air in disgust. "*Now* you tell me. If you're going to stride around tackle-out, then I'm gonna look. Besides I saw it last night....sawit, touched it, tasted it," she said, voice changing from suggestive to slutty in six little words.

He froze, jeans in hand. Thoughts and feelings swamped him. Jack pushed them aside, forced himself to keep moving. He was not going to be thinking with his dick.

"You don't want to talk about it?" she said, taunting him.

He sent her a malevolent glare, hoping it would unsettle her as much as she was trying to unsettle him. Actually, she wasn't trying. She'd succeeded. He was fucking unsettled. "I don't remember it, so what do you want me to say? It doesn't seem like something you should brag about, getting someone who was 'near-death' as you put it, to bone you. Congrats. Good work. I'm sure I had an *excellent* time. Now where the fuck is Valerie?"

He found his shirt and pulled it on.

She pursed her lips. "Do you see differently? Smell things slightly oddly? Your senses are enhanced because you're a werewolf now. You're stronger too. You could rip a human's head off without breaking a sweat. When the full moon comes, and you're looking for outfits to coordinate with your pelt, we can talk about the wolf thing." She laughed and it sounded bitter. "No rush. But the more important thing is that we need to leave. And *now*."

Jack finished lacing his shoes. So many questions, so many things she was telling him, and yet it wasn't quite right. "Where is Valerie?"

"Hmm. So, you're not going to make this easy, are you?" Rachel asked. She closed her eyes and took a deep breath. *"Get up. Follow me. It's time to go,"* she said, voice thick with command and power.

Jack stood. *What the fuck?* Suddenly, they were walking out the door, and Jack didn't remember putting one foot in front of the other. He tried to stop walking, but couldn't. All he could do was follow her as she walked down the hall.

"What did you do?" he growled, rage suffusing him as he followed her down the corridor. It wasn't a slow burn, but instant combustion. It scared him, thrilled him, and made him look up at the woman in front of him and want to do something terrible.

And Rachel ignored him. Unimpressed with his fury. She led him up a staircase, and they stopped before a door. A shining iridescent glow seeped out from underneath. She turned the handle and stepped inside. *"Take my hand and follow me,"* she said.

But it was a command. Something he couldn't stop himself from doing. Like falling asleep against one's will. He thought about freezing in place, about objecting, and still he was moving forward. She stepped into the blue light, and he did too, and then it was gone, and they were back in the Roanoke Forest.

"Thank God," Rachel said.

"No. You didn't...you didn't just take us out of there." He wanted to throw up, he wanted to kill someone, he just couldn't believe it. "We...we have to go back! What about Valerie? Christ, what about Lucas? You can't leave them there. I will kill you if you don't get us back there right now, do you understand?"

Rachel chuckled and came closer. He wanted to strangle her. Something inside of him snapped, and he surged towards her with an inhuman snarl, the reaction primal and...*perfect.* He slammed her up against a tree and had the satisfaction of seeing shock on her face that he'd managed to move on his own. No longer following her around, and doing what she bid like a little puppy dog.

"It's done. Fey is far behind us. If you want to go back and help Valerie, then you'll come with me and tone down the alpha bullshit." Her gaze locked on his lips.

"Where is Valerie?"he demanded and shook her hard.

Rachel jerked away from him. "You're a broken record, you know that? She's trapped with Cerdewellyn. Lucas is his prisoner."

With a snarl, he took her down to the ground, rolling her on to her stomach. He used his weight, his strength, and a new hidden reserve of power to keep her there. He could smell her, smell himself on her, and it pushed the anger back, made lust rise in its place so that he felt himself hardening as he rested on top of her. He shifted, cock settling between her cheeks as he ground into her.

She stilled and his hands moved, pinning her wrists above her head, his hands on top of hers, twining their fingers together. He put his lips next to her ear, took her flesh into his mouth and bit lightly. Fuck, he needed to say something to her. There were things he had to know, but all of it was fading. All of it was unimportant and forgettable as she lay beneath him. She said his name, and it made his cock pulse in his pants.

"I want to be inside you," he said, and his hand went to her waistband ready to rip them off her.

"Think, Jack. Shut it down. I can help you, but you have to be on board too. Valerie is stuck in Fey. I'm Rachel…you kind of hate me…and as impressive as that erection is, we have to go."

Her words were a slap, and he felt the peace coming from her, travelling down an invisible connection, like an umbilical cord between them. All he had to do was take it, accept what she was offering, and he'd be able to think. Some part of him conceded, rolled over and off her, back on the ground as he hauled in breath after breath. Fuck, even his breathing was angry, and he wasn't sure that was possible.

"Why am I like this?"

She pursed her lips and put her hands on her hips. "What's the last thing you remember?"

He frowned, tried to puzzle it out. Walking down the path, being in the cabin, the certainty that Valerie was lost to him forever, deciding he would kill Lucas. The fight, watching as Lucas was about to be torn to pieces and then…nothing. Haziness.

"Lucas. I was about to kill him."

She laughed, but it wasn't happy. "Great. Yeah, I hate to tell you, but stronger, less human men have tried and guess what? 1600 years and they didn't win. Shockingly, you didn't either. He gutted you, and you almost died. I saved you. You can thank me later. I take cash, visa or flowers."

He couldn't take his eyes off her, the way she moved, the way her breath went in and made her breasts swell. "Why do I want you like this?" he asked.

She snorted indelicately. "Who are you kidding? You have always wanted me."

"No. Not like this. Not like…" He needed to have her, needed to sink himself inside of her before he could worry about anything else. His voice was low, filled with need and pain, "Like I'll die if I don't get inside of you."

The need in his voice snuck through her, and she felt her body respond. His hands moved, one arm around her rib cage, his hand covering her breast tightly. Her nipples pebbled against his palm, and he growled in response. His other hand slipped around her hip and settled between her legs.

"Spread your legs for me. Let me in," he commanded her, and she felt light-headed with desire. She whimpered and shifted, his hard length pressing more firmly between her cheeks. His hips bucked against hers at the move. The length of his fingers rested against her core, and he rubbed at her hard and fast, his only goal to make them both come.

"This isn't good enough," he said darkly, and then his hands left her, and she heard him unbuckle his pants, take down his zipper, and as she turned to look back over her shoulder, he took his cock in hand and stroked it from root to tip. His eyes burned as he looked at her. "Pull your pants down or I'll rip them off you," he threatened.

She tried to turn over, and felt his hand on her lower back keeping her on her stomach. "Not this time," he said.

Her body spasmed in response, and she lifted her hips awkwardly, unbuttoning the snap of her jeans. His hand landed on her ass as she raised her hips, and then he was pulling her pants down, only to mid-thigh; her legs trapped in the material. And then he was on her, his hand back under her body and between her legs, spreading her open to take him while the weight of his chest kept her on the ground. He thrust inside of her sharply, his hips instantly taking up a furious rhythm. He circled her clit with his finger and worked her hard, her body gushing in response to the passionate attack.

Jack was wild, lost to his desire for her, and she came hard, her body milking his shaft. His body froze behind her as his orgasm swept over him, and she felt him coming deep inside her body. They lay there for a long minute, and Rachel could hear Jack's heart beating.

"We have to go," she said, voice trembling. That mating and loss of control had been a primal thing, and made Rachel feel disgustingly emotional. He never would have taken her like that if he hadn't been under the wolf's influence.

He was going to kill her. "What did you do?"

"I saved your ass. Valerie is in deep shit. You were going to die unless you had an anchor, someone to tie yourself to."

"And so what? Did you hurt her?"

She looked confused for a moment. "Who? Valerie? No. I'll have you know you chose me of your own accord. Good thing too, because I wouldn't have taken no for an answer." Her look was suddenly fierce. "And *then* she would have gotten hurt."

"I chose you?" His brow furrowed, and his lip hurt as he bit down on it hard, trying to think about what had happened the night before. "I love Valerie. Like a…well, it's not really definable—"

"Bullshit. You love her like a sister. You were undergoing a transition. Becoming *Other*. That is about power, passion and death. When the choice came, you didn't choose comfort and family. You chose revenge and death. You chose me," she said, fiercely, keeping eye contact, willing him to see the truth.

He drew in a ragged breath. Speaking in a gentle tone, she said, "You were infected by a werewolf bite. I had enough magic to bring you back, but it was too late. You're a wolf. Wolves are bound to someone. Always. They go nuts otherwise. Like Fido, but psycho. Maybe Old Yeller. Valerie wanted to bind you to her...but Jack, she's stuck there. With Cerdewellyn. You would have belonged to him. Or maybe Lucas would rescue her, and then Lucas would have had you through Valerie."

"So what you're saying is that you were the best of a terrible bunch of choices?"

"Yeah. I guess I am."

He needed to move, couldn't stay here any longer. He felt like his muscles were going to explode. "Let me the fuck go."

She arched her hips up, rubbing herself against his hard length. A promise. "You sound so dangerous when you talk to me like that. Are you going to hurt me, or fuck me again, Jack?"

He made a noise, and was happy it was mostly rage, and only a twinge of frustrated lust. "I am not your—"

"Bitch?" she interjected happily. "Cause that would be funny if you said bitch now that you're gonna be a dog."

He threw himself backward, commanding his body to move off her, to escape her and respond to his will. His pinky didn't even twitch.

Her tone was carefully neutral. "Listen, Jack. Here is the plan. You and I are going to—"

"I'm not going with you. I have to help Valerie."

"That's not an option," she said flatly, and then she reached behind her, and the next thing he knew she had a knife. She brought it to her wrist and then flashed him a coy look, as if they were teenagers, and she was about to take off her bra. She made the cut slowly, slicing lightly, but he knew the moment her skin parted and her dead blood hit the air because he could smell it. It made his mouth water, made his cock weep with need. If she hadn't been controlling him, he would have ravaged her...again.

Nothing.

He'd never wanted anything so much in his life. It scared the hell out of him.

"This isn't real," he said, as his mouth filled with saliva. He didn't know if he wanted to fuck her or drink her or both.

"It doesn't matter, Jack. Just drink and then we can go."

"What happens when I do?" Not 'when', but 'if' he told himself sternly.

"It'll put hair on your chest. All the kids are doing it."

"No," he said.

She stared into his eyes coldly, pitilessly. "Drink now, Jack. And then we go. You're fighting me is not good. I need to feed. You need to feed. Don't push me, or I can promise you we will both regret it. No more worrying about Valerie. Don't ask me to go back there and get her. Valerie is fine," she said, voice trembling.

He believed her. Was she making him believe her? Did she control him that much? There were dark circles under her eyes, and the wrist she held out to him trembled slightly. Was it hard for her to keep control of him? Or was it just her hunger? And then it didn't matter; her wrist was at his mouth, he was sucking her down greedily, and the only thing that mattered was her.

CHAPTER

5

The silver shackles were tight. No slack. Lucas pulled with all of his strength, but didn't feel the slightest give. His chest was tight with panic. Should he scream? *Do not scream you fool, that would be pathetic.* But the urge was there, even tighter than the bonds. Strangling him, chanting to him that death was not the worst thing that could happen to him.

Lucas had woken up in a dungeon, chained to a wall. Alone. He hoped that Valerie had escaped, left him here and disappeared back to a mortal life. Against all odds and all reason, he wished for that.

Helpless. He laughed and couldn't stop. It had been a *very* long time since he'd been at the mercy of another. He jerked against the metal and hated himself for doing it. He knew it was useless, so why did he keep struggling? *Because you are weak.* He exhaled shakily, aware that he was breathing fast, close to hyperventilating.

Emotion. It would kill him. He couldn't do this. Lucas heard the sound of footsteps as someone came down the stairs towards him. And who would show up to pay him a visit this time, he wondered, and forced himself to breathe evenly.

Lucas stood straight, his expression that of a mask, hiding the torrent of emotion that burned through him. Still bluffing. *The game is still playing. Nothing is over yet.*

"Your empath is stronger than she looks,"Cerdewellyn said as he rounded the corner. He tossed that scrap of information out to Lucas and waited for him to bite.

Do not respond.

Cer was watching him, wanting to know just how much Valerie's blood had altered him. How many weaknesses were now exposed. Cer was tall, almost the same height as Lucas, but leaner, perhaps more graceful. In almost every respect, they were opposites. Lucas was light, and Cerdewellyn was dark. Cerdewellyn had been regal, born to wealth and privilege. Whereas Lucas had been little better than an ignorant peasant, graduating to a ruthless upstart who was willing to kill to get to the top.

Cer crossed his arms and took a step closer. "I did not understand how she could fight so hard. I had broken her, you see. Every bone smashed in. She was almost dead. Weak. Vulnerable. But now she is not. It is amazing," he said. But it was clear that he wasn't amazed; he was furious.

Lucas felt his heart begin to pound in what had to be terror. He wanted to lick his lips, avert his gaze, do something. He looked past Cer's right shoulder instead, hoping the tiny gesture gave nothing away.

"She is still fighting. It might go on for hours. I feel a bit ridiculous that it took me so long to figure it out. You drank her. She drank you. You are giving her your strength, so she does not give in to me."

Cer wanted answers. But he was always so bad at getting them. The man just didn't know how to torture. That struck him as funny, and he couldn't help but laugh.

Cer smiled derisively and made a tsking noise. "You know the dangers of feeding her. And of feeding *from* her. Has nothing changed in all these years, Lucas? You still cannot resist an empath? How important is she to you right now? Will you die to protect her?"he asked quietly.

"Are you jealous?"Lucas asked. *Stop provoking the captor.* His fists clenched. Cer smiled.

"Over the centuries, there was one constant. The empath died, and you survived. But, this time will be different, do you know why?"

"I assume you are going to tell me, and the asking is rhetorical," Lucas said, voice raspy. It shamed him.

Cer sighed. "The bravado of you, Lucaius," he said, like a father disappointed in his son. "This time will be different because you are in my land, at my mercy, and stripped of all defenses."

"You will make me blush."

Cerdewellyn moved back a few steps. A chair magically appeared, and Cerdewellyn took a seat, stretching his legs out, crossing them at the ankles, as if they were friends in a drawing room sprawled out by the fire at the end of a long night of whoring and gaming. "No. I will make you *bleed.* I will rip you limb from limb. It is nothing less than you deserve." Death and promise in every word. Lucas wondered why Cerdewellyn waited. Why he didn't torture him or kill him?

"1540 was a very bad year," Cer said in a bored tone.

Lucas lifted his head, peered out under a halo of dirty-blond hair. "Believe me when I say that 1540 was a *very* long time ago. Time has left you behind, old man."

Cer nodded slowly, taking the comment at face value and ignoring the sarcasm. "It was, wasn't it?" He shook his head slowly, his gaze distant as though he were reliving a bad dream. "I had a sense of time passing while we were here…a knowledge that things were changing and that we were growing ever weaker…" Dozens of heartbeats passed, and then he leaned forward and said, "1540 was a very long time ago, but for me, it is as close as yesterday."It was as though he were confessing a dirty secret.

"You need to let Valerie go. I endorsed her, Cerdewellyn. A representative of my kind to yours."

Cer's black eyes glittered in the guttural light. "There are no representatives when there is no one to represent. There are no more rules, Lucas. And over the years, I have learned one lesson at last—honor has cost me everything. My people, my lands, my queen. Your empath made a deal for you." His expression conveyed how stupid he thought Valerie had been. "I do not think she would make the same deal again. Do you want to know what it is?"

"She cannot bargain for me. She is mortal, foolish and inconsequential," Lucas said, his tone conveying how unimportant Valerie was to him.

His smile was roguish. "You drank from her. I can see it, Lucaius. That it is so very hard for you to keep it together and not go wild. I think you feel for the girl. I hope so."

Lucas shook his head, saying nothing.

"You should be happy that I will make her mine. Be happy, because I will still be treating her better than you ever could. And you will get to see it. *That* was her price. I will not kill you for a period of time. And I will listen to *any* offers you have," he said snidely. "I promised her I would not kill you. But that doesn't mean someone else cannot." He walked to Lucas and inspected the cuffs binding Lucas's wrists absently. He suspected it was more to taunt him, than actual concern he might escape.

"My queen was young. Close to your Valerie's age. I kept her out of the politics and orgies, preserved her innocence. I sheltered her from everything, and it was a grave mistake. Annika had her killed rather than give up the throne."

"I saw Annika as we came in. Time has not been kind to her."

Cer's eyebrows raised in mock inquiry, "You speak of the desiccation? Indeed. We do not all grow old as gracefully as you. Virginia was to be my queen, but Annika would not sacrifice. She was so weak. My gravest flaw is idealism...and assuming that other people share it."

"I believe your gravest flaw is that you will not shut up," Lucas said, and strained forward, pulling with all his strength.

"Virginia was young, Lucas. Just as your Valerie is young." Cer stared into Lucas' eyes, as though he was looking for the truth. As though he was genuinely interested in what Lucas might say in response. "Do you think if they were wiser, more aware of the world, that they would want nothing to do with us? Wisdom is the great equalizer. Your Valerie will be wise." He took a step back from Lucas.

"What do you want, Cer? Do you want power? Do you want to come back to the world? I can give you that. The world has changed. It is a wondrous thing to behold. Things we could not have dreamed of. They have machines to take them into the heavens, and means of traversing the world in hours rather than months. The invention of the wheel has nothing on the advances of today."

"I do not need you, Lucas. I have Valerie, and she will restore us all. I will kill you and yours. I will take your Valerie, and I will make her mine. No more mistakes, Lucas. No more idealism. It is life or death from here on out," he said, and turned, walking back to the steps, ready to leave Lucas here in the dark for some unknown amount of time.

"Then why are you here?"

Cerdewellyn didn't stop walking, his voice carrying from the stairwell. "I have not had a good conversation in ages. But I will take what I can get."

CHAPTER

Valerie's pillow was lumpy. And it prickled her cheek a little. She opened her eyes, lifted her head and looked around. Cerdewellyn's castle. She knew because of the dust, the bed curtains that hung in shreds—and the man who sat in the corner of the room, one leg crossed over another, staring at her with dark eyes.

"Cerdewellyn," she said, and really wished she had some water.

"I am glad you awaken. I was worried about leaving you alone, yet time is marching onward. How do you feel?" he asked.

"Like shit. Thanks for asking. Like some *psycho* shoved me over a cliff, and I'm lucky to be alive."

He sighed as though bored. "You are fine. Better than fine. You are now a full empath."

"Voila? That's it? It's that easy?" Her arm burned, and she rubbed it, trying to make the pain go away. Out of all the places on her body that were in pain, the arm was somehow worse. She looked down at it, seeing nothing but a faint scratch. *The sign of a true wuss.*

"No. It is not easy to turn you into an empath. All I have given you is costly. And that is the problem. I can feel a change in the realm. I must see what that is."

He stood up, came towards her, lips pressed tightly together. "Stay here and get well. When I return we shall talk about the future."

"Wait. What...happened? I'm not Fey, right? And where is everyone else?"*Did I go to an island? How come I didn't wash up on shore?*

He shook his head. "You are not Fey. Not yet. As for your companions..." He sat on the edge of her bed, and she wanted to kick him off it. "Do not concern yourself with them. Lucas is alive as I promised you, and shall not harm you further. Stay. Rest. And then we will talk." He stood and tugged on the cuffs of his ivory shirt.

"Who is Virginia?"

His gaze was searching, voice quiet. "Why would you ask of her?"

"Did you love her?" *Cause she loved you.*

Cer smiled, but it seemed sad. "Our fates were so entwined that love did not matter." A pause. "But yes, I did love her."

"And she's...dead."*Because knowing that I had a conversation with a ghost would really top this off as the trip from hell.*

Or to hell.

Both suck.

"Once upon a time, I could have brought her back. I would have called forth her remains; the earth would have given them to me, and I could renew her."

"You can bring people back to life?" she asked, surprised, Maybe he *was* someone worth hanging around.

"There was nothing I could not do. But that was millennia ago," he said, looking towards the door as though desperate to leave. Men seemed to give her that look a lot. Curse the lot of them.

"You men and your millennia," she grumbled. He gave her an odd look, and she realized he didn't get it. Didn't think it was odd to say the word 'millennia' the same way she might say 'decade.'

"Yes, I could have brought her back to me. But the way things are now, no. And perhaps I will never have that much power again."

She touched the silk bedspread, resisting the urge to pull it up her body and hide away. "Does that make you…a god or something?"

She could practically see him thinking about what to tell her. "You will know soon enough. Stay here. Food and drink is there." He pointed towards a table that held a silver platter with a few cheeses and a mother of pearl knife beside it. There was also bread, fruit, and a silver pitcher with a beaten silver goblet next to it. *Great. This again.* She bit her tongue to keep her mouth shut. No need to tell him he could take his food and go fuck himself.

His voice was firm with resolve. "You will eat and drink eventually. I have given you a great gift, transformed you to more than you ever could have been. I hope that one day you will be grateful."

"I'm sure you do, and I'm sure I won't. I want to leave," she said, loud and proud.

Cer turned away from her and headed to the door. Almost as an afterthought, he said, "Do not go searching for Lucas. Do you understand? I know the bargain. He will live until you tell me otherwise or the requisite time has expired."

"Where is he?" Val asked, feeling so conflicted about him that just saying his name made her nauseous.

"Is it not enough to know he is alive? Is that not more than he deserves?"

She'd been betrayed by her father. By Jack. By Cer. But Lucas...maybe his betrayal hurt the most. He had lied to her, taken her memory, wiped away her free will. "What have you done to him?" she asked, her fingernails digging into the palms of her hands.

Cer rubbed his brow tiredly. "The tenderness of empaths. He brought you here, betrayed you, and still you cannot let him go. I have him, yes. And I have *hurt* him. Nothing that will kill him. He has destroyed my people. Nothing that I can do to him will balance the scales. He is alive. Leave it at that."

He opened the door, but Val couldn't let it go. "Where is he? I want to know what you've done to him."*Because I am a huge fucking moron.*

"He betrayed you," Cer said tonelessly.

She laughed unhappily. "Everyone betrays me. I'm not going to *go* to him. I just want to know."

Now he looked at her. "Lucas is no longer your concern. Your concern is *me*. My people. What I have given you. And maybe you should start being more concerned for yourself. I have expectations of you, Valerie. My world is falling apart. I made it worse by giving you such powers. Reconcile yourself to staying here with me and being my consort. Drink the water. Eat the food. For when I return your life will start anew."

He shut the door behind him hard. Not slamming it. She suspected he wouldn't slam a door no matter how riled he was. He prided himself upon his control.

The pitcher of water caught her eye, and she was so thirsty she thought she could smell it. This was the waiting contest. How much longer could she go without food or water? Valerie got out of the bed and went to the mirror. Her face was pale, and she had deep, black smudges under her eyes. *So,* that's *what haggard looks like.*

Her skin felt raw under her shirt, and she lifted it up, exposing her stomach, then her bra, wanting to see what the damage was. Thin black lines were on her chest, radiating outwards from a central point. Her heart began to pound. She leaned forward, looking closely at the lines and patterns, noting that they looked like vines. *Don't freak out. Don't scream. That's what they do in the movies, and that helps no one.*

"It will settle down. It does not hurt for long."

Val jerked her gaze up, saw movement in the mirror behind her. Virginia was there, walking past the bed, trailing one finger along the coverlet. Valerie whirled around, but the room itself was empty.

"I am not really standing behind you; I am in the mirror. Sorry, did not mean to scare you."

"Really?" Somehow Val doubted that.

Virginia smiled prettily. "Really."

Val licked her lips, fingers still tracing the pattern on her chest. "What is this?" she whispered. It felt smooth, and if she couldn't see it, she wouldn't have known it was there. Somehow that made it worse, like her body wasn't even fighting this terrible change. This was just happening to her, and she couldn't do a damned thing to stop it.

"I am not your enemy, Valerie. We are both women whose lives have been determined for us by men. Whose lives have been taken by another. Not much separates us." She gave Valerie a look of compassion. "Do you want the vines to disappear? So you do not have to see them?" she asked, her voice kind.

Before Valerie could speak, the vines vanished. "How did you do that?" Val demanded. But the image of Virginia was gone. She looked behind her and back to the mirror, searching in vain.

Val's heart was pounding, and she decided to get the hell out of that room before Cer or Virginia came back. She had to find Jack...which meant finding Rachel, unfortunately, and she had to get out of here. What would she do or say? How could they leave?

One life-threatening problem at a time.

What if he was in the middle of boning Rachel? The thought of it made Val want to hit something. Not just because her feelings about Jack were so messed up, but because their lives were in danger. And if she was going to put hers at risk to find him, instead of leaving like a smart person would, then the least he could do would be to put his dick back in his pants and try to escape.

Maybe I should leave him here.

Although, the sad truth was that Rachel had a better chance of getting him out of here than she did anyway. She was an idiot leading the blind. She didn't know anything about Fey, escaping, or witchcraft.

Val opened the door and peered down the empty hallway. This was a different floor than the one she'd been on with Lucas, Jack and Rachel. There was a runner on the ground, and the hallway she'd left Lucas in didn't have a carpet. She remembered his shoulders and head hitting the floor. The tear sliding down his cheek. The sound of pure, desperate joy when he'd swallowed her blood. It made her shiver in desire, confused her, and made her want to cry; all at once.

Distracted by her thoughts, Val found herself on the ground floor in front of a stairway that continued down another level. It was dark, and she could feel a cold draft. *Great. Cold, pitch black, freezing and kind of scary.* Of course, that was the way to go.

Some people just had all the luck.

CHAPTER

7

Val walked down the stairs, and all she could think about was how nervous she was. Her legs were shaky, and she held on to the wall, in case she fell down the stairs. Lucas was here. She knew it. She could feel him as if there were an invisible rope leading her to him. All she had to do was follow it. *Isn't that the premise for Hansel and Gretel? Right before they get eaten?*

She stopped a few steps from the bottom. Once she turned that corner, she would see Lucas again, and she needed a game plan. She'd betrayed him. And Lucas wasn't the sort of guy one could betray, and he'd let bygones be bygones.

Val thought of why he'd wanted her. How he always would have. Thought of what he'd taken from her—her free will and her memories, and she felt fury. She nursed it, kept it close, and prayed that when she saw him, the fire would still burn. There were several ways that seeing him again could go wrong. One—she could get really angry and yell at him. Two—she could cry. Three—maybe he'd be angry, or now that he was emotional, he'd cry...*Nah.*

Plus, she wanted him. Still! Even after all that he'd done, there was some stupid part of her that thought he was worth a damn.

Isn't that just cause he's gorgeous and the sex is insane? She took a shallow breath, imagining the flash of hunger in his eyes as he sank to his knees before her in the hallway. He'd given in, let down his defenses, and she didn't even want to think about how good it had felt to be inside of his head. *Then don't. Just get it over with.*

Their last moments together had been so personal and intimate…and yet, it had ended in betrayal. He'd betrayed her, and she'd left him there like a present for Cerdewellyn. It wasn't the stuff Disney made movies of. *Too much blood and violence for Cinderella.*

And she had seen his secrets. Those were not even his bad secrets. No one was murdered or even tortured. What had made them awful, was that they were his secrets about *her.*

Val went down the final steps quietly. *Why? Not like I could take him by surprise.* She made herself stand up straight—like people did before they went to the guillotine. The room looked like a dungeon. No, it was a dungeon, she corrected herself. She was in a genuine castle, so this was a real dungeon. And it felt like one too. Dark, cold, a weird smell, and a feeling that this room had seen bad, bad things.

There were a few torches lit and Val reached up for one, taking it down off the wall, so she could see into the gloom. The fire was so bright that it made everything more than a few feet away impossible to see.

As he came into view, the first thing she could see was his bare chest. Always a good look, it was true.

But not like this.

His skin was streaked with black. Soot or dirt were the good options; blood the bad. His hair was lank and matted with dried blood. Lucas was shackled to the wall, his wrists and ankles in manacles, so he couldn't move, let alone escape. Cer was taking no chances it seemed.

"Wow. Look at you, rocking the chained look," she said, voice not as confident as she wanted.

His gaze landed on her, and she felt the weight of it. Heat, anger and passion. *Might be all in my head.* He looked away, and she mentally slumped in relief. Somehow, it was a relief not to see his face.

"It is my confident attitude,"he said, in that emotionless tone he had. She wondered if it was an affectation because it wasn't always there. "No matter the role or the attire given to us, we must embrace it with confidence."

She nodded. A joke. He was joking with her. She wanted to hit him. "Don't pretend we are friends, or can have a civilized conversation. Not after what you did to me."

He raised an eyebrow, and the force of his stare came back to her. "What about lovers?"

It felt like a hit. *I let you into my body; I cared for you, and you did this to me.* It took everything she had to ignore him and not start screaming about what an ass-hat he was. "I need to get out of here," she said.

He gave a faint nod, and looked around the dungeon as though it were a hotel room not quite up to snuff. "Yes. You do." He looked behind her. "Where is your pet wolf? Cerdewellyn will not be pleased if he marks the furniture."

"Really? You're going to insult Jack?" *Would he mark the furniture? How dog-like would he be?* Val dismissed it from her mind;

she had to find the jerk first. "I don't want you to say his name. If you'd had it your way, he'd be dead."

Lucas shrugged awkwardly. His shoulders lifted, the muscles in his arms contracting. But there was no slack in the chains, which made it hard for him to move. He twisted his wrists, hands flexing as though he was uncomfortable. The smell of decay, of something burning, reached her nose. It was similar to the smell of human hair, and she gagged.

He continued to stare at her steadily. "Jack has wanted me dead for years. Why am I the one that is punished?"

"Because you knew what he meant to me! And you knew he couldn't harm you. He was nothing more than a pest." She took a deep breath. *Dammit.* She didn't want to talk to him; she just wanted to get out of here.

His head cocked to the side, and he peered over her shoulder into the dark. "Where is he? Why are you not with him? He is bound to you, and you have each other. Correct?" She couldn't bring herself to tell him Jack hadn't chosen her. She'd been so sure he would. She'd been a fool, and to see his condescending smile if he found out...screw him.

"It doesn't matter," she snapped at him. Her hands were shaking, so she crossed her arms. She saw him note the movement. He frowned fleetingly, and then his expression was back to being bored. Except for the intense focus of his gaze. It was his posture, the cadence of his words, and even his expression that seemed to say he was business-as-usual-Lucas. But the intensity of his stare made it a lie, she thought. Val decided to go on the offensive. "What about you? I thought you'd be sobbing like a little girl and atoning for past mistakes."

"Why would I do that?" he asked, sounding genuinely interested.

"I don't know...you had my blood, and you were all teary."

He laughed. And it was definitely *at* her. "Yes, you are a great terror to vampires everywhere. All powerful, and I am trembling in fear," he said.

Jackass. "You jerk. You spent all that time worried about my blood, and then you get it, and it doesn't affect you in any way? Is that what you're telling me?"

He shrugged. "Where is Jack?" he asked again.

"He's waiting for me upstairs." She lied. "I thought you'd be more willing to tell me if I saw you on my own. Just tell me how to leave."

He was looking her over piece by piece, as though she might be injured, or on the verge of growing a third arm. She felt like there were some understatements in there. "You are exhausted, and your emotions are everywhere. You are not attempting to shield at all," he said.

He tried to lean forward, and his eyes were bright, shining. As if he were emotional. His biceps flexed, and she couldn't help but admire them. Remembered how she had touched him as he made love to her. *No, Val, that was fucking.* Because he couldn't have made love to her and treated her the way he did.

"What if I say no? That I have no interest in helping you escape," he said.

She shook her head. "Then I will make you tell me."

He laughed, nodded slightly, staring at the ground. "You will force me...I suppose you would." But he didn't sound worried about it. He made it seem impossible. Like she said she was about to climb Everest in a swimsuit and on her own, and he was indulging her by saying she might be able to do it.

"You owe me," she said, and a little sadness crept into her voice.

His response was soft. So low and dark that it should have pitched the room in blackness and put out her torch. "What do I owe *you*? All the things I gave you. How I took care of you. Money, information…pleasure. I denied you *nothing*. If I could give it to you, I did."

She took a step closer, anger forcing her near. Dried blood was flaking off his cheek like paint. "You gave me things that cost you nothing. It certainly didn't seem to be a hardship to fuck me."

He raised an eyebrow. A condescending look on his face. It meant there was a small smile on his full lips, and a narrowing of his blue eyes. "No. Never a…hardship."

"Yeah, you're a fucking genius at double entendres. I want out of here. Tell me!" She closed the distance between them and hit him on the chest. "Money!" she said, almost shouting. "You gave me *money*? What, when you put me up in an apartment so you could keep an eye on your pet? How fucking dare you tell me you gave me money as if it means something! The literal cost was nothing, as rich as you are. And what *information*? I know what you did to me, what you took, everything you stole. You gave me information you wanted me to have, and if I found out something you didn't, you took it away. How many times did you do that to me? Tell me!" she demanded.

He looked away from her sharply, as if he were flinching.

"My mother, the memories of you with the wolves as you slaughtered the village, even that you wanted me to love you. You're pathetic."She swallowed. Felt close to crumbling. "Just…tell me," Val said, suddenly feeling weak. She didn't meet his gaze and stared at the floor. *Please give me some sign that there is a part of you on the inside that matches the beauty on the outside.*

"There are so many things you want to know, and alas, I am not good enough to tell you for nothing. Not even now. Where is Jack?" he said. And he waited.

Should she just get it over with and tell him? He probably already knew. Maybe that was his revenge. He wanted to humiliate her. "Jack is with Rachel. What the hell—you were right. Rachel, totally not trustworthy. She threw me out of the room and bonded with Jack. Cer showed up, chucked me over a cliff and now..." A harsh laugh. "I may be even worse off than when I was with you. What's your price, Lucas? You want me to find an axe and get you out of here?"

"Will he come for you soon? I assume he does not know you are here?" His tone was cold. The power of his anger washed over her, his emotions sweeping over her and then disappearing again.

She shrugged. "I don't know. He's got a problem with his realm or something, and he said he'd be back. He said he made me an empath...a full-blooded one...like a thoroughbred, and there was a cost to that."

Lucas shifted in his chains as much as he could, twisting his wrists.

Val moved closer, peering at his wrist. "Youch."

He glanced at his wrist and then shrugged, as if his flesh was burned off him all the time, and it was a petty annoyance. "As far as dungeons go, it could be worse. What has he said of his plans for you?" Lucas asked, inclining his head towards her.

She raised the torch and peered to the side of the silver cuff, so that she could try to see the damage clearly. His wrists were wet, covered in what looked like dark gel, a mixture of melting skin and blood, she thought and gagged again. "It's like some kind of skin sludge. How bad is it?" Val took a step back, and felt as if she might faint. She reached out to keep herself upright, and her hand landed on his bare shoulder.

His skin was cold, but she didn't let go. She instantly felt better, the terror and stress, the fear, even the hunger and desperate thirst receded. She wanted to put her arms around him and pretend that none of this was happening. He was so imposing and strong, that even chained up and helpless; she felt as if she'd be better protected if she could just cling on to him. Her throat clogged with tears. *I am so pathetic.*

"Do not touch me," he said, voice hoarse. "Your grief is cloying."

She jerked back and blinked fast, hoping tears wouldn't slide down her cheek. "What did he do to your wrists?" she asked numbly.

"It is not fatal, simply irritating. If the manacle came off, I would heal instantly. Tell me more about being Cer's horse."

Val smiled weakly. "Thoroughbred. He told me that if I gave in and did what he wanted that…it would be easier for me."

"What did you say?" he asked very quietly. As though he was afraid of the answer. His brows were pulled together, and he was staring intently at her face.

Her voice was hard. Being reminded of this made her angry. Anger was better than tears, so she went with it, letting him see how pissed off she was. "I told him 'no.' That I had learned it was best to demand more than words from a pretty man." She blinked quickly and turned away from him, wanting distance between them. Being near him hurt like an open wound.

"Look at me," Lucas commanded.

She didn't want to. It would hurt her to look at him. *I can't be a coward anymore. Someone who can't deal with reality and the truth.* And she certainly couldn't be weak because of him. She wouldn't be vulnerable for Lucas anymore. Their relationship was over.

She turned back to him and tried to convey her feelings to him with just a look. Her resolve and disgust. She was here for a purpose, and she'd learned. *Damn it.*

"There is nothing more dangerous in an Other than a pretty face," he said. "They have power. And they want to control you with it. Looks are a weapon and a deceit. A means to make one vulnerable. Words mean nothing. Beauty means *nothing*," he said, voice like ice. "All that matters is blood, bargains and proof. Make no promises and give nothing to anyone, for they will betray you. Do you understand me, Valerie Dearborn? So Jack and Rachel are together. Cerdewellyn has nefarious plans for you...and I am stuck in this infernal dungeon. It seems unlikely, but things have begun to look up for Cerdewellyn."

She struggled with what she wanted to ask. "Can you...tell that he has done something to me? Do you see it? Or feel it? That he has made me different?"

"Do you mean, can I tell you are now more powerful than you were?"

She nodded.

"No. But I would not know unless you decided to...try it out. Examine your powers, and play with them. Then I would feel it. Through the connection we already have."

"He's waiting for me to eat or drink," she confided, and realized she was close to him again, her feet taking her near without her being conscious of it. She took a step back, not bothering to make it casual.

"Then do not do that," he said blandly, and put his head back against the wall as if he were bored out of his mind.

"I know it's been awhile since you've been human, but time is running out. I am so thirsty and hungry and tired. I'm so..." *Heartsick. You took out my insides and left me a little broken.* She wanted to tell him. Confess it. Like the words might hurt him. 'Look what you did to me, you should be ashamed of yourself!' But that was not how it worked. He was evil. He would probably laugh or something. And maybe she would deserve it.

"Keep your feelings to yourself, Valerie," he said, coldly, as if he had read her mind. "You are vulnerable here. You cannot risk trusting anyone. Your shields are down and your thoughts clear. Try again. Think of a wall. With you inside of it, and me outside. You do not want me privy to your thoughts."

Was that how pathetic she was? That he was willing to tell her not to wear her heart on her sleeve? "I know that! I hate you. Do you understand? I *hate* that I am here because of you. That I did those things with you. I knew what you were, and I ignored it. I was *stupid*. You are violence and death and—"

"You could not have avoided me, Valerie. I put myself in your way, and it was only a matter of time." His tone was distant, and she thought she could see him becoming more inhuman with each word. As if he were creating a barrier between them since she couldn't. He was paler. And when he spoke, his words had more of an accent and a lilt.

"They all succumb. Every woman I have ever wanted. I am as you say, too beautiful as well as evil. And if my own magnetism is not enough, I can read you like a book. I have lived it all, experienced it all…turned my back on all of it. Life is a game, little Valkyrie. A toy. I always would have used you. Count yourself fortunate that if you are careful you may do what no other woman has."

He waited for her to ask. And of course, she did. "And what is that, Yoda?"

He gave her his full attention again, but he looked like a vampire. Pale, flesh hard, and inhuman. She realized how little she saw him like this, how much effort he put into making himself as human as possible when he was around her. Now he wore his predator's smile, the one she'd seen when he killed vampires in front of her. The smile he had given her when she was sixteen, and he saved her life. "You might survive me."

She heard him take in a deep breath, and when she looked back to him, his head was against the wall again, eyes closed. "I know you hurt. I am not sorry. Tell me you understand that? That I am *not* sorry."

"Yeah, you're a jerk; I get it." She watched him because she couldn't help it. He was ignoring her, and so she could. Maybe it was the last time she would ever see him. She saw a tear slide down his cheek, and he turned his head as if to hide it. *What the fuck?*

His voice was gruff with conviction, maybe even anger. "Do you know that if I get out of here that I will come for you? If you were smart, you would pray that I die here. You would find a stake and kill me yourself."

"I don't need more encouragement to hate you. I got it. I hate you. I hope—"*I hope you die here.* But she couldn't say it.

He said something in a language she didn't know, probably a swear word or two, and then gave her his full attention. His face was wet with tears, and he looked furious. "You will not stay mad at me. You will not hate me forever. We are connected now. You will want to come back to me, just as I will want you. You will believe you can change me, that you can control me with your abilities. But, I will always be *exactly* the same to the very core."

She screamed at him. "I know! I know what you are! Just tell me *how* to leave you here to die, and I will!" Her voice echoed off the walls, bouncing around them, and for a moment, neither of them said anything. As if they were both waiting for her angry words to dissipate.

Finally, Lucas said, "It is only you here, Valerie. Rachel came by to pay me a visit; she was going to leave with Jack. You must assume that they are gone."

Her lower lip trembled. "No, he wouldn't leave me."

His voice was soft. "He would not have had a choice. He is bound to her; right now, her will is his will. And she wanted to leave."

Her mouth was hanging open, and she snapped it shut. "So why did you ask me if Jack was bound to me? Just another game? A way to pass the time?"

She saw his chest expand in a deep breath, the rippling muscles of his stomach bunching. "I do not know," he sounded tired. "I suppose I just wondered if you would be honest with me." He cleared his throat and shook his head as if he were coming out of a fog. "In regard to leaving, your options are limited. Dismemberment is one, but I have a hard time imagining you hacking Cerdewellyn into pieces, even if you had the strength. Bone is...difficult."

She ran her hands through her hair, feeling nervous. *Yeah, that's what's keeping me from dismembering him, pulling a muscle as I cut through bone.*

"Your second option is to cut him, bleed him, and then you anoint yourself with his blood. Think of it as a warding. You ward yourself against his magic with his blood. And thus it will allow you to leave."

"You know, it would be nice not to have 'blood' be the answer for once." Her heart started to pound at the enormity of the task before her. "Both of those options suck! He's strong and fast. How the hell am I going to cut him?"

"Bide your time until you find the right moment. And in the meantime, of course, do not drink nor eat. How long can you go without food?"

"An hour," Val grumbled. Afraid she wasn't really joking.

He shifted a little, moving his weight from the left foot to the right. He sounded tired, voice a bit slow, words careful. "You need to stay strong if you are to get out of here. Cerdewellyn can fight, and he has abilities you do not." His fists clenched and released, a sign of his agitation. "I will give you my blood. But it is not free." He caught her gaze. "Not without a bargain."

Her mouth went dry. What the hell would he want from her? "You are not in a position to bargain," she said. She stalked closer and drew out her knife, so he could see it.

He chuckled, and his expression was her own personal nightmare. He looked...human.

A trick of the light.

"Where did you get the knife?" he asked.

"It's Jack's. He wouldn't mind me using it. And if he knew I was using it on you, he'd probably want a photo. You don't have to *give* me the blood. I can *take* it. I don't need to bargain."

Unless.

61

She berated herself, knowing it was stupid to ask. To wonder. But she did, because this was the last time she would ever see Lucas. "You took my memory away." The words were whispered. That's how painful they were.

"So?" he said loudly, uncaring, his head going back against the wall with a light thunk and a harsh exhalation.

"You stole my mother's memory from me."

He swallowed, and she closed her eyes, reaching out to him, wanting to know what was going on inside of him. She couldn't feel anything, so she walked forward, put her hand on his chest. He seemed surprised, flinching at her touch.

His emotions slammed into her, and she gasped and stepped back, recoiling from the shock of what he was feeling. Emotion churned inside of him like a storm, sloshing and moving around, trying to escape. He had a lid on it, barely. And now that she knew, the physical signs were clearer. That he was not nearly as in control as he wanted her to believe.

He pushed himself forward, pulling against the shackles, "Do not think to play with me. Do not pity me. I am Lucaius Tiberius Junius, King of the Vampires, slayer of all the Others. Do you think me weak because of your pathetic emotions? Do you think it gives you an advantage? You are but an empath. I killed the others, Valkyrie. Emotions will not break me, nor will they sway me."

"Tell me why you took her memory away from me." She wanted to know. She would get out of here, and she didn't want to look back and think about him for any reason.

"Let us hope that you will leave if I tell you. You had *nothing* left of her. Only pain. Only fear. The memories were destroying you."

"You want me to believe you helped me? Isn't that convenient."

He shook his head, mouth in a hard frown. She wanted him to tell her, and she had only one threat that might work. "I will make you drink my blood again, unless you tell me the truth."

He shot her a look she couldn't decipher. "You were afraid and miserable. You did not sleep. Your father was going to send you away. It was easier to hide you away and pursue his grief, than deal with a daughter who was teetering on the edge of mental collapse. I did nothing except allow you to be...who you are. It was there but buried underneath the fear. I moved that aside."

Was it true? Had he helped her, taken it away because she was a wreck and her father was going to get rid of her? Tears coursed down her cheeks, and she didn't know what to do.

"Valerie. You are an empath and emotional. You must be rational to leave here. I saved you for myself. The last of your kind. What good would you have done me if you were insane and locked away?"

She nodded. That was a reasonable explanation, wasn't it? Why he helped her? Not because he cared for her, but because she was a commodity.

For the briefest moment, she wished she'd never found out about his trickery, that he would have taken her from here, escaped the Land of Fey, and she could have loved him blindly. He would take her to bed, keep her safe, be kind to her...and she would have loved him. He would have protected her. Kept her and cared for her. Wouldn't he?

He shook his head back and forth looking at the ground. "Take my blood and go, Valerie. There is nothing for you here."

"You don't dismiss me anymore. I'm looking for reasons to forgive you. Why? Why do I...still want you even when I know what you are?"

"The futility of your interest in me is truly ridiculous," he said angrily. "But if you are so desperate then come, undo my clothing, and we will be together one more time. You do not need to romanticize your desire for me. Do not try to turn it into something pretty. You crave me. You want to be with me. Let us see how bold you really are. Take what you want. It is nothing more than lust. An *itch*. Do us both a favor and scratch it."He smiled at her malevolently. "After all, this could be my last chance before I die."

She wanted to slap him. Deny what he was saying. Lust? "I think it's more than lust. I think you—" Rage rose within her sharply. It blinded her and overwhelmed her thoughts. Rage she had never felt before. It was a storm surrounding her, and she wanted to hurt him back for all the terrible things he had done to her and all of his victims.

She was suddenly before him, her blade at his neck, her body an inch from his. She pricked his throat, and he did nothing to stop her. Held still while she cut him, and his blood trickled down the pale column of his throat. He turned his head to the side, granting her access. She leaned forward, ready to drink him down.

He deserved it. After everything he had done, she was doing nothing he hadn't earned. The pleasure of her fury arced through her, made her hesitate because it was so...*strange,* but familiar at the same time. And then she remembered the ring, the I-want-to-fuck-you-and-kill-you ring, as she thought of it. He had put it on her the night of the vampire ball, and it had been made with Fey magic. It provoked the wearer to act. Just like she felt the need to drink him down right now.

She was acting, but the motives and drive were not hers. She watched the spill of dark blood slide down his flesh. *I cut too deep;*

I hurt him. Hunger slammed into her again, blocking out any concern for his precious neck. She hungered…like a vampire.

This isn't me.

"No!" she cried out and stumbled backward, falling hard on her ass. The feelings clung to her like cobwebs, something sticky and elusive. "You did that to me. You pushed those emotions at me. Why?" she asked.

His voice was harsh and gravelly, his breathing as fast as hers. "You truly are a full empath now. Good for Cerdewellyn. Do you understand that I can manipulate you? Just as you can manipulate me. We shared blood. Consider yourself warned. Now hurry, Cerdewellyn might return, and your angst is exhausting." He sighed. "You are like a puppy gnawing at my shoes. You make demands with no reason, no strength to back you up. Come. Take your blood and go. What happened in that corridor was an aberration. If you try to control me, try to break into my mind again, I will fight back. I have more experience than you ever will, little girl. More experience in everything. I could own you if I choose to. I could have you on your knees servicing me like a whore," he said in a low tone, his gaze raking over her indecently. "Take my blood and leave my memories alone. Do you understand?"

"I don't want your memories."

He made a noise that was part growl and part exasperation. "You lie to me and to yourself. You ripped through my mind and left a mess in your wake, pulling out what you wanted to know, shoving your fears inside of me as you left me on that floor—uncaring whether I lived or died.

"You deserved it."

He smiled, shook his head. "No, Valerie. We *never* get what we deserve. We get what we bargain for. And I am bargaining with you now: I will give you my blood freely, but you need to stay out of my mind.."

Val was shaking. She stepped forward and touched his chest, felt his flesh under her hand. His jaw was hard, and she could see the muscles of his jaw locked tight. Every muscle tense as she invaded his personal space, a scant few inches separating their bodies. Of course, it reminded her of kissing him, being with him.

She nicked his neck with the knife and leaned forward, really wanting to get it over with, feeling her stomach heave in revolt at the idea of slurping up his blood, putting a damper on the instant lust that always arose when she was near him. Her mouth filled with saliva, and not in a good way.

She made a sound of distress and began to pull back. And then she felt little tendrils of hunger snaking around her, coiling tighter: blood lust. He was feeling it, letting it rise to the surface, and her bond with him was bringing it forward, giving it to her, making her own grow.

Suddenly, the blood was not revolting. Was nothing beyond a connection to him, and Val realized she didn't have to hate him for the next few moments. She could lean her weight on him, kiss him, and it was for her survival. *Oh yeah, I'm totally pathetic.* She kissed his chest and then again, near his shoulder. The blood a few inches away.

Dimly, she heard him say 'no.' He did not want her affection, or for her to get caught up in him physically. She kissed again and pressed closer. Inhaled deeply. The smell of him, his blood and strength, was like an aphrodisiac. He was evil. But for this moment, he was hers.

Valerie licked his smooth flesh, closed her mouth over the wound on his neck.

There. It was like a lock. A connection. Like two huge pieces of metal fitting together. A car crash at a hundred miles per hour.

He was not hers. She knew that, but it fell away. For this moment, when her body was flush to his, when she could feel his erection against her stomach and hear him sighing her name, he was hers. She wanted to weep for the loss of him.

And I will never get over him.

That was the brutal, inescapable truth. He was like a crippling disease. Even if she left here and lived a normal life, she would dream of him, remember him, and want him. Wonder what he was doing tucked away in Cerdewellyn's dungeon waiting to die.

When she was old and he was still here, perfect and alone, would she sense him? Dream about him? If he died, would she feel it? She might be dust, and he would still be down here, perfect and golden, waiting for Cerdewellyn to put an end to him. The thought of it broke her heart.

CHAPTER

8

Strength returned to her, infusing her limbs with energy, making her feel more alive and awake. As if she had just downed a triple espresso and a candy bar. She wished happiness had come with it. She stepped back from him and couldn't face looking, didn't want to see what expression he might have. Be it condescension or boredom, she didn't want to know.

She could not get him out of here, had to focus on herself. A pang went through her, but Jack and Rachel were gone. Sure, Lucas said Jack couldn't fight her, but she didn't believe it. Part of her thought that if Jack really cared about her, he would have found a way to fight Rachel and stay.

So that was it then, she thought, as her newly energized body went up the steps. And what kind of goodbye could she say to him anyway? 'I really wish you weren't evil' or 'we had some good times, thanks for the orgasms.' But walking away from him was hard, it was as if the magnetic force of him was trying to pull her back. Valerie opened the door to the dungeon, lost to her own thoughts as she stepped into the corridor.

"Following directions is not one of your strong suits I see."

Valerie whirled around, startled half to death. "Cerdewellyn," she gasped. Cerdewellyn wore brown this time. Brown breeches and some sort of riding boot. As if he'd just stepped out of a Regency Romance and had been inspecting his property all morning. There was no denying that Cerdewellyn was attractive, his thick black hair and olive-colored skin. He was tall, graceful and athletic, and he wasn't as ruthless as Lucas, either.

And yet he scared her more.

Perhaps because she was a commodity to him, and nothing more. She sensed a barrier within him. That he wouldn't let her or any woman in. Would he have been the same way with Virginia?

Maybe that was one of the problems with these men who lived forever, they'd built up an immunity or resistance to affection. Perhaps because when everyone they knew and loved continued to die, they realized the value of distance, of not losing one's self completely to love.

Did one have to be mortal in order to love?

He gave her a small nod and looked at the closed door. "No matter. You look well. Better than before," he said, solicitously. As he looked her over, again as if she were a prime piece of equestrian flesh, she tried to get herself together and figure out what she was going to do. She didn't have a lot of time to make plans.

"Come," he said and led her to the library. The place where she'd learned all about Lucas and his treachery. He walked to a small table. Poured a drink of what looked like brandy and offered it to her. "Drink?"

"No. Still no."

He raised an eyebrow. An expression that playfully said he had to try to get her to drink even though he knew she would say no. It was *almost* a joke. Except that it was her life on the line.

"What's the deal, Cer? You're just going to wait me out and then what? I don't want to be your queen. You have to let me go. You promised you would let me go." She cleared her throat, trying to orient herself to this moment. Part of her was still in that dungeon with Lucas, and she needed to be here. Cerdewellyn was a threat. He wanted to harm her. This was her chance. She took a deep breath.

He tossed the drink back, held the liquid in his mouth for a second before swallowing hard. As though it burned all the way down. "Lucas cares for you. Not forever you understand? But for now. Your blood runs through him, and it's clear he feels for you. Harming you will harm him."

He came towards her, and she backed up. She bumped into something and whirled around. A table had come from nowhere, blocking her in. This was her moment. And it was coming upon her a bit faster than she'd expected.

Cerdewellyn was closing in on her. Valerie drew her knife and stabbed outwards, slicing his arm as he jerked away from her slashing blade. He grunted in pain. "That will hurt you more than me," he said, and his hand covered hers, wrapping around the handle of the knife so fast that she hadn't seen more than a blur. Damned supernatural freaks with their speed. He squeezed her hand hard, her bones shifting in excruciating pain as he ground them together.

"I will break your hand if you do not let go," he warned her.

She screamed and threw her head forward, trying to head butt him, but he jerked back, and had the gall to chuckle at her. Despite the pain, she held on tight, unwilling to let it go. She needed to break free, stab him, and then go.

Cerdewellyn yanked her forward and to the right, using his weight and superior strength to force her body to move, slamming her arm into the table. Her hand went numb, fingers opening, the knife falling to the ground, and suddenly she couldn't breathe, as if the air was liquid and too heavy to drag into her lungs.

Her chest burned, and the blood vessels in her head, heart, and then her entire body, seemed to throb. Before she could scream or even fall down, the pressure dissipated, flooding out of her, taking all of her borrowed strength from Lucas with it. It was as if a fundamental piece of her soul dissolved.

It was a strange and unpleasant feeling, having her strength and vitality leave her. It didn't hurt per se. It just felt like she was becoming exhausted. It was hard to stand upright, to keep her eyes open, muscles she took for granted protested at working. Would she die, she wondered? Would her heart stop pumping too?

Valerie fell forward, and Cerdewellyn caught her. As he hauled her up in his arms, she saw a vase of flowers behind her change. It had been a container full of sticks, brown and dried out, but now they were blooming.

"He fed you; he made you strong, and now I am taking it back. Do not fight it, do not try to attack me again, or I will chain you like a dog, and there will be no more pretense of civility. Do you understand? Now go to sleep," he said, voice dark and hypnotic.

And so she did.

CHAPTER

9

Valerie moaned and shifted on the ground, coming to slowly.

Her head was killing her, and she covered her face with her hands, her body curling into a fetal position. Without opening her eyes, she knew she was back in the dungeon. It was cold and smelled bad, and just to confirm her guess, Lucas spoke to her.

"You are weak. What did Cerdewellyn do?" he asked.

"He sucked me dry like a sorority girl with a Jell-O shot," she said and opened her eyes, seeing him several feet away. Her eyes met his, and she felt that same electric charge between them. That current of knowledge and desire that she'd only ever felt with him.

His eyebrows raised. "For a moment, I was uncertain where you were going with that metaphor."

She wasn't sure what the hell he was talking about. Although it could just have something to do with the fact that she'd been drained and tossed aside, and was now in the midst of what felt like the worst hangover ever. What had she said? Oh, she'd been sucked dry. *Cause a sorority girl might suck other things.* She laughed weakly and felt herself blush. "I wish you weren't funny."

"I am not," he said to her gravely. "You are in a desperate situation. If you think I am amusing, we truly are one step away from certain death."

"Great." She rubbed her forehead and sat up slowly, whimpering at the pain that flowed through her body.

"Can you stand?"

"Just a minute," she said.

"Then let me tell you the story of the Sard. At least what I know of it. It is a jewel. One that Cer covets. The legend is, that once upon a time, there was a prince who walked out of the sun. That, I believe, means he came from Fey to Earth. He was very powerful and was revered as a deity and king."

"Wait. Where and when is this?"

"Egypt. Probably, six or seven thousand years ago."

"That's what you have narrowed it down to?" she asked, unaccountably irritated.

He blinked slowly. "I cannot see why it matters. Cerdewellyn exists. That is fact. The point is that it was a very long time ago. The point is, the Sard, which Cerdewellyn wants back, and *why* he wants it. Not whether or not his father was Horus or Narmer."

He waited for her to argue. She shrugged. He sighed and continued. "The prince who walked out of the sun, was Cerdewellyn's father. He fell in love but was immortal. His beloved was not."

Uh oh. "So she got older, and he stayed young?"

Lucas gave her an odd look. "It is a frequent problem when mortals and immortals mix," he said, conversationally. "But no, she became pregnant. And the child was killing her. She was going to die, her womb still distended with child; and the king called all the sorcerers and wise men and women in the land to her bed-side. They told him there was nothing to be done. The midwives explained to him about life and death, and whatever they told him, convinced him to try to make her like him. He bled himself, feeding her his blood again and again. For whatever reason, it did not work, and she died. Perhaps he waited too long. And then her body disappeared."

"So he loved her but couldn't save her. That's kind of sad. How do you know she didn't get up and wander away?"

"If you stop interrupting, I will tell you," he said waspishly.

"Temper, temper," she said, and in a different situation, it might have been amusing to see him irritated.

"I am not irritated; it is just that the day is wearing on, and I have so much in my schedule."

She squinted at him. Yeah, another joke. "The story is that her body was divided up without the king's knowledge. Some ate her flesh; others drank her blood, and yet another group took her bones and made talismans of them. For their king was much feared and much beloved. When he found out what had been done to his love, he cursed them."

"That must have been quite a damper on the beloved part."

He ignored her. "Those who ate her flesh, were consumed with the desire to eat flesh forever, and turned into wolves. Those who drank her blood became vampires. And those who took her bones, were witches, their magic twisted so that when they used their newfound powers, they paid a great price for it."

His gaze slid to hers, and it was so empty, his eyes so dull, that she was suddenly scared for him. Scared for him, even though he was superhuman. As if the biggest danger that threatened him was internal rather than external. "What the king did not realize, was that the blood he gave was still linked to him. As the curse spread, and more creatures were created, he became weaker and weaker. All those that he had cursed were draining him, taking from him to sustain themselves. He worried he would perish, and that he would be forgotten and unavenged. He sent out his followers to kill all those that were accursed, and created the Sard—a repository for all the power to return to, until he could find a way to reabsorb it into himself. But he still wanted to punish those that had stolen from him, and so he created one more group of accursed beings…those who could make the cursed feel remorse for what they had done. They would remind all the Others what pain the king had endured. I assume you can guess—that was the creation of the empath."

He lowered his gaze. "And the king…retreated. Beset by grief, he hid, and centuries passed. Then, one day, Cerdewellyn appeared. He came from the deserts; some say from a tomb in Egypt where he buried his father. But that part of the story was never quite nailed down."

"How do you know this?"

"I tortured a lot of people a very long time ago. Witches. Empaths. The wolves. They all knew snippets of it. And as I killed them, I came to believe it, that all of our magic came from Cerdewellyn's father and this realm. As the Others have perished over the centuries, Cerdewellyn's strength has waned. Until now, when there is very little left."

"So if someone could find the Sard and use its magic, they would have a lot of power?"

"Perhaps. The legends say that anything is possible with the Sard. One might have their heart's desire. But there is a book as well. The Book of Life and Death. It has only been seen here. A thing one hears rumors of."

"So you need the book and the jewel?"

She took his silence for a yes. The pieces all fell into place. Why he'd brought her here. "And what did you desire?" she asked.

He shifted, adjusting his arms in the cuffs. "The relevant question is, where is the Sard now?"

She couldn't help but wonder what he had wanted all that time ago. *Whatever.* She needed to get over him, not discover he'd always had a hankering for Geng his Kahn's hat or something. "Fine. Where is it now?"

His voice was very bland. "It was turned into a necklace in the twelfth century."

"And then?"

"And then it languished. It could not be used. All who came near it knew that it had great magic, could almost touch it and yet, they couldn't access it. Everyone tried. Everyone, except Cerdewellyn of course. It is very dark in here," he said, sounding almost whimsical.

"Where is it?" she asked.

He laughed, and it made his stomach muscles ripple. "You flatter me."

"No, I *know* you. You have it, where is it?"

A sudden light filled his eyes, an animation that wiped away the casualness. "You do not *know* me," he said, voice near a hiss. She took a step back, and he leaned forward, straining against the bonds. There was a calculated detachment to him, a look that said he would kill her if she came closer, that every scrap of emotion she had ever thought he might be capable of having was a lie. That evil could never be good. "If you *knew* me, you would kill me. If you *knew* me, you would not let me into your body. Would not have let yourself be used by me. You would have run away."

Her voice was hard. "Okay, I have terrible judgment. If I picked up a hitch-hiker, she'd turn out to be a serial killer. I get it. Don't worry. I have learned not to trust. And if I ever get out of here, I will be sure to live by that until the end of my hopefully long and senile days. So where is the necklace?"

He took a long, uneven breath.

"I gave it to Marion a very long time ago."

"Marion is in a box." Her stomach flipped unpleasantly.

Lucas gave her a rakish smile. At least, that was what she'd always assumed rakish meant: a little insolent and a lot smug. "Are you not glad I let her live? If it had been up to you, she would be dead."

She pursed her lips. "I'm pretty sure I still want her dead." She kind of wanted to blow chunks.

His next words were noticeable by their blandness. As if he were trying too hard to make them sound nonchalant. "You must feed again."

"What?"

He didn't repeat himself.

"Cerdewellyn will just take it out again." *See how I avoided using the work suck?* she almost said.

"There is no other option. That is the plan. It is very...him."

"You don't sound impressed."

His muscles flexed as though he was shrugging, but he was so immobilized it was hard to tell. "Cerdewellyn is not direct. Even now, he behaves surreptitiously. Weakening me in the shadows. He sends you to make me weak. A great villain does not act timidly."

She swallowed hard, stuck on one thing he had said. "Do I make you weak?"

"Come and feed. Then go. Find Cerdewellyn, attempt to attack him."

She nodded. "This has a certain Groundhog Day quality to it."

He looked at her blankly.

"That's the Lucas I know. Inscrutable and out of touch with pop culture," Valerie muttered.

"Yes. It is one of my better attributes."

"You mean compared to the bloodshed and plotting for world domination?" she said, sarcastically.

For a moment, he looked sad, then his expression cleared, and he was his cold, distant self. "Do not be a fool for me, Valerie Dearborn. It is one of my better attributes, because my personality is one of death and violence. Soulless. You keep trying to forget it."

"No, I don't." *Yes, I do.* "Okay. Maybe you're right. I do get that you've done bad things and that you are evil, but—"

His voice was loud, angry, and he leaned forward, making sure she caught a flash of fang as he growled the words at her. "You do not *get* it. I know you will come back for me. I see it in you, Valerie. You are not the first girl to become enamored of me. I have bedded more women than you can count. And you still look to me with hope that you are different. You are so desperate to believe that I protect you because you are special. Because you have reached my dead, black heart. It makes you a *fool*. Cerdewellyn uses us both. Take my strength and try to leave. You do it again and again until you succeed—or he does. That is the end. There is no plan where we leave together, no happily ever after. You and I have no future beyond your death or mine. You keep seeking to redeem me. You keep looking and hoping. Painting me in emotions I do not have, nor can have."

That was the last straw. She was sick of his bullshit. "You know what? You go to a lot of trouble to reassure me how evil you are. And yet, here I am, and you keep offering to feed me. If you're so evil, then shouldn't you just snack on me instead of warning me away? You're a contradiction wrapped in a hot package. But I'm onto you now." She stood up shakily and went towards him. She saw his eyes widen in surprise, and then his jaw hardened, and she knew he was trying to get his shit together, keep his emotions to himself.

She went forward and wrapped her arms around him, holding tight to him in a moment of desperate weakness, a piece of debris in the middle of the ocean. Valerie reached out to him mentally, trying to touch his emotions and see what he was really feeling. His words said one thing, his actions and body language something entirely different. But she didn't have to take him at face value anymore. He was chained up, weak, and emotional as all get-out. She could touch him, and know what was truth and what was a lie.

Inside, Lucas was like a hurricane, churning up everything, all of his emotions whipping through him. But there was a calmness in the middle, the small eye of the storm where he knew what he felt with certainty. She focused on that part of him, wanting to know what he really felt.

He was filled with grief.

His voice startled her. "Get off me."

"No," she said, and tears filled her eyes. He drew in a breath that was ragged, and she wondered if he was crying. If she looked up, would she see the real him?

"There is no real me. You think to be my savior? Hope that you are different from anyone else?" A pause, she heard him swallow.

His body relaxed, and he took a shaky breath. Calmness went through him, tinged with resignation. "I know where this leads."

She felt his body relax, as though he were done with pushing her away. His tone was low, barely more than a whisper, and she felt like what she had in this moment was the real Lucas. The one she'd hoped for, but only imagined. She listened hard, wanting to memorize every word, so she wouldn't forget. "I have cared, Valerie. I have cared, and I have tried, and it always ends in death. Sometimes I fear I will *never* die. The world will end, and I will still be here. It scares me. As much as it can, it scares me."

She rubbed her cheek against the smooth skin of his chest. Was this was what crash survivors felt like? She just wanted some human contact before the end. He rested his cheek on top of her head. If he could hold her, he would. Right now, he seemed vulnerable enough that he would.

He spoke very quietly, like a small boy confessing his sins. "How cursed am I that I can cause so much pain and death and yet live on? What sort of demon is hated by the heavens so much that he never gets his due?"

She held him tighter. She could feel the pain coming from him. The misery. His self-loathing.

Lucas laughed. A hard sound. Maybe the worst sound she'd ever heard—worse than fingernails on a chalkboard, worse than Marion screaming before she'd been put in that box. Maybe worse than the sound of her mother when she….*No.*

"If I am not evil, what am I? There is no devil inside of me. Nothing to exorcise or pray for. I am a fluke. A cosmic affliction. Something perverse and dreaded. *Get* off me."

She took a step back. His voice was seductive, with a hint of a blade underneath it all. "I make you come. That is the hold I have over you. And that is not real. It is not a man and a woman it is one monster to another. It is power coursing between us, pleasure and control. That is not a pure desire or love. It is lust. Consumption. Danger. That is what you want from me."

"And you don't want to give me that much. Do you?"

"No. I cannot. My time here is done, Valkyrie. I will continue to feed you, and try to protect you, for as long as I can, but the day will come where he will break me, or he will kill me and…that is right."

She drew back, looking at him through a haze of tears. "So you've given up?"

"I gave up long ago. Drink from me and leave. My anger did not sway you; my evilness is something you brush aside, so let me show you the worth of my affection. What happens to those that I love. Then perhaps you will finally let me go."

"I don't understand."

"My memories. I will let you see them as you drink from me. And then…then you will be happy to see me dead."

What would he show her that he knew would make her not love him? And oh, she didn't want to see it. She wanted to stay here, hold him, and pretend he could be other than he was. She wanted to be the ostrich.

With a last look, as though she knew things would be forever altered after she saw his memories, she brought the knife to his neck, nicking him lightly. The taste was immaterial, the idea that blood was gross was irrelevant. She was too deep into him now, into the end of *them* to care that his blood was disgusting.

She leaned in and drank.

"And when you wake up your mama will be here. We will do something fun. Go to the ocean. Shall I tell you of the ocean?"

Margaret's cornflower blue eyes were dull, struggling to stay open, and he knew the end was close. He would talk for a little longer and then... He knew what would happen then. He heard Marion screaming in the hallway, demanding to be let in, to see her little girl, swearing she would kill Lucas if he did not open the door this instant.

Margaret would slide away. Into the ever after. To another world in the sky, and he would still be here. Another beloved child whom he would outlive.

Was this his punishment, Lucas wondered, to see the end come for an innocent while he continued on? Healthy and evil. And one day he would not remember her: the little bow shape of her lips, how she could go from smiles to tears in an instant over the slightest thing. But she was little. And that was what little girls did.

He wished he did not know that.

Grief made it hard to swallow, even to speak.

He would forget her. He longed for it and dreaded it. Any moment now she would die, and who would remember her pure innocence, but two monsters forgotten by the devil? Although she was not his flesh and blood, she was still his. A child he would forget.

"I will remember you," he said, vowing it. Lucas was ashamed to realize he had said it aloud. Her eyes focused on him, trust shining through the pain. She loved him because she did not understand evil.

She thought he was good. Her savior. The father she had never had. Was it wrong to let her die when he could save her? When, even now, Marion's desperate shrieking demanded he save her?

He would let her die rather than become like them.

Again.

Just like his children centuries ago. History repeating itself. He was making the same decision. Was it wrong? Was this villainy or kindness to let her go when he could make her open her eyes again?

He leaned down and kissed her on the forehead. Margaret's hand squeezed his. "The sun is out," *she said weakly.*

It was bright outside. So bright that the world should be embarrassed. As if a god or the gods or nothing were happy that a child was dying. It was a torment to know that great tragedy could come, and yet the sun could shine. The world would not be affected by this small death.

Lucas blinked away tears, and found Margaret staring at his hair. Her hand lifted, touched it, her fingers sliding through the heavy mass. "It looks like the sun. Mama won't stop crying. Why?"

"She wants you to get better," *he said.*

"Have you told her what you are? She would not cry if she knew."

He froze—heart, limbs, emotions, everything. "What? What am I?" *She couldn't know.*

"An angel. You came here for me, didn't you? To take me away. And that is all right, because you will stay with her, won't you?"

Even now he could not be better than what he was. So he lied to her. "You will be fine. You will stay with your mother and I."

"I don't want to leave mama and you. Where will I go?" *she asked, voice trembling. Lucas almost took his own dagger and stabbed himself through the heart. As if he knew or could tell her.*

"You will stay here with us." *But they both knew it was a lie. He felt incapable of saying it with conviction. Should he compel her? Was that a kind thing to do? She knew she would die. The sores that covered her flesh looked like the ones that covered the dead bodies heaped in a pile by the side of the road as they had fled Blackfriars.*

She had clung to him, and he had pressed her head against his shoulder, so she would not see. Would not smell the death. But she had seen it, taken the rot inside of herself, and even though he wanted to shelter her, she recognized her own death marks on her soft skin.

And again, the question was there, like a ghost knocking on the door, pounding through him to the beat of his own heart. Should he save her? Should he change her?

But he couldn't do that to this little girl anymore than he could have changed his own. Damn her soul for all eternity. Make her life one of blood and death. Take away the sun and friends. There was no greater curse than immortality. She would never grow up, never have a family, a young man to love. If he changed her, she would stay a child. Stunted and dark.

No, if he loved her, he would let her go. And yet, somehow that seemed impossible; that death could ever be the right answer.

"The ocean is blue. The pond out side is dark and green. But the ocean is blue with white tips. Water rushes outward to meet you and tickle your feet. Then it pulls away, wanting you to chase it. When I was a boy...we played chase with the ocean. But it was very cold, and our feet would lose all feeling from how cold it was." Maybe he should walk into the ocean and let it cover him too. Make him numb, take him away. "The ocean is also loud. The water makes a noise as it beats against the rocks and the shore. If we had a boat, we could sail into the ocean for days, weeks, even months and see nothing, but a vast land of blue water."

"Where does it lead?"

What should he say? "It goes..." He had to get it right. It was important. What would his daughter have wanted to hear? "It goes to heaven. You sail on it; you keep going and going. And then you reach heaven."

He could hear the relief in her voice. "*That is where you will take me.*"

He nodded clumsily, thought he could hear God laughing at him. "*It is.*"

"*You will come see me. Angels always come to heaven, don't they?*"

"*Of course I will. I can't think of anything I want more than to see you...*" he stopped. Choked on the feelings. The nightmare shoved in his throat. "*Of course I will see you. I will stay with you. Your mother and I will get a boat and come find you.*"

She smiled. And that was how she died. With a small smile, listening to his promise that he would find her. That what he wanted was to be with her. A final lie. For he couldn't be with her. Not a devil like him. He could sail the seas until the day he died, for a hundred years, maybe a million. The sails would shred to nothing, the boat rot away beneath him, and still he wouldn't find her.

Not someone damned like him.

He opened the door, and Marion stopped screaming. Her eyes were wild, and whatever she saw on his face was enough. Marion screamed, and she flew at Lucas, fingers raised like claws, scratching down the side of his face. He let her hit him, made himself touchable, vulnerable, and felt her fingers dig into his skin and shred it.

A small punishment. Something he deserved. He felt the marks healing already. Too soon.

"*You could have saved her! I could have saved her! I will kill you, Lucas. You will die for this,*" she swore.

Lucas reached into his pocket, and pulled out a heavy jewel that fit neatly in his palm. It was on a chain, surrounded by gold. It winked in the light. As white as an opal, but inside of it *were ribbons of what looked like diamonds running through it. It glowed softly, illuminating the dark hallway.*

"It is Fey. Pure magic. If you find the book and the spell, you can have anything you want. You can make one wish, and it will come true, Marion. You can have Margaret come back to you. Alive and well."

She blinked at him slowly, confusion leaving her pale face, replaced by a zeal and desperate need to believe him. "But where is the book then?"

He shook his head. "Not here. It is guarded by Cerdewellyn. He wants this back. Believes it would restore him. He does not know that I have it. He believes it was lost a long time ago with the Irish witches."

"How do you have it?"

"They gave it to me," he said, voice quiet. He didn't have to say he had killed them all, and that was why they had given it to him. A last-ditch effort to save themselves.

"You will help me. We can be a family again," Marion said.

"No. It is not my quest."

Now Marion did look up, peering into Lucas' face. Searching and searching. "But you love her. Like her own father. Why will you not help me?"

"It does not concern me. She is dead. If you wish to bring her back, you do it." Lucas turned on his heel and left, watching each foot land in front of the other until he was outside of the castle and squinting against the bright light. Pain seared him. The sun on his skin like pin pricks from a thousand needles. It had done nothing but rain for weeks; the world around him was mud and yet now the sun shone.

He hated England. Hated the wet. And the cold. It seeped into his very bones, and made him want to die. Made every muscle ache.

Margaret was gone. Not even a young woman. Still a child, and gone. And it was his fault. He had reached for something he should not have. He was damned. Cursed. He needed to live like the damned. Not pretend to be a man. Pretend to be something good. Fate, the Gods, even the Christian God, all of them would peer down at him from the heavens above, see him reaching for something that he did not deserve, and they would take it from him. Over and over again until he learned.

Now he had learned.

Because he was evil. And he was death. Who was he to want the world? To have such vanity and belief, that fate would let him get away with murder? He had tried, and Margaret had died. His love for her had killed her. Would Margaret be alive if he'd never met her?

Maybe Marion could do it. Maybe she, not steeped in evil like him, would be able to find the book and bring Margaret back. The gods might let her. He would ignore it. He would never mention it again. Never think of her again. If he did not care, perhaps it could happen.

This was a reminder of his purpose. His goal in life. Kill the Others. Kill Cerdewellyn and every last creature he'd spawned. And then he would kill the vampires. And when at last there was no one left but him—he could die. Finally kill himself, as he should have done all those centuries ago when he discovered his murdered family.

Someday, he vowed, the world would be free of the Others, and be grateful for it.

Valerie stepped back, the memories fading, returning her to the present. Lucas put his head back against the wall, turning away from her. Eyes closed. Not seeing her or anything beyond his own private hell. She reached up to his cheek, wiped away a tear.

"It made her insane. The death of her daughter. That is what did it," he said.

"And you blame yourself for that too?"

His voice was sandpaper rough. "Marion was like me. Periodically, she would become a zealot, and seek something beyond her own selfishness. She would try."

"Is that why we came here? To get the book so you could get Margaret back? Because you loved her like a daughter?"

"No. That is long past."

"Then what?"

"Time is passing. Go, Valerie. Attack Cerdewellyn, flee from here."

Tears filled her eyes. How could she leave him?

He snarled at her. "I am a monster. I fucked you like a gentleman, and you want to read into it things that are not there. The best thing I can do is die. And you should beg for it. Because I do feel remorse, and I hate it. It is a burden I cannot endure. That is the lesson you were to learn by seeing my memories. I will be sick to death of my shame and self-loathing, and I will kill you. Do you not see it? The truth? I am a weak man, Valerie Dearborn. I always have been, and always shall be. The day will come when I know that I shall break because of the things that I have done, and instead of ending my own life, I will take yours. You are the last of your kind. The only one. I would never feel like this again. Hatred, lust, anger and fear. A longing for things I have no right to." His words burned her, his expression a deadly promise.

"That is why I will kill you. So that I don't have to remember the man I wanted to be. So that I don't have to hate myself and care about my failure. That was why I never wanted your blood.

Because I did not want to feel *this* again. You signed your own death warrant by giving me emotions."

She slapped him hard across the face, and it echoed throughout the cavernous room. He spit blood and turned back to her.

"Maybe you will survive the day yet."

She stumbled away from him, and towards the stairs. He didn't try to stop her, didn't shout taunts after her or try to apologize. The truth of his words, the bitterness and sincerity in them were impossible to ignore. It was hopeless, she realized.

She opened the door to the dungeon, and took two steps forward before realizing that the corridor was different. With the next step, she was suddenly back in the dining room. Cerdewellyn was standing next to a chair that held a corpse, his hand on the woman's shoulder; eyes closed.

The body began to shrink in on itself, the sound of bones snapping loud and wrong in her ears. The rib cage collapsed as she watched, shattering in on itself. The skull went next, cracking in half, the jaw breaking and caving in at the occipital lobe. And with a sudden flash of light, the body was gone. The other chairs were empty, and she knew he had done the same thing to the rest of them. Valerie wanted nothing so much as to get the hell out of there. She didn't want to be involved in this supernatural bullshit. In love with a monster who promised to kill her, stuck with another monster who wanted to make her his queen.

His eyes opened, and he looked at her; a weight to his gaze that was somber and distant. "They are gone. They were barely alive. Their survival required energy I could not give them. And so I took it back. Took it all. Their flesh. Their souls."

"You killed them," she said, and wrapped her hand around the handle of her blade, as if for comfort.

"No!" he suddenly shouted, his face filled with fury. "*He* did this. *He* has chased me across the world and killed everyone I knew and loved! I have no choice, but to make these decisions…to be like him," he finished, misery and rage in his tone.

"It should bring me pleasure that I need you to make things right. That I have the greatest means for bringing Lucas to his knees living under my roof, and yet it does not. You reek of him, do you know it? He let you bleed him. Gave you power to stay strong. The hold you have on him will save me and mine yet," he said, and the room they were in shifted and changed. The walls blurring and changing from stone, to the walls of her bedroom in San Loaran.

Suddenly, he was behind her, his hand gripping her neck in one hand and her arm with the other, keeping her still. *Shit!* She was supposed to be fighting him! She hadn't done anything yet.

It looked like her room down to the last detail: beige carpet, light pink walls that her mother had painted when she was a little girl, pink bedspread and a heap of decorative pillows. And yet there was something too still about it.

The curtains to her room were closed, and she had the ridiculous urge to pull them back, look outside and see what was there. It was important somehow. He pushed her down, and she fell to the ground, crumpling like a doll, her strength nothing compared to his.

He knelt behind her, hands steady on her, her whole body beginning to tingle and weaken. He was feeding off of her. Taking the power Lucas had given her, and keeping it for himself.

Again.

Her arms became heavy and wouldn't lift. He lifted her in his arms and laid her on her bed. The familiar feel of her pillow cushioned her head, and the solid weight of her comforter being placed upon her lulled her. Made his using her, harming her, seem almost irrelevant.

She didn't have the strength to care.

CHAPTER

10

Valerie awoke, but this time, she wasn't in the dungeon. She wasn't even in the castle, but back on the rock with Virginia Dare sitting next to her on the ground. She could hear the ocean all around her, feel the mist of the water as the waves crashed against the rocks. Her clothing was damp, and for the life of her, shecouldn'tfigure out how the hell she got there.

"What are you thinking?" Virginia asked, and she put her cheek on her knee; arms wrapped around her legs. It made her seem young and naïve.

"How did I get here?"

"We are Fey. We are Masters of Illusion. It is our greatest magic. When all else fails we still have this. Surely, this is not the first time you have wondered what is real? How you get from one place to another?"

Valerie frowned and sat up carefully. She thought about the events of Fey. Wondering which of them were real and fake. She'd gone from the castle to the cliffs with Cerdewellyn in the blink of an eye. He'd pushed her into the sea, and she'd been hurt, almost died. Only saved by Lucas.

Virginia laughed. "You think he saved you?"

Valerie knew she hadn't said that aloud. How many people could read her damned mind, she wondered?

"We are like sisters you and I. I can read your mind because I am a part of you. Why do you think I helped you, Valerie Dearborn? Not much separates us. Especially not now," Virginia said, and looked at Valerie pointedly. Valerie couldn't help but look down;her hands were covered with vines, almost like tattoos. With a cry, she pushed up her sleeves, then lifted her shirt, seeing them everywhere, thick and black, curling over her entire body.

"Your face? Oh yes, they are there too," Virginia said sweetly, and suddenly Virginia changed, her face shimmering, and she looked exactly like Valerie—the same clothes, same hair and expression, but on her face were vines, almost like scars.

"Make it go away," Valerie demanded.

Virginia smiled at her with Valerie's smile. A downward tilt to the chin, and a quirking of her lips; It was bizarre.

"It's too late for that. You are too far gone. My Cerdewellyn," Virginia hesitated. "He will never love you. Even if you do become his queen."

"Well, I'm damnedsure I'm not going to love him either. You can have Cerdewellyn. I don't want him."

Virginia laughed and shifted back to herself, wearing a pale green ball gown that looked familiar.

"You wanted it. It was once your mother's. She wore it in a play. The play where she met your father. He put it in the attic after she died. After Lucas' vampire killed her."

"How do you know that?" she whispered, heart thudding sickly.

"I know everything about you, Valerie Dearborn. I know you want to escape, and yet," her eyes flashed down to the ground coyly, "I do not think you try hard enough. I think you cannot fathom the idea that your vampire will stay here while you leave. Do you think you can save him? When you know that he has no hope. No desire to escape with you."

Valerie knew she couldn't tackle all those arguments. She stuck with the first one that was easier to answer. "That's not true. He's a fighter. 1600 years and he always wins."

"But he's not trying to escape."

"He's chained to a wall!"

She waved her hand dismissively. "Yes, but if you could free him? Or if I freed him, because it is something that I can do with a flick of my fingers, would he leave with you? Do you know what I think? I think he would take you to a portal and push you free, and then he would stay behind and let Cerdewellyn kill him. I think he is done."

"No," Valerie said. Which wasn't even an argument. Nothing more than a vague denial. A flat refusal to examine the issue.

Virginia sighed and moved, extending her legs out, the dress rustling. Her calf showed, the white stockings underneath tied at the knee with a ribbon. "And then there are your other...companions. Rachel who wants to see you dead. Jack who followed her out of this realm without a single glance back. No hesitation. No concern for your welfare. And yet again, you believe he cares for you. That his devotion to you is as constant as your own.

"Jack and Rachel are gone?" Valerie asked, shocked that it was true. Part of her hadn't believed it.

Virginia laughed, her gaze locked on Valerie, as though trying to show her the sincerity that lay inside of her. "Oh yes. They left a while ago. They were…amorous, and then they left. Do you want to see it? I can show it to you. That they left, and he didn't care to ask whether you lived or died."

"Ouch. You're really going for the low blows."

Virginia looked confused.

"You're being a bitch. Saying things to try to hurt me. Did you have the word bitch back in 1500?"

Her expression turned malevolent, and then it was wiped away. Back to pleasant, sweet and naïve. "Truth is a luxury. What I could have done with the truth had I known it. Had I known that the queen would kill rather than give up the throne. *You* should be grateful. Do you know what she said to me? She said that I was a fate that never was. That was the last thing I heard as I died. But I know the truth." She crept closer to Valerie, her lips shaping each word precisely, delivering them with venom and promise. "I am nothing small and insignificant. I am elemental. I am *raw.*"

She had the look of a zealot on her face. "I am the cold wind that slams the door shut on a winter's night. I am the biting rain that soaks one's flesh, and when I have to be, I am the hurricane that destroys everything in its wake." Her eyes gave her away, showed what she was going to do next—touch Valerie. And it didn't take a genius to figure out that it was a bad idea. She'd tried to touch her before, back in the ocean.

And now again.

Valerie kicked out, her shoe connecting with Virginia's wrist. Virginia cried out in pain, and the world wavered. The rocks disappeared. The ocean grew quiet. And she could see flashes of the dungeon illuminated at random.

"I'm in the dungeon," Valerie said, and suddenly she was. Virginia was nowhere to be seen. And Lucas was staring at her. She stood and walked towards him. "Do you see them?" she asked, almost hysterically.

"What?"

"The vines. Am I covered in vines?" Her voice rose.

"No. I see nothing," he said calmly, as though he were dealing with the lunatic.

She went up to his cuffs and touched the one closest to her. Willing it to open.

"What are you doing?" he asked.

"I have a hunch. This is Fey magic, right? Only Fey magic can open it, and I think there is something in me—" the cuff opened. And she wanted to cry, for if she could open the manacles, didn't that mean she was Fey?

"Quickly, then," he said.

Valerie went to the other cuff and opened it. He moved away from the wall, flashing her a piratical grin. "Give me your blade," he said.

She handed it to him, heart pounding in fear as he grabbed her hand and led her out of the dungeon. She was used to him lacing their fingers together, but he didn't. He held her hand gently, as though he were worried about harming her. As if he'd never held on to someone for dear life and didn't know how to start now.

It was strange, and she wasn't sure why.

He took her up the stairs, down corridors and then to a last staircase where a blue light shone from under the door, moving easily, as though he'd been here before.

"That's it? That's the way out? But, I thought you said I couldn't leave unless I had his blood." Lucas ignored her, walking up the stairs so quickly she struggled to keep up. He threw the door open, and she couldn't help but gasp at the room. It was filled with gold and jewels, priceless pieces of art.

"He didn't lock it?" she couldn't help but ask. Maybe he wasn't a very good villain.

"These are things of tribute to Cerdewellyn. Gifts worthy of his station," Lucas said in an oddly impressed tone. Didn't vampire kings get jewels?

"Go ahead. You go first, and I will be right behind you," Lucas said and gestured towards the portal. Virginia's words came back to her. That he wouldn't go, would let Cerdewellyn kill him.

"Are you going to come with me?" she asked.

A flash of a smile. "Of course."

"Go," he said. "I will see you on the other side." He took a step back as though giving her space and crossed his arms. Valerie took a step forward and paused, turning back to look at Lucas. His expression was...predatory, somehow.

Almost anticipatory.

His eyes a dark blue and close to glowing. She blinked, looking again, and they were light blue, the color she was used to. She studied him from head to toe, heart pounding in fear, suddenly wishing she had that knife back. And then she looked at his hands, and realized what was stopping her. What had been so odd since the moment she'd freed him. He had no scars.

He was watching her patiently. "Go, Valerie. I hear Cerdewellyn. Quickly now." But he made no move to come closer.

"You are not Lucas. What happens if I go through that doorway?" The form of Lucas dissolved, replaced by that of Virginia, who looked at her with an angry sneer. As if she couldn't stand to be in her presence for one moment longer.

"What do you want from me? Whatever you're trying to do, it won't work," Valerie said, edging away from her and towards the door. She tried to think of the common denominator, what Virginia's real agenda was. Choice. She wanted Valerie to make a decision. To agree to things, or to go through the portal. "I have to agree to this," she said.

"I was trying to be nice to you. But you are not interested in my kindness. I asked you the value of your life, and you had no answer. I have an answer. I need a body. I am inside you now. I will take you over, and if you go willingly, it will not hurt."

"Go fuck yourself," Valerie said, and reached for a golden goblet that was on the table. It disappeared before she could touch it. Fine, no weapon to beat her over the head with? She'd find another way. But then the room shifted again.

She was outdoors, at that same stupid outcrop of rock over the ocean that Cerdewellyn had taken her to before shoving her into the ocean. "Do you want to go in again? Do you think that Cerdewellyn's seas still have no life in them after what he has stolen from you and Lucas? You thought you felt monsters before; this time, they will consume you." Virginia's long hair was caught by the wind blowing out behind her in a long auburn stream, two smudges of pink on her pale cheeks.

"This is the end of your time, Valerie Dearborn. Choose wisely." Virginia lifted her hands and shards of rock pushed from the bottom of the ocean, an earthquake shaking her tiny patch of earth. She fell to her knees, sinking her fingers into the ground, and trying not to fall off and into the ocean.

The cliff crumbled, becoming nothing more than a tiny needle of rock in a vast ocean. As the earth continued to shake, more rocks rose up, making a ring around her, like spokes on a wheel with her in the center. And then people appeared on each cliff. Her father, her mother, Jack, Lucas, Rachel, and on the sixth spoke was Virginia.

"Choose one, Valerie Dearborn. Choose your savior."

They were impossibly close. All she had to do was take one small step from where she was, and she would be safe. The ground began to crumble away, so that reaching anyone would soon become impossible. She had to decide quickly. As the ground sunk in, decaying around her, her island of safety shrinking, Valerie didn't know what to do.

"You can trust one of us. The question is who? When everyone you love has failed you, when no one can help you, one of these people can save you. Do you know who that is? I know. Choose and jump or die. Your time in Fey is over." The ground shook again, rock crumbling, sounding like an avalanche.

Who would help her? Who could save her? Was it a trick question? The images of everyone she knew, and some that she hated were stationary. Looking at her soullessly and dispassionately.

Choose?

Who the fuck was she supposed to choose? Her father who had never cared for her? Her mother who was dead, but had loved her? Jack, her ally who would die for her? Rachel, who….no, she couldn't think of a reason to choose her. Or Virginia, who clearly wished her harm. And then there was Lucas. And yet none of them was right. She knew that. Her foot slipped and as the earth beneath her crumbled, she jumped.

Virginia watched as Valerie's mind collapsed in on itself, praying she would not see out of the trap. And she did not. The moment came where the ground fell away from her, where she had to make a choice, and she did...thinking one of *them*, the people she loved, could save her.

Weak girl. None of them could save her. She had needed to be strong enough to save herself.

They were still in the dungeon. Virginia had taken Valerie nowhere, simply created place after place hoping that she would wander into Virginia's trap. Valerie's mind shut down, sending her body into shock. Her heartbeat faltered, stuttering in her chest. She saw the vampire Lucas, who was staring at the ground, look towards Valerie, an expression of horror on his face. Perhaps he heard her dying. He screamed and pulled with all of his strength, futile against the magical bonds.

The tiny scratch on Valerie's arm had been her way inside. Now she took over, filling her organs, her mind; taking her over completely. But she couldn't breathe. Valerie's heart did not start beating. She couldn't give up this body. Couldn't let go of this one chance to be with Cerdewellyn. She tried to gasp, tried to scream. Nothing came from her, from the dead body she was trying to inhabit, only the terrible screaming of the vampire to keep her company.

And then she heard Cerdewellyn's voice as he appeared in the dungeon, lured by the screaming vampire. She felt his touch on Valerie's cooling flesh, felt the thrust of his magic as he poured it into Valerie's body, life cascading through her.

She breathed deep, the sensation of air in her lungs odd after all this time. She made herself do it again.

Breathe. And then it became automatic.

She felt Cerdewellyn's hand on her cheek, stroking her skin. She opened her eyes and gazed at him, letting him see the love she felt, the joy she felt in knowing that she had done it. Managed to return to him.

He frowned at her expression, and she tried to speak, but the coordination was hard, and she moaned instead.

"Cerdewellyn," she tried to say. Not in the flat American way that Valerie said it, but the proper way, so that it sounded like ker-de-win. His frown deepened, and he put both hands upon her face, stroking her cheeks with his warm fingers.

"What happened?" he asked, and Lucas answered.

"Her heart stopped. She should have woken up, but she did not. She is mortal, Cer. You will kill her if you are not careful. You need her."

Cerdewellyn scooped her up into his arms, carrying her out of the dungeon. "That would be a shame for you," he said to Lucas as they left.

Virginia said his name again, and this time got it right. She wrapped her arms around his neck clumsily and held onto him. She touched the skin of his neck with her nose, inhaling his scent. He smelled of the earth and life, like power and magic. It resonated within her, and she clung to him tightly, kissing his neck as he carried her up the stairs. And between one step and the next, he took her to his chamber, placing her on the bed and backing away from her.

"Are you well?" he asked her.

Virginia was thirsty, starving actually, and seeing food in the corner of the room, she stood on her new legs and walked towards it. The girl's clothes were certainly comfortable. If obscene. Her feet were cushioned in the strange and silent shoes. So silent, she could walk and make not a sound. But she did not like the lack of corset. She felt exposed.

She drank the water, ate cheese and bread, and after a moment, turned back around, needing to see his face.

His arms were crossed over his chest, one hand up near his mouth as he looked at her with a careful and closed expression. She took a bite of apple, giving him a slightly wicked smile.

"What is this?" he said, voice taut. He watched her as though she were a poisonous snake.

"It is I," she said, and did not know how to behave all of asudden. He had been imposing for so long, and yet now she was here. He had never bedded her; they did not have the familiarity of lovers or the comfortableness of equals. She had been a child; he had been her world, and to him, she had been...what? Another queen? And so she did not run to him as she had always thought she would, but stood there waiting, feeling sick and out of sorts.

"Virginia?" he asked, coming towards her hesitantly. And then she was overcome with emotion. With grief for the loss around them, for the pain that she had felt for all these centuries, and the death that she thought she would never escape. She ran towards him, throwing herself into his arms.

"They are all gone, Cer. What do we do?" And then she was crying into his hard chest while he held her, his large hand cupping the back of her head. He made shushing noises, spoke to her in the Old Language and promised her...everything. The future, amends, and the only thing that really mattered. That he would never let her go. She couldn't say how long that went on for. His holding her, her weeping. The joy of their being together again. But finally, she stopped, and he gave her some more food and sat her down at the little table near the window, even though it was dark outside, and there was nothing to see.

"What is the time, Cer?"

He sat opposite her and drummed his fingers on the table for a moment. "Time is irrelevant now. My love..." He took a deep breath as though trying to find the right words. "I cannot believe that you have come back. I cannot fathom my good fortune, to have lost everything and have my very soul returned to me. But I must know where she is. What happened?"

"Do you want her back?" Virginia asked, sharpness creeping into her tone.

He shook his head and spoke softly. "You know me better than that. But it can be difficult to maintain possession of her form. So, how have you done it, so we may ensure she does not return?"

Virginia flushed, feeling ashamed at her doubt in him. "She is asleep now. I altered her perception of reality, like laying a trap. She is still here, but unaware."

"Then the danger is in her waking. Do you know her? Can you see her mind and her memories? Her emotions and wants?"

Virginia thought of Valerie, the woman's whole life lying before her. Her childhood, Lucas, her want of another life. "I see it all," Virginia said. "It is like a series of portraits that run together behind my eyes."

He nodded. "Good. Now you must replicate it for her, so that when she wakes, what she sees before her is reality. She cannot question it, do you understand?"

Virginia nodded. "When she awakes…she did us a great service, Cerdewellyn. I do not want to hurt her."

Cerdewellyn reached out, twining his fingers with hers. It made her heart skip a beat. The affectionate look he gave her, the electricity of his touch. "You are tenderhearted, Virginia. It is one of the things I love the most about you. But we do not have the luxury of kindness. You must be wise first, do what is best for you and *us*. And whether it is ruthless or kind cannot enter into the balance."

"Is that hard for you, my love?" she asked, and hoped he would answer her. That their situations had changed enough, he would no longer treat her like a child and shield her. "I am not a child, Cerdewellyn. As you say, I do not have that luxury. There is no time to...wait. Not for anything." He cast her a look from under his thick, black lashes. A knowing look, one that said he understood what she was saying.

"You want to be my queen in truth? You want there to be no more prevarications. My mistakes are ever at the front of my mind. Every mistake I have made is based upon my ego and desire for...chivalry. There is no more time for dreaming like a man, for ruling like a king. I must command like a despot for us to survive. You are my right hand. My true destiny, and neither of us must ever look back."

In that moment, she would have followed him anywhere, performed any task to be worthy of his love.

He stood and came towards her, leaning down, kissing her lightly on the lips. She opened to him, letting her lips part, feeling the light lick of his tongue at her lower lip. But then he stopped, kissed her lightly with closed lips and stepped back. "I want you to prepare for her awaking. Make sure your world is complete for her, so that she does not fight you or try to return." He reached for her hand and kissed the back of it and then turned it over, kissing her palm and then releasing her.

Virginia lay upon her bed, staring at the faded red canopy above her. The last time she had seen it, the fabric had been new, vibrant and beautiful. This was truly a place that time forgot. She did not blame Cer for their downfall, even though he did. But their extinction would stop here. They would rebuild.

The monster who had done this to them was downstairs, at their mercy, and he would get none of that from her. He would pay with his flesh and his tears. Pay with his pain and his terror for the things he had done. She did not want to lay here; she wanted to live. To be with Cer, to punish the vampire.

But first she had to take care of Valerie. The girl who wanted nothing but a normal life. Whatever that meant.

Virginia did not understand the concept but Valerie's idea of it was clear. Why not give it to her? Give her that as a gift for losing the game of life. For not being desperate enough to claim her destiny. She closed her eyes. That was exactly what she deserved.

CHAPTER

11

Rachel opened the door for them, and Jack was surprised when it didn't creak open ominously. This was where Rachel and Marion lived...*together*. It was a surreal moment to be standing here with her. Bound to her. And to be so blatantly reminded that she had a history with the woman who had ruined his life and taken his parents. What the fuck had he been thinking? Or not thinking, apparently.

"The apartment is Marion's. She bought it...before me," Rachel said, voice trailing off as she looked around. Almost as though she were embarrassed too. And frankly, that was the least she should feel. Crippling remorse. Guilt. *Really? Is that who you think she is?* Deep down, past the ever-present lust and need for her, did he honestly believe she had remorse for anything? He didn't even know if she could *have* remorse. Vampires were evil; the earth was round. Those were facts. He had always known that. Lived that. Until now. *Which just makes you a fucking idiot.*

Jack stepped over the threshold and looked around. His stomach was filled with acid, and he wanted to leave. Wanted to undo the last few months of his life. Before Nate died, before this Fey crap, before all of this. His life was turned upside down.

Jack had been ruthlessly in control for years. And now he wasn't. He was at Rachel's mercy. Why had he done this? Why had he chosen *her*? Was this any different than belonging to Marion? He had to trust that it was, and Jack wasn't someone who trusted.

Even Valerie, the only woman he had been close to since the death of his parents, would say he didn't trust her. It was part of the reason they could never have a relationship. The rules were too well-established between them: he was in charge, he would keep her safe, and he knew what was best. Even though he wanted to change that dynamic and let her in, he hadn't been able to.

A dark part of him wondered if he had ever really believed he could let Valerie in, be open to loving her and being vulnerable. Perhaps that was why things had never worked between them. Because it would have had to be a conscious decision on his part, and when it came down to it, he just couldn't let down his guard enough to let her be his equal.

And he was pretty sure that made him a douche.

Now he was chained to Rachel. Forced to be vulnerable, forced into a position of letting someone into his heart so that they had access to his deepest secrets, maybe even his soul. He didn't know what it said about him that the only woman who could get through to him was a monster.

At best, she was cold, and at worst, homicidal. His life would have been easier if he had chosen Valerie. For one, it might last longer. It seemed all too likely Rachel would kill him. The only question was whether it would be sooner or later.

He remembered his papa telling him how he had met his mama. And the look of surprise that had always flashed across his papa's features when he spoke of falling in love with her. It was something that just happened he said, like seeing a rainbow after a storm. Love was something one couldn't choose.

He bit back a laugh. Lust, desire, *something* had hit him, but he wouldn't call it love. His relationship with her had nothing to do with rainbows. It was more like a meteor slamming into the surface of the earth and causing mass extinctions.

The few windows were covered and blacked out. She turned on lights as she passed through the living room, going straight to a bedroom with a giant king-size bed dominating the room. The ceiling and walls were covered in mirrors; handcuffs draped casually on a bed post.

"You've gotta be fucking kidding me," he muttered.

Rachel ignored him, disappearing into the closet. He followed close behind, desperate to see, wishing he didn't have to. He didn't know what to think, and he encouraged the blankness in his mind, suspecting he was pretty close to losing his shit. She opened drawers and boxes, rifling through things, trying to find the gem. After a few minutes, she stood back up, looking at the ceiling like the answer might be written up there.

"Fuck."

"It's not here?" he asked, voice sounding surprisingly conversational. As if he weren't having a crisis on the inside. His hands were shaking so he crossed his arms. He could smell Marion's perfume. It was like she had just left this room.

Eerie and surreal. Jack felt like he might turn around and see her at any moment. The urge to turn around, to know for certain that she wasn't here, just waiting to pounce on him was overwhelming.

"No, it's not here. That's it. There is nowhere else to look."

Jack nodded, turning around, half-expecting to see her in the doorway.

Rachel looked at him sadly. "I'm sorry."

"Why?" he asked, voice guttural. Did she know how fucking afraid he was? Could she have any idea just how horrendous it was to be in Marion's personal space? Would Marion have brought him here if she'd succeeded in abducting him the night she killed his parents? Perhaps he would've died in this room years ago.

Maybe Rachel would've been the one to kill him. He felt hysterical in that moment. What had he done? Was he really tied to her? Part of him wondered if he should just kill himself, do it to himself; it seemed like the final outcome.

Rachel's voice eviscerated him, demanding he come back to the present. "I'm sorry because there is no other choice. I thought we could find it on our own. But I can't. It's not here, and I have nowhere else to look. I have to ask her where it is," she spoke the words quietly, as if she were a doctor delivering fatal news.

He leaned back against the wall, using it for support, so he didn't fall down. He heard her wrong. He must have. "Get her out?" he said stupidly.

Rachel nodded but didn't move closer to him. Thank God for that.

He licked his dry lips, his tongue feeling like sandpaper. "You want to get Marion out...of her coffin, so we can ask her where she left her fucking necklace?"

"If there was any other way, I would take it. I'm sorry, Jack."

"Why?" He gave into the emotion choking him, unsure if he was laughing or sobbing. "Maybe this was always going to happen." This was his fate.

She squeezed her eyes closed. "No. I thought she would be… unconscious when the end came. We'd open the coffin, and you'd stake her. I didn't expect…I have to see her again too."

"Now you can give her a goodbye kiss."

"*Don't.* I don't—" Rachel swallowed hard, eyes wide, as though she was shocked too. What had she been about to say?

He stepped in close to her, demanding she give him her attention. "I'm going to kill her. You promised me. If it doesn't happen…." He was a god damned idiot. There was nothing he could say. They would go get Marion out of her coffin, and she would either kill him, or he would kill her. It was that simple.

CHAPTER

"Don't forget permission slips for tomorrow, and the debate tryouts have been moved from B-1 to the cafeteria. Have a good weekend and don't do anything stupid." There. That was tactful, right? Valerie had a habit of speaking first and regretting instantly after. It was on her list of things to sort out.

Someday.

Her students jumped up, slinging bags over their shoulders as they bolted from class. Conversations started up again, picking up where they left off an hour ago without missing a beat. Val sat back down in her chair, and waited to see if anyone would come up to her to ask a question about the homework or what they had discussed today.

But it was Friday, so no. Although they didn't usually ask on any other day either. They all filed past her without meeting her gaze, as though she might assign them work if they made eye contact.

Val smiled. She liked her job. She really did. Val shut down her computer and grabbed her purse, hitting the lights on her way out. Next stop the gym. And then home to a delicious Lean Cuisine. Again.

She'd managed to run two miles last time. Frankly, she never wanted to run again. And she didn't quite trust these people who said they ran ten miles on the weekend. Were they liars? Should she be lying? Was the endorphin high a myth? Tonight she'd go, run two miles,

Add one minute and see what happened.

As she locked the door behind her, she wondered what would be on TV tonight. Big Bang Theory? A Buffy repeat? If she were lucky, maybe she could find Game of Thrones. Yes, this was her life, and it was pretty good she thought, and then gasped in outrage as she realized she'd parked her car under bird-crap-tree. Her car was now covered in shit. *No,* that's *my life.*

CHAPTER

$\mathcal{A}$s the hours passed, Virginia became more confused about Cerdewellyn. She had spent centuries longing for him and cursing her fate. Now she had been given another chance. No, had taken it, and yet she still was not with him. Where was he? What did he expect of her? If he cared for her, truly longed for her, would he not be here, right now?

And now all she could think was that time was passing. They had spent hundreds of years away from each other, and she was still alone. He was close, two rooms away was all that separated them, and yet she was not with him.

Even the queen was no impediment. Virginia was not a girl who waited. She rose from her bed and went into the hall, its barren emptiness a tragedy. There should be Fey bustling up and down the corridors. Everyone who had seen her had bowed.

There was no one to bow to her now.

The door to Cerdewellyn's chamber was open, the man himself standing at a window and looking out at the world below.

"I want to kill him," he said.

"He deserves it."

"It scares me how much I want to hurt him." He turned to look at her, gaze empty of the Cerdewellyn she loved. This was a hollow shell of him, whatever was animating him now based in darkness. "He is our salvation, my only chance to get back the Sard and have enough power to slay the vampires, and yet I am afraid to be alone with him." He smiled at her sadly, "I fear that I will give in to my murderous impulses and destroy our chance. That is not who I am. He is the impulsive one. Not I. And now here I am at the edge of utter ruin with one last chance to save us, and all I can think about is cutting him open and consuming his beating heart."

She walked to his side and wrapped her arms around him, pressing her ear to his chest. She could hear his heart beating, the intensity of his desires quickening his breathing.

"Soon, my king."

He made a sound in his chest, and she squeezed him tighter. "This world is almost empty of magic. I may never find the Sard; in which case, the only power I will have, is what I siphon from him."

"Does he know where the Sard is?" Virginia asked.

He pulled away from her, not meeting her gaze as though he were ashamed. "I have not been able to do more than ask him. This world is so weak that I fear that if I leave it, it will collapse. I need you to help me, Virginia." He came back towards her; expression filled with pain.

"Anything," she vowed. She was filled with joy at the idea of helping him, becoming more his equal.

"I need to know once and for all if he has the Sard. I need you to take his strength and stay here, so that we do not lose this world. Your presence will keep it alive."

"Where will you go? What will you do?"

He kissed her lightly on the forehead. "There were Others who stayed behind when we came to this new world. I need to make sure for myself that they are gone. And perhaps one of them will have left some clue as to the location of the Sard."

"But it's dangerous," she said, and instantly regretted it. She could see his features harden, knew she had pricked his pride.

"I'm not so weak that you must fear for my safety like a child loosed from its mother's skirts."

"No! That is not what I meant, and you know it." She reached up to kiss him on the mouth and his jaw, desperate to show him that she did not think of him as weak. She still saw him as perfection, as her God, even there was no one else to worship him besides herself.

She felt his hands on her arms, the strength he so carefully kept in check as he began to set her away from him. She made a noise similar to a sob, emotion overwhelming her. "No Cer, please! I am sorry. So sorry. It is only us; I love you. I swear it!" She found herself crying, and he stopped, wrapped his arms around her instead and pulled her close, sheltering her in his embrace.

"It is all right, Virginie. We will find a way back from this. I swear it to you." She would not let him go again. She would not be put off again. He was hers, and he would be hers—*now*. After several minutes, she composed herself and pulled back, looking up into his omnipotent gaze. Truly, he seemed to be more than her. More beautiful, more powerful. Different and above her. *But mine.*

He inclined his head, an invitation to tell him what she was thinking. She didn't know where to start. His eyes moved over her face, from lips to eyes, and then he squeezed her hand in encouragement. Unaccountably, she had an urge to cry again.

"This is not how I thought it would be," she said.

"You are here. It is wondrous in our eyes. That is all you need think upon." He leaned in and kissed her gently on the lips.

She had been demanding he lie with her when the queen attacked them. It had been all she had wanted in the world. Like a fool, she had spent days planning the perfect way to make her dreams come true. She had worn a thin shift, one that would show her body when it was wet, let her hair down because he had always liked her curly hair...*but this is not* my *hair.* On the outside, she was someone else. Could he love her enough to see beyond the exterior? To remember who she had been? Perhaps he preferred Valerie Dearborn's olive skin and dark eyes. Her larger breasts and...she could not think that way. There was no point.

She blinked back tears.

"Virginie, my heart. What is wrong?" he murmured, lips trailing up her cheeks to her tears. He kissed them away and pulled back, licking the last hint of them from his lips.

"I love you. That is all. I am...grateful and beyond amazed that we can be together. But...it is so selfish." She shook her head, the words stuck in her throat.

"What?"

She stared at his doublet, at the fine gold stitching that edged the collar, unwilling to look into his face as she told him her petty problems. They were the only ones left in all of Fey, and she was worried about something utterly trivial. "You look at me and... this is not me. This is *her.* Another girl. And I wonder...when you take me to bed, finally, will you see her or will you see me?"

"Always you. You are the most beautiful girl I have ever known."

"No. I know that is a lie." Annika had been beauteous beyond wonder.

"You do *not*. You are my queen. My destiny. A balance of souls. The exterior does not matter. It is you I see. You I saw for hundreds of years as I thought of my failure. That I did not protect you." He dropped down suddenly to his knees and took her hand in his, pressing the back of her hand to his forehead. As though he didn't deserve to touch her, and expected her to stop him at any moment. He looked up at her, and her heart broke to see him; his strong features, those penetrating eyes, shining with tears. "I failed you. I failed everyone and everything. I am so sorry, Virginia. Sorrier and filled with more shame than you could ever know."

She sank down next to him, wrapping her arms around his neck, squeezing him fiercely. He did not hold her back, seemed too aggrieved to respond with affection. "You did not fail me. And it does not matter. We are here now. We are together, and we can start again. We will take from the vampires, eradicate them all, and then we will begin again. The Fey will return, Cerdewellyn."

He drew back and stood, holding out his hand to pull her up. "My queen does not belong on the ground."

She let him pull her up, but gripped his arms as though he might try to run away from her. "You are honorable, Cerdewellyn. A good leader, and a gentle king. Ruthlessness is not in your nature, and that should not be a cause for shame, but joy. It is only because of *his* ruthlessness that you must change. You know your mistakes, and you are changing to fix them…" Words failed her.

His voice had a rough edge to it. "Not being ruthless is a weakness. It is shameful when it means I cannot keep my people safe."

"I will be ruthless for you," Virginia said, and she meant it.

Cerdewellyn laughed. His hands came up and cupped her chin, his words low with promise and devotion, "I swear to you that I will keep you safe. That no one will ever harm you again. That I will do anything, to keep you." And then he kissed her, hard, his arm around her waist as he pulled her close. He kissed her deeply, and she wrapped her arms around his neck, trying to push her doubts aside. It didn't matter what she looked like. It mattered that they were together. That he loved *her.*

The kiss slowed, gentled, and he pulled back from her with reluctance. She could feel his desire for her, and a part of her could not believe that the time had finally come where he would take her. And yet….

She frowned.

"Virginia," he said in a low tone, demanding that she tell him what was wrong.

"I am sorry. But, this, this is not me. None of it. I look in the mirror, and I see her. I speak, and I sound like *her.*"

He made a noise deep in his throat.

"No, I am dead. Maybe that is the truth, Cerdewellyn. I am dead, and there is nothing for it, but to accept it."

"So maudlin all the sudden. Why, my heart?"

She looked up into his bottomless black eyes, and knew she had to tell him. No matter how stupid or embarrassing. She had to tell him. "It won't be me. The girl you take to bed and perform the right with. I will be her. Do you love her? Do you want her? Expect your children to look like her instead of me? With her dark skin and hair."

"I do not see her. I see you."

She shook her head. She wished she could believe him, but she knew the truth.

"Come." He held out his hand, and she had no other option but to take it. He led her towards the mirror. "You are Virginia Dare. You are the one I waited for. The one I grieved for, and now you are back. Because you were strong enough to fight for us. You are not her." His head descended, lips making the barest contact along her neck. She shivered and felt the shudder all down her. Felt her body open, ripen, and wanted to lean against him, offer herself to him. He was her king, her protector. Her destiny.

"You did not give up. And you shall be rewarded. The king of the Fey is not without resources."

His fingers traced her cheek, slid into her hair. And as she watched, her face changed, shifted from Valerie's to hers. Her hair color changed to a lighter brown; her eyes lightened to her own mossy green.

"Your beautiful hair, Virginia. I always imagined it, what it would feel like sliding down my body."

She shivered. Was transfixed, as his hand slid down her neck, the color of her skin changing before her eyes. She'd had a tiny mole on her neck, and it showed up as his hands slid past. "Change all of me. My legs, my arms, my chest—all of it Cerdewellyn."

He gave her a faint smile and did what she asked, both of them watching in the mirror as her body changed and shifted, illusion overcoming everything, so that nothing was left of Valerie Dearborn. The last to go were the clothes. Indecent, exposing clothes, made of rough blue fabric that showed her bottom and outlined the front of her body. Her clothing was replaced with a dress, her own. Light pink with black satin trim.

She stopped his hand on her stomach, lacing her fingers with his, heart beating with the triumphant sound of destiny. "No Cerdewellyn. No clothes. Not now." And she turned in his arms, bringing her mouth to his, absorbing his kiss inside of her, hands restless on his chest, wanting to touch, feel, and be with him. She was making up for lost time. For all the things she would have done had she known that her life was about to be cut short.

But now she was back, and she vowed that nothing would ever keep her from Cerdewellyn again.

CHAPTER

14

Virginia felt Cerdewellyn slip out of bed quietly, heard him moving about the room, preparing himself to go back to the mortal world. She watched him through sleep-laden eyes, enjoying the sight of his strong body before her. She wanted to pretend that everything was fine, at least for a little while.

As Valerie did. And look what it got her.

Cerdewellyn stood before her in unrelieved black. "I will go, and when I come back, we must know for certain if he has it. Can you do that?"

She smiled at him, even blushed. Could she torture the vampire who had ruined their lives and make him talk? "Oh yes, I do not imagine it being a problem at all," she said, and then he kissed her and left.

Virginia dressed and ate a plum and some bread that was in the dining room. She was too nervous to eat much, and eager to see Lucas. As she walked through the castle, saddened by the signs of decay and loss, she couldn't help but think of the woman whose body she now inhabited. She had needed a body and Valerie, well;

the woman was confused and weak. Valerie didn't deserve everything she had been given, and didn't appreciate the gift of life. Virginia did. She dressed in her own clothing, a robe to ward off the chill, and went down to the dungeon, needing to see her foe.

She would kill him. Not today, but soon. Her king would have his vengeance, and if she could be the instrument of it, then that too was just.

His head was bowed as she entered the dark dungeon. She used magic to light the torches, hearing them splutter to life with a whoosh. He raised his head, and she was struck by the intensity of his gaze. *He is a predator.* It was the first thought that came to her mind. She knew he was confused by her lighting the fire and displaying magic. Knew that when he looked at her; he saw Valerie still.

How could meek Valerie have kept company with this monster? How had she wondered if she might be in love with him? Nothing human looked out of his cold eyes. "What is wrong?" he asked her. She almost jumped at the sound of his voice. It was dark and beautiful. "What happened?" he said, unable to take his gaze from the robe, knowing that she was naked beneath it. Did it disturb him to think that Valerie had lain with Cerdewellyn?

She frowned. He saw her as Valerie. Not as Virginia. Had Cer made the illusion for her alone? And if so, why? But that was something for later. She was here to be ruthless.

"You do look imposing," Virginia said, her voice was soft, light and musical. She ignored his question. What Lucas wanted was irrelevant. "Certainly fearful. But I had always imagined you would be regal. You are not regal. You look like a filthy beggar," she said drawing the words out, wanting them to echo in his mind. There would be no misunderstandings. She studied him as though he were subhuman. "Someone I would have crossed the street to get away from. If Cerdewellyn was in chains, covered in filth and beaten like you, the world would still know him for a *king*."

She saw his gaze sharpen; lips flatten as he studied her. "Valerie?" he asked, and she thought she detected his unease. She closed her eyes and reached out, touching him with the empath's power that remained in Valerie's body. She heard him hiss and retreat, mentally staggering away from her.

"Your heart courses with fear," she said flatly.

"What is this?" he asked and looked beyond her. "Where is Valerie, and why do you pretend to be her?"

"I am Virginia Dare. I am Queen of the Fey. Valerie Dearborn is gone."

She felt him reach out, psychically touching her, almost tasting her, in an effort to understand what was happening. "Where is Cerdewellyn?" he asked.

She smiled at him, huge and radiant. Then her look turned coy. "You do not treat with Cerdewellyn. Not now, and not anymore. I am the one who will save us. And I will use you to do it."

"Where is Valerie?" he growled at her.

"Here," Virginia said, hand raising to her head. "Or here," she said and touched her heart. "She is not dead, but she is…away. And this body is mine now. I am Virginia Dare. Know my name, for you will say it when you die."

His expression was so filled with menace, that even though he was chained up and could not hurt her, she had to stop herself from moving back a step. "I do not deal with you. Leave her body, then go and fetch your master."

"Cerdewellyn is…sleeping," she said, letting him infer what he wanted. She saw his face go pale, felt the shock run through him; that Valerie's body had indeed slept with Cerdewellyn. His grief and horror rolled out of him like a wave, but his expression stayed calm. Such control, she thought, and she knew that the control would have to go. She would break him.

"I wanted to meet you, Lucaius. I have heard about you from everyone. You are the bogeyman I was told stories of when I was little. And Valerie, she talked of you too. I find it ironic that I must thank you for giving me this life. If it had not been for you, I would not be here." Virginia wanted to touch him, wanted to cut him open and see inside of him, open his mind and rape out every memory, abusing it and him so that he was nothing but a shell: partial payment for all the wrongs he had ever committed.

But patience was something she had learned. She had grown up watching Cerdewellyn, learning from him, how best to behave. *Patience.*

"Tell me what scares you, and I will make it real,"she whispered, as though she were a courtesan asking him what filthy things he fantasized about. "I will punish you for the world. For my Cerdewellyn and the death of my people. For the death of the Others, and even for Valerie and the hurt you caused her." Virginia stepped close, extending her hand, ready to touch his chest.

"Touch me and I will bite your hand off."

She grimaced as though he had told a bad joke. "You cannot harm me. You are in too deep with the empath's blood. Soon I will own you. You will not even be able to speak against me because I will have such a tight hold upon you."

Lucas laughed at her. "You think you have won because I drank her blood a few times? You know nothing of me and my strength."

"I know that I will take it. I know that I will make you drink my blood over and over again, and that a vampire is susceptible to empaths. That with repeated blood exchanges, the vampire can become enslaved. I know that I have you tied up in a dungeon with the ability to go nowhere. And I know that you will not hurt me. Not this body…not *her*. She did not know how you felt. But I know. As someone who has loved their entire life, I know. Hurt me and you hurt her. Kill this body, and she is gone forever. You would not do that even if you could."

"What did you do to her?" voice low and strained.

"I ate her," she laughed as his jaw clenched, "Not literally, but in every way that mattered, I have consumed her. Her body, her spirit, everything. She was very sad, Lucas. You weakened her. She did not have the strength to fight. I think she was relieved. She is buried deep inside of me, six feet below the surface and…happy. For she has left her reality behind."

She watched in satisfaction as he pulled against the cuffs. As if his reaction was to physically fight her words. She withdrew a knife from her robe. Wickedly sharp and honed to harm. Silver to burn. She showed it to him, and before he could blink, she slammed it into his stomach.

She withdrew the knife, twisting it as she pulled it out, and he grunted, then gasped. "Does Cerdewellyn know you are down here playing torturer?"

"He cannot harm you. He promised your empath." She smiled chillingly. "But I have made no such promise. Where is the Sard?"

"I do not know," he said, and his body tensed for the pain that was surely coming.

"I will rip you open," she said dreamily. Virginia trailed the sharp points of the knife down his chest, leaving a narrow trail of his own black blood on his skin. "Shred you from the inside out. One day I will. I will make you pay for what you have done to me and mine. To Cerdewellyn, and all who have been cursed enough to encounter you. But for now, you may live. While Cer keeps his promise to Valerie, while we have need of your strength. I cannot hurt your body, not really, but we do not need your mind. You should think about what you have done. The people you have harmed and the lives cut short. How many people have you killed?" she asked, conversationally.

She didn't wait for an answer, but continued talking, tracing her fingers through the blood on his side, absently. "How many were never born because of you? You do not understand the gravity of your wickedness. But I can show you. Let's start at the beginning shall we?" And she raised her finger to her mouth, sucking his blood, activating the bond between them and sliding into his thoughts.

The dungeon receded and became the outside world. A frozen landscape filled with snow. She brought forth his memories, and it was as if they were real, happening to him now. A village…he remembered it.

It was the first village of Others he had found. He had been a vampire for less than five years. His feet trudged through the snow to the first hut, smoke curling out of the chimney. He drew his sword, felt the rightness of what he was about to do, and the desire to kill. Slaughter. That was what she wanted him to see, to live again, every face he had killed throughout the years. He sliced deep through a man's shoulder and felt the pain of it in his own skin.

Lucas screamed in agony.

Virginia's words came to him from a long way away, as if they were carried on the cold wind around him. "It is not real.

It just feels real. The beauty of it is that I can still torture you, but you will not weaken. There will be no marks, no loss of power, but you will still *hurt*. Not enough. Never enough. But it's a start," she said.

He watched her leave, walking away from him, the dungeon falling from view as he was washed away by his past, death after death soaking into his mind, coursing through his body and crunching his bones. And all he thought, as the tears flowed, and he cried out in pain, was that he deserved it.

~

Valerie felt sick.

She was sweating and clammy, and she felt as if something bad were about to happen. Like the world was about to end, or she was about to die. She took a deep breath and went to the air conditioner, trying to make the classroom colder.

Her students were taking a test, and after that she could leave, go home and do what? Freak out in private? Have a panic attack or scream hysterically?

The bell finally rang, and she went home; the sense of fear, dread and pain, consuming her. She lay down on her bed and was glad for the dark. She didn't remember closing the curtains, but she must have. *You must always keep the curtains closed,* she thought and didn't question it.

She closed her eyes, and a vision, like a flash of lightning, sizzled behind her eyes. A man: tall, broad-shouldered, golden and beautiful. He was shirtless, covered in blood; body bowed outwards as he screamed in pain. His hands were fisted, and tears coursed down his cheeks. Her sense of wrongness and fear increased so that she wanted to scream or cry—suddenly willing to do any thing to make it stop.

She jerked upright and turned on the light. It wasn't real. It made no sense. She needed to get her shit under control. Go to the doctor and get some Xanax. She could just imagine what she'd say—she felt panicky, and when she closed her eyes, she saw the hottest man ever, bleeding and half-naked; being tortured.

Had she suddenly become a sadist? Read too many kinky S&M novels and this was the price?

She got up and walked to the windows, ready to open the curtains and let some light in.

Suddenly, she was in the kitchen. *What am I doing here? What am I looking for?* Valerie went to the cupboards, opening it up, hands shaking. She must have come down here for water. That was the only explanation.

She grabbed a mug, and had an urge to throw it, to take everything out of that cupboard and destroy it, smash the whole house to pieces. She gripped the mug tightly, so tight her fingers whitened, then went and opened the back door, walking out onto her patio.

"Don't do this. It's insane," she muttered. She lowered the mug, breathing deeply. She was a sane person, right? "Except for the talking to yourself, you're great," she said aloud.

All at once, the feeling of wrongness and pain—that she was failing someone—came back and overwhelmed her. With a scream she threw the mug, watching it shatter a few feet away from her.

It wasn't enough.

She ran back inside and grabbed more glasses and mugs, taking as many as she could carry in her arms. She began throwing them, smashing them all to pieces, bits of glass and pottery stabbing her in the calves. Her lower legs were covered with blood, and she stepped backward, went back into her house and started to cry.

CHAPTER

Lucas had no idea how long the memories had gone on for. Hours? Months? Hundreds of years he had relived for some unknown period of time, and his voice was gone. He'd screamed it out long ago. If he hadn't been chained upright, he'd have fallen. He could barely think. All he knew was death, and that he was the cause of it.

He heard Valerie's steps on the stairs, and had a moment of irrational hope that she was back. That Virginia had lied, that the whole encounter had been some kind of ruse. But when he saw her, he knew the truth. It was Virginia come to see him, and Valerie was gone.

She smiled at the dried blood on his skin and his lost expression. She chuckled when a shudder ran through him. She was wearing different clothing. A sapphire blue dress and he decided that was an indication that time had passed.

"I like your tears," she said and touched his cheek with her finger. "It is time to drink. You drink my blood, and I will drink yours." She held Valerie's wrist out towards him. His heart thundered; his mouth was dry, and his head pounded as if someone were striking it with an axe.

He needed blood.

He needed to stay strong.

But every time he drank Valerie's blood, they became closer. How many more times could he feed Virginia and stay himself? Not become a total junkie, or have her so rooted into his mind that he would be nothing more than her puppet?

Maybe the next time.

Maybe it is already too late.

His eyes were closed, and so the pain of her blade at his neck came as a surprise. She sealed her mouth to his neck and drank his blood for what seemed like a long time. Everything about her was familiar but different. She stood differently, touched him differently. Even her scent was different. In a way he could not define and did not want to.

Valerie's wrist was in front of his face. A small gash parted her skin, and red blood glinted in the light.

He felt himself at a crossroad, and wished that he felt sensible enough to look left and right. But his mind and his emotions were in upheaval. As if they belonged to somebody else. Someone desperate and frantic. Someone who would rush across the road and hope to make it rather than look around them.

The scent of *her* blood turned away his restraint. This was Valerie. This essence and sweetness. This lightness and purity. What was there that was worth fighting for if Valerie was gone?

The answer was simple: Nothing.

If Valerie was not here, then he wanted nothing. He'd been dying, fading away out of boredom. Losing time for decades and all he'd felt was relief. Valerie changed that. She was fresh, exciting, funny and caring. So caring and emotional, that he had wondered what it was like to live that intensely. He'd wanted to warm himself by the fire of her soul, and now that chance was gone.

Time had had no meaning for him, and so he had dithered. He should have acted sooner, given himself more time to be with her. The weight of his mistake brought him low. He was not thinking. He was only feeling.

And so he drank.

The power of her blood washed him away, left him open and defenseless. He heard her laugh, felt her inside of his mind, preparing to harm him further, wondering what the best way was. He wasn't fighting her. He was open, waiting and vulnerable. She spoke again, but the words meant nothing. Time meant nothing. Her hold on him was everything. Lucas felt himself falling, shattering to pieces—and then his world changed.

CHAPTER

$\mathscr{A}$s Valerie stepped out the door of her classroom and locked up, she saw James, the science teacher, coming towards her. He was tall and handsome, and he seemed to like her, which was nice. *It should be more than nice, right?*

"Are we still on for Pinkberry?" he asked, his keys already in hand.

"Yes. But I'll meet you there. I've got to run a few errands afterward," she said with a distracted smile.

At Pinkberry, Val ordered coconut yogurt with strawberries and kiwi on top. She also decided to 'go big' and ordered this strange chocolate sauce that had crunchy rice bits in it. It was waxy and weird, yet strangely addictive.

James ordered watermelon yogurt and then paid. Maybe she should have stopped him from paying for her. He was always asking her out, and although he was cute…he just didn't do it for her. Whatever 'it' was.

But he was nice, and she thought she was supposed to want a nice, dependable guy to ask her out. Should she tell him she was insane and see if it scared him off?

They sat at a table near the door, and Val looked around, goose bumps rising on her arms. She had the distinct feeling that someone was watching her. *I'm just paranoid.* She tried to ignore it. It was probably because she was on a diet. Convinced that everyone knew she was blowing it with the chocolate sauce.

James reached out and touched her hand. "Earth to Val."

She couldn't help but look over her shoulder again. *Still no one looking at me.* And then a man came into the store. She hadn't seen that part; she'd looked up, and it was as if he'd appeared out of nowhere.

He was tall and...godlike. Too attractive to be walking into a normal store in San Loaran. He belonged in a photo shoot. His hair was blond and thick, his shoulders broad. And he was ridiculously tall. And that jaw...hard and square. She wondered what it tasted like, how it would be to kiss his skin.

Her heart jumped as she looked at him, feeling a certain connection, almost a recognition. He was staring at the yogurt shop in shock. As if he were an alien that had just been placed on earth and had no idea where he was. Admittedly the décor was a bit loud. Lots of neon colors and white retro chairs and tables. Then he saw her, and he took a step forward, then checked himself and looked around again. Val jerked her gaze away; no need to ogle the beautiful man. Until his back was turned, then she'd ogle.

James was saying something, and she wondered what the hell it was. *Cars.* He was talking about cars. Val snuck a glance back at the gorgeous guy. She didn't know anything about cars and didn't want to. The man was walking up to them, and Val felt herself filling with panic at the sight of him. *Panic? Is that how little I get attention, that a beautiful man looks at me, and my first reaction is to panic? Pathetic!*

She set the yogurt down on the table and waited, staring at the white surface. Maybe he wasn't coming up to them.

He is. And he's even better up close.

"Valerie." His voice was deep and had an accent. He said her name as if he knew her. Laughter, a little bit hysterical, rose up inside of her for no reason. She bit back a giggle and knew she was blushing like a moron.

She looked up and into his pale, blue eyes and forbidding expression, and whatever she saw in those depths wiped the laughter away from her. She had the oddest feeling that she knew him.

"That's me," she said and waited. Was he a parent of one of her students? He looked young to have a high schooler, but there was a certain hardness to him, a weight and presence that made him seem like he'd lived a long and hard life. It belied his age. If she had to guess, she'd say 30. Maybe he'd had a kid at 15? While it wasn't impossible, somehow it just didn't seem right.

"What is this?" he asked, arctic gaze flicking from her to James and back again. But it was barely a question. More like an accusation.

"You mean the yogurt shop?" she said, confused by the question.

"No. This…" His nostrils flared as he exhaled hard. And then he turned and looked at James. James stood, as though he couldn't meet a guy like *this* sitting down. His inner caveman demanded he stand.

"I'm sorry, do I know you?" Val asked. *I wouldn't forget you.* He laughed, and it sounded bitter. It raised the hair on her arms, made her feel like she was suddenly in an electrical storm, and everything was crackling around her.

"You heard her, who are you?" James said, sounding slightly belligerent.

The stranger ignored him, attention honed in on Valerie. "Your life is in danger. You are toying with death by being here. And what about Jack? Will you let him roam the world tied to Rachel?"

James cut in, "Are you threatening her? You need to leave or else I'm going to call the police." Val felt the breath leave her. What was he talking about? Who was he?

"Who are you?" she asked, and felt a buzzing in her ears like she might faint. *Jack. Rachel.* Should she know those names? They flew around her mind like they were familiar. Birds with razor-sharp wings that sliced open her mind as they tried to escape the confines of her skull.

"You know me. You know my name. Do not play games, Valerie Dearborn, or we will all perish."

"Oh, Jesus!" James exclaimed, and he held out napkins towards her. "Your nose is bleeding. Are you all right?" Val blinked and looked down, blood dripping all over her shirt. The buzzing turned into a steady ring, and she put her head down on the table, hoping that if she fainted, she would stay in the chair and not fall on the ground.

And then everything went dark.

∾

Lucas looked at Valerie in horror, heart pounding in fear. This was his fault. But seeing her here, knowing that she was alive, his first impulse had been to walk up to her, take her into his arms and kiss her.

And then he'd seen the man she was with. It was clear that he cared for her. Where the hell were they? He could hear some part of him screaming, knew that Virginia was torturing his body, and yet he felt as if he'd left that behind. His immortal coils, as it were.

Valerie was alive. Some part of her was alive, and their connection still held. That knowledge made him feel strange, almost breathless. Valerie's eyes were closed as she rested her head on the table top, blood pooling in front of her, dripping off the white table and landing on the ground. This was not simply a nosebleed. He grabbed the napkins from beside Valerie, shoving the man out of the way and tried to stop her bleeding.

She was limp as a ragdoll, unresisting as he tilted her head and pinched her nose. It could not be a coincidence. Remind her of the past and have her bleed all over the table and pass out.

Was it internal? He had a sudden fear that she might be hemorrhaging, and wondered if they should call an ambulance? Wait. That didn't make sense. This wasn't reality. Sure it looked like reality, felt like reality…but this was a mirage. An illusion.

But he did not know what the consequences would be if she died here.

His hands were covered in bright, red blood. His heart started to pound for another reason, human emotion making him feel shame and disgust at the blood lust that would hit at any moment. She was dying, and he would want to drink her blood.

Any moment now.

Wait. He should be feeling it already. But he was not. Lucas jerked backward, tripped over a chair and fell to the ground. Which hurt!

Hurt?

The situation was utterly bizarre. A quick survey of the shop showed that the workers and customers were frozen, as if this were a movie halted. They all stared at Valerie but did not move. And Valerie was still sitting at the table, unconscious, blood coming out of her steadily while the room around him began to darken.

As if he were at the theater, and this was the end of the act.

"Valerie!" he yelled, and the response was pain.

Sharp and close.

A knife slicing through the muscle of his arm greeted him when he returned to reality. Valerie was gone and Virginia stood before him, still wearing Valerie's flesh. She held the blade in her hand and smiled at him. His body felt flayed alive.

Then Virginia hunched over, one hand at her head as if it hurt, and the other covering her face. The scent of blood hit him, blood lust rising within him sharply. Blood dripped through her hands, coming out of her nose and even her eyes.

"Cerdewellyn," she called weakly and then again, in a louder voice as she dropped to her knees.

Cerdewellyn appeared from nowhere and went to Virginia, dropping down next to her, forcing her to look at him. "It hurts," she said with a whimper.

"What happened?" Cerdewellyn asked her.

"Nothing. I don't know. I was here and then there was just… pain. It is coming from her. I can feel it." Virginia started to cry. "What if she comes back? What if I can't keep this body?"

Cerdewellyn pulled her close, and he could hear the man whispering in Fey, telling her she would be all right. At least, that's what he assumed Cerdewellyn was telling her.

"Once I have the Sard, no one will be able to harm you. Your body will be restored to you, and we will start again. I am close, my love. Come and rest for a while. He is not going anywhere."

"I can make him tell me where it is. I just need a little more time," Virginia whispered.

Cer kissed her on the forehead. "Of course. Tomorrow. Hundreds of years we have waited. What is another few hours? You must stay strong so that Valerie does not awaken and fight you." And then he scooped her up and carried her out of the dungeon, ignoring Lucas utterly.

Tears coursed down his cheeks unbidden. In fact, he hated himself for it. It made no sense to be emotional in this situation. How did people do this on a daily basis? Live and function while their feelings were just waiting to consume them. It was dreadful. He turned his attention to what was important.

Valerie was alive. He had found her once, and he could find her again. It was also clear that what hurt Valerie also hurt Virginia. There must be a way that he could use that to his advantage, but how?

He suspected that Virginia knew nothing of Valerie's little world. He thought of it almost as a bubble, a little place somewhere inside of her where Valerie was...living? Hiding? Recovering? Perhaps even regrouping so she could make a return.

He didn't know, couldn't even guess, but the fact that she had almost died, that the world she had created for herself began to crumble as soon as he forced the truth on her, worried him. Mental pain caused physical harm.

And she knew nothing of her past. So what was she doing? Was it a defensive mechanism that her mind had created to keep Virginia from taking her over? And a scarier thought, one he did not know how to deal with, what if she had just run away?

What if that man who'd been so concerned about her and eaten sweets with her was what she really wanted. Human, boring and in love with her. If that was what she truly wanted, how would he ever convince her to come back?

CHAPTER

17

Virginia returned to him all too soon, coming back for more blood and his strength. She tortured him, made him weep, punished him for his past and his mistakes; but he never went back to that place, that nirvana, where Valerie was.

He did not know how to get there. And as the days passed, and he became more and more dependent upon the empathic blood—he wondered if he had imagined it all. Perhaps he'd never seen Valerie at all. What if seeing her again was something he had wanted so dearly that he had lived a fantasy.

Virginia was becoming stronger, using his power, her own, and undoubtedly Cerdewellyn's to gain strength. All he had now were the moments she appeared. If he became free and she called him, he would respond. If she sent him nightmares, he would dream. His chance at free willor freedom was almost gone. The only chance was to get Valerie back, but he did not know how he had gotten to her before. He'd been…abused by Virginia, more vulnerable and susceptible to pain than anytime since. The shock that Valerie was gone had left him defenseless in a way he had not been since. Was that the answer? That he had to succumb to the worst torment, let her plunder him and break him down, in order to get to Valerie?

There was an unfortunate element of justice to it, if that were true.

A terrible idea took shape in his mind, the rightness of it making him feel light-headed even as fear made his limbs tremble. Virginia had no pity within her. She wanted his death, and he could see the desire for it shining out of her eyes with the brightness of love.

Do it. Do not be weak now. And yet he did not want to say it. He wondered if he would survive what she would do to him if he told her his weakness. If he opened himself up, became unable to keep her out.

He did not know if it were the only way to see Valerie again. His only chance to bring her back. And then a moment of recklessness and peace overcame him, as if he'd been touched by the hand of God and offered a way to salvation.

The truth was that it did not matter if he saw Valerie again, for that was what he wanted. One as wicked as he, had no business wanting things, or aiming for his own self-interest. He would do this, because sacrificing himself to try to get Valerie back, was the right thing to do.

Virginia was humming, touching him lightly, almost petting him as she contemplated what torture to inflict upon him next. It took him two tries to get the words out. "I can give you the keys to my soul."

Virginia rolled her eyes. "I have that. I have your memories, have subjected you to pain after pain. I already own you," she said and ran her hand down his cheek possessively. Did Cerdewellyn know how much time she spent down here, torturing him? The thrill she got from it?

Lucas caught her gaze, saw her breath catch. "You are young, so let me inform you about remorse. We all have it. But it is unequal. You make me relive things that were wrong, and I feel the physical pain of it. But the emotional toll…I did not care for those people. I weep for them, but those memories will not destroy me. But everyone, even the worst villain, has something that will destroy them. Some memories they cannot survive."

She tapped her finger against her lip. "What you are afraid of the most? Your grief? Why would you tell me that?"

"You do not need my reasons."

Virginia smiled coyly. "Very soon I shall have them anyway. Whether you tell me or not. Did you love her? Is that why you are giving up?"

"I am dead. I do not love." *Is that what is happening? Am I giving up?*

She squinted at him. "You are lying to me. You think to trick me somehow."

"Vampires do not love, not really. We desire, and we covet. We become infatuated and jealous, but it is not love. If I were…mortal, I believe I would love her. The secret to my soul? The reason I have killed for centuries? Vengeance. For my family. My wife and daughter. My son. All of them were killed by vampires. I vowed that I would avenge them. That is what set me on my path of destruction. Not hate, but love."

Her eyes glittered like twinkling stars, and an anticipatory smile quirked her lips. She did not care for his motivation; all she wanted was to cause him pain. He looked down at Valerie's wrist and felt fear slide through him.

Fear.

Lucas bit deep and swallowed. The time for regrets and hesitation was over. Lucas felt her thrust inside his mind and gasped at her strength. He could feel her in his mind, ripping through doors and breaking windows into his soul, all the time looking for it, plundering, and wanting to find that last door, the final one that he had held so deep inside of him that he'd forgotten about it.

He was nothing.

Lost.

Virginia pawed through his mind, and his every instinct was to fight, to build up his mental walls and keep her out. Shield himself from her attack. Snarl in return and declare war.

But he didn't. Lucas left himself open, used every ounce of willpower he had to let her do what she would with him. She reached that door and opened it, filled up the cavity of emptiness inside of him. He saw his daughter, Anna, flash by him, saw her joyful smile and blond curls, and it made him flinch.

"It is true," she said, and he heard the satisfaction in her voice. She was like a murderer in a house at night, pausing, listening for the slightest sound, wondering if she had gotten them all. He was the last survivor. He was the faint sound in the dark, like a child's plea, begging to be spared. She found that innocent version of him, the good man he'd once been, and she studied him curiously.

And he heard her clear as a bell, as she passed down judgment upon him. "That is the totality of your soul, Lucaius Tiberius Junius. The moment of your grief that you never healed from and that stalks you like a pestilence. You grieve for your children. Who are so distant that no one would know their names, could find no hint of bone or flesh. Have you thought about that, Lucaius? How time treated them when you were the one to carry on? Beautiful, strong and deadly. Each and every day you became more so, and every day they were lying in the dark, underground, decaying, and they did not know what had become of you. The monster you let yourself become. From the moment they were born to the moment they died and became nothing but earth. Think of all the things you could have done differently so that they might have lived. Live it, Lucaius. Live it until breaks you."

Lucas was there: He could smell the closed up room and smoky fire where his daughter was born. Hear her first cry, and how small and light she was when he held her in his arms. The soft skin and blue eyes. Love surged within him, followed closely by pain and grief. He could see it all, feel it all, and he wanted to leave, and he wanted to stay more than anything in sixteen hundred years.

They aged and grew before his very eyes. Happy and loving, and all the time the danger was coming closer, looming and growing in the shadows…And then the night came where they died. They were in their beds, and he saw them die, felt the dirt under his fingernails as he pawed through the earth and laid them to rest. But this time was different. He didn't get up and walk away, didn't become a creature of the night, soulless and savage, determined to slay every creature he encountered until the world was safe again.

Instead, he stayed there, buried in the earth with them. He saw the bugs come for them, saw their clothes disintegrate, saw them return to a state of dust, and she made it last, made their loss go on for an eternity. A torture even he would have shied away from.

"I liked that," she said from very far way, and he smelled his own blood on her breath, as his mind and body pitched. "I want you to do it again." And she set it up, from start to finish, his children being born to the moment they were beyond ruin, until Lucas wanted nothing else but to die, to have it stop. He would have given everything to make it end.

But he had nothing left to give. Nothing to fight with, no means of defending himself because he had given every last piece of armor to *her*. So she could forge it into a weapon and stab him deep. His lips shaped Valerie's name, wanting to say it, hoping he wouldn't forget that he'd made this gamble for a reason. But his children caught him with dead arms and kept him in the earth with them, stole his words and his senses, his plans and his memories.

His children lay back down in the earth and took him with them, holding him there with nothing but grief, as the bugs returned, nibbling away, growing strong on his children's death. And he cried, and he prayed, for the first time in hundreds upon hundreds of years—Lucas prayed to die.

~

Valerie stumbled to the faculty bathroom and splashed water on her face, wetting a cloth and going into one of the stalls. She put the lid down and sat, body trembling. She wanted to cry. She wanted to scream. She closed her eyes, and she saw *him* again. The mystery man who had shown up once before.

You know me, he'd said.

You toy with death, he'd said.

Then what was his name if she knew him so damn well? Valerie put a wet paper towel against her forehead.

Death.

She could see him, trapped behind her eyes. See him in a dark dungeon and chained to a wall, but he wasn't screaming anymore. He was limp, body fallen forward as though he were dead, and that was too much. It made everything impossible, made her want to rush out into traffic and end it all. Which was insane. And so she sat here instead, hoping to get herself together, hoping to make the panic end.

I have to help him. That was stupid. He wasn't real. He wasn't being hurt, and he wasn't dying. *It's just a symptom of being crazy. Just a little unwell like the Matchbox Twenty song.*

She didn't know him, all she knew was this—school, her house and how none of it felt quite right.

But he's mine, she thought irrationally, and she found she was crying. You know me, she thought again. His voice accusing, demanding of her. You know my name. Did she? Did she know his name? Did she know him?

He was hers and he was in pain, and she wanted him. Wanted him here with her, wanted to save him. *Dammit.* Her nose started to bleed again, blood coming fast and steady. She grabbed toilet paper, but kept bleeding through it. She could die here, she thought suddenly, and she wouldn't see him again.

You know me.

You know me.

You know me.

She let the blood fall, gave up on trying to stop it, and thought about him, about what she knew, what she'd seen. "Lucas," she said, and felt as if a spike were driven into her brain. "Lucas," she called again, voice getting weaker.

"You're mine," she said, and the floor rushed up to meet her as she started to convulse.

CHAPTER

*J*ack's heart pounded, and he felt sick. No, he felt like a kid again. One who was defenseless. Helpless. *Fuck that.* He wasn't helpless. Jack heard a noise, the barest scrape of sound, but it took him back to his childhood, made him feel like he was there all over again, being carried by Marion, the way her bony shoulder had dug into his stomach and ribs, the sound of her skirts as she carried him slung over her shoulder.

Oh God.

And then he had a peculiar thought. Peculiar because it was clear. It cut through the paranoia and the terror that were swamping him. *This is the moment you've been waiting for your whole life.*

Vengeance.

He had dreamed about it and sacrificed for it. He'd given up Valerie, given up life and love. He had isolated himself from everything, in hopes of getting close enough to kill Marion. And now it was here. His big chance.

It's about fucking time.

Rachel was staring at him, hands on her hips, head cocked. "Look Kujo, I know you're ready to slaughter and run, but we have a purpose here. We have to get the information. Killing her comes later."

Jack crowded close to her, knew he was vibrating with anger. He hoped she felt it, like ants crawling on her skin. He wanted her to understand every word as if he were shouting it at her. "*She* is mine." His voice was gravel, scraping the lowest register.

She swallowed, dropped her head. "I know."

He grabbed her chin and forced her to look at him. "Promise *again*. Promise now that we are bound, and I can feel your sincerity."

She looked into his eyes, and Jack wasn't sure what he saw there. If she were being honest or not. She was either good for him, or she'd kill him. He prayed his baser instincts had chosen right. That for some damned reason, he had seen something worthwhile in Rachel and that it was *real*.

She nodded jerkily, licked her lips, voice thick. "I promise. You can kill Marion when we get the information that we need."

His shoulders drooped, tension flooding out of him. He stepped closer to her, putting his head on her shoulder, resting his forehead against her neck.

She shivered.

"That's not the hard part. The *decision* is nothing. Now we have to do it," she said.

"Funny," he replied, lips brushing the column of her neck. "That's the only part I feel confident about. What comes after, I have no idea. But killing her...I know that part."

He drew back, saw her lashes were wet with tears. "I'll get her...up, and hopefully she will tell me immediately."

"Make her tell you," Jack said, as if it were the easiest thing in the world.

Rachel smiled. "One doesn't *make* Marion do anything. Marion is her own entity. Twisted, crazy and stubborn. She doesn't mind pain. If she doesn't want to tell me and laughs when I try to hurt her—don't underestimate her. I don't want to get into some long drawn-out bullshit about why you are with me. She's suspicious and smart."

"So, what am I supposed to do?"

"Man the door. Make sure it stays locked."

"Won't they just materialize in?"

"No. It's warded. Lucas had the witches do it centuries ago. No one can come in without breaking down the door. And it's a big fucking door. Lucas didn't take any chances. *Fuck*. Okay. I have to go in. The sooner we do this, the sooner we can...forget about it." He wondered what she had been about to say. Move on? Was she afraid to say they would move on because it implied they would be together?

"I want you to say nothing. Be weak and cowed. Like I beat the crap out of you in places that don't leave marks."

Because she undoubtedly did that. *That's my girl,* he thought harshly.

"Won't she ask about why I'm here? She will know it's for revenge."

She gave him a quizzical look. "No, she'll think you're my bitch. Bound to me and under my control. She won't be expecting the, 'You snacked on my parents. Now prepare to die approach.' Okay Inigo Montoya, let's go." She opened the door and switched on the light, illuminating the dark room with harsh florescent light that added to the morgue vibe.

In the huge stone room sat a single coffin, wrapped in silver chains.

"Table for one," Jack muttered, really not wanting to go into that room and get close to that coffin.

"Yeah, Lucas isn't big on second chances. You're going to need to help me unwrap her. I can't touch the silver chains," she said and grimaced.

It bore repeating. "You want me to...unwrap the woman who slaughtered my parents?"

Rachel scowled. "Yeah. That's what I want you to do. It's no big deal," she said with an airy wave.

"If you don't see how fucked up this is—forget it." Jack blew out a harsh breath and moved closer. "There's no padlock," Jack said, and pulled on a chain, the sound echoing off the stone walls as the metal hit the ground. The noise startled him, and he wondered if he should try to be quieter.

"The silver chains were symbolic. More for my torture than hers." He wondered if Marion could hear them. If the noise had woken her up. Or maybe she was already awake.

Rachel put a hand over his and squeezed gently, careful not to touch the silver. The irony of the moment was not lost on him. Here he was, digging up his parent's murderer to set her free. The last loop of chain slid to the floor, and Jack couldn't stop staring at the unwrapped coffin. It looked new and had flowers carved into the top of it.

"Why the flowers?" he asked, needing a moment to steady his nerves.

"Lucas got it on discount," Rachel said, and then she looked at him with a scowl. "How the fuck do I know? It's probably part of his flair for the dramatic. Okay, stand back. I'm going to crack this baby open like an oyster. Come on this side; stand next to the wall behind her head."

Jack walked around the coffin. How many steps was it? Eight? But he felt his shoe touch down with each step, heard the small noises of his footfalls blaring in his ears like gunshots. *Fuck.*

Rachel sighed, and then with one hand, she grabbed the lip of the casket, ripping it off and throwing it aside. Jack bit his lip to keep from making some kind of noise. This was happening too fast. He could see into the coffin. See Marion laying there, eyes closed, looking like a corpse. As though she had fought a long illness and hadn't survived.

Her collarbones jutted out in harsh relief. Rachel brought her wrist to her mouth, biting hard. Jack thought he heard the flesh tear, and it made him tense. Made his world narrow down like he was in a combat situation, surrounded on all sides and waiting to die.

This is really fucking happening.

Blood dripped over the white satin interior, a drop landing on Marion's jaw. Then Rachel's wrist was over Marion's closed mouth, forcing her lips apart. Marion swallowed instantly.

Ravenously.

Jack jerked back a step. As though his legs were trying to escape, whether he wanted to or not. He saw her heart beat once and then again. She was so thin he could see the pulse of it under her skin. He wanted to stake her. He'd burn anything that was left even if it were just dust. Just to make sure she never came back.

"Now you," Rachel said, and withdrew her arm from the coffin.

He couldn't move. "I can't," he said hoarsely.

"You can and you will. Give me your wrist," she commanded, and he responded. He *had* to obey that tone. He walked forward despite himself. Rachel cut his wrist with her teeth, and he held back a sound of distress, felt her tongue on his flesh as she swiped at the wound, the lick oddly reassuring.

Then she pulled him closer, so his wrist was above Marion's open mouth. Her eyes were still closed, but there was such a sense of impending doom, that he knew she was close to wakefulness.

"How much?" he asked through a fog. When he was little, his Papa had given him a Jack-in-the-box, and he had hated it. He'd hated waiting for that stupid puppet to jump out at him. This was a million times worse.

"Not too much. I don't know what effect your blood will have on her. His blood dripped on to her mouth for several heartbeats, leaking in grotesquely.

"That's enough," she said and let him go. He took a step back, unable to be so close to her. "If she doesn't wake up in a minute, we can try it again, but I don't want her to be too strong. Your blood might be different now, because of the bond. Plus, you're a werewolf."

"Different how?" he asked numbly.

He heard Marion say softly, "It tastes like magic." She sat straight up, as if she had hinges instead of bones. She took in a shuddering breath and then looked around her frantically, eyes filling with tears.

"I'm in a coffin! I don't want to be in a coffin! Get me out, Rachel. Help me!"

Marion reached for her, and Rachel leaned in, letting Marion wrap her arms around her neck as she scooped her out of the coffin. Rachel carried her to the corner of the room, and he knew the exact second Marion spotted him. He felt it inside of him like a ghostly touch.

"Fear," Marion said. Then she smiled, the action making her skin crinkle like old paper, and for one horrendous second, he thought her skin would split open.

"I'm thirsty. Bring him to me."

Rachel stroked the hair back from Marion's face. "Not yet, my love." She sounded tender, and Jack noticed that she was crying, holding Marion tightly. Like she loved her. Rachel was lying to one of them. But who? "We can't drink him. Lucas ordered us to leave him alone," Rachel said, lying to her.

"Lucas," Marion whispered, filling his name with venom.

Rachel nodded. "He's willing to let you out. He made me an offer, and I accepted on your behalf."

Marion blinked at Rachel in confusion. "Why would you do that?"

"Because he was going to kill you, and I couldn't let that happen. I love you," she said, and kissed Marion on the lips.

Marion smiled and looked fondly at her, raising a weak hand to brush down Rachel's porcelain cheek.

"Lucas wants the Sard," Rachel said, voice sounding loud in the small chamber.

Marion frowned. Scooted back a little, and almost fell off Rachel's lap. Rachel tightened her grip, holding her close. "No. It's mine. He gave it to me. Why would he want it after all these years?" she paused and took a breath, then asked slowly, "How long have I been away?"

"Not long."

Marion looked down at her lap, smoothed her hand down her silk dress. "Why does he want it?" she repeated.

"I don't know. He just said that if you gave it to him, you were free."

Marion nodded, slowly. She looked up at Rachel with emotion in her eyes. Love, trust and something else. Maybe sadness. "He gave it to me to bring my Margaret back. He has never wanted it for himself. Where is he? He loves Margaret. He just needs to be reminded."

Her smile was tremulous. "We will go get it and take it to him. Then you can convince him. If you go empty-handed, he will be angry. We cannot give him an excuse to send you back into that coffin."

Marion gasped, "I can't! I cannot survive in there."

"I know." Rachel kissed her on the lips. "Where is the Sard, my love?"

Marion blinked a few times, as though she were processing the question. "The Paris flat," she said quietly.

"I looked there," Rachel said. Marion flicked a glance at Jack as if he were the only unpleasant item of food left in a barren cupboard. Alarm bells went off inside of him, but he stayed still, trying to do what Rachel wanted.

They left the room and went to the antechamber. Rachel took Jack's hand, and he saw Marion track the movement, a frown on her face. "We will meet you there," Rachel said. Rachel and Jack disappeared. The three of them appearing in Rachel and Marion's Parisian love nest at the same time.

Marion sat down on a blue velvet couch. Her cheeks were pale as a sheet. She patted her limp black hair. "Call down and get me a snack, dear. Any delivery boy will do. Or girl." She looked at Jack. "I'm not sexist, you know."

He couldn't speak. He hated the sound of her fucking voice.

Rachel was standing near the fireplace looking tense.

"And make me a fire, will you?" she said to Rachel, but her gaze was fixed on Jack. Not just her gaze he thought, but it was as if every fiber of her being was attuned to him, and was examining him for weaknesses, strengths and signs of treachery.

After all of these years, Jack had thought that he had grown, left the past—if not behind—then locked away deep inside of him. But seeing Marion, having her close enough to touch, having her words directed at him with such cool hauteur, smashed open that dark place inside of him and made his life a living annihilation.

She would destroy him.

She did not believe them.

He knew it.

"It's boiling outside," Rachel said, throwing up her hands in disgust.

Marion shuddered, the move exaggerated. "It's cold, my love. I want to ward off the chill. It must be from being stuck in that coffin for so long. Please?" Marion pouted and slumped back against the couch weakly.

The fire was already set, and Rachel took the matches off the manteland bent down, lighting it easily. The room was all pale purple and gray, except for the blue couch in the center of the room. Beautiful and modern, but cold.

So cold.

"Marion, tell me where the gem is and let's get you free. Then we can work on everything else," Rachel said, still kneeling down by the fire.

"I'm already free. What's the hurry?" she said petulantly and reached behind her, pulling a gray silk blanket off the back of the couch and arranging it around her.

He feared Rachel paused a moment too long. "Lucas said he wanted it immediately. He won't wait."

Marion arched an eyebrow. "*Now* he's impatient? Just like a man. Does nothing for centuries, and then suddenly we are supposed to jump and do his bidding. Fine," she sniffed, "Bring me my jewelry box."

Rachel pursed her lips and frowned. They had looked there. Was there a hidden drawer or something? Jack shifted on his feet.

"Send your wolf out. I don't want him here if I can't eat him."

Jack clamped his jaw tight. He wouldn't screw this up. Rachel nodded at him, and he moved towards the door. How far should he go? When should he return? Rachel was already out of the room, so he couldn't ask her.

He had to walk past Marion to reach the door, only a few feet between them. Her voice caught him, stopped him in his tracks "She gets bored you know. I see that she's interested in you. But what we have…love, death, passion—it's a once in a lifetime bond. And I mean *my* lifetime, not yours. You are a passing fancy, and the day will come where she won't want you around, and then we can finish things, all right? Maybe we can go back to that sad little hotel your parents owned. I'm very nostalgic that way." She rubbed a finger along the coffee table as though looking for dust; Jack apparently dismissed from her mind already. "I'm glad the maid kept up with things. How long was I in there anyway?"

She waited for him to speak, the moments spinning out, until finally he cleared his throat and managed to respond. "Not long enough."

She shrugged. "It felt like longer," she said flatly. "Terrible hunger. Now leave. Let me go through my things without an audience that wishes me ill."

He walked past her, out the door and down the hall. He wouldn't leave. He couldn't, but standing here, waiting for something to happen, for Rachel or Marion to come and get him, for one of the three of them to die...

It was almost over. His big moment was almost here. She would die. He just had to hope she didn't take him with her.

CHAPTER

19

Valerie hit Save and leaned back in her chair, rubbing her eyes because they burned from staring at the computer screen for so long. Who knew teaching required so much computer work? Tiny numbers on a tiny screen dealing with big kids.

"So this is where you work," she heard a deep voice say, and her breath caught in her throat.

It was him again. The beautiful guy who'd accosted her at Pinkberry. Who'd bolted when she started bleeding. And now he was here. *Leave it to me get the most gorgeous stalker ever.*

Unless he really was someone's dad. Why did she dismiss that? Assume that his interest was for her, in particular? His skin seemed darker than it had when she saw him in Pinkberry. As if he'd been outside all weekend. And he had the faintest crinkle lines near his eyes that made hot men seem wise and as if they enjoyed life.

But the eyes themselves, and maybe even the set of his mouth, were not young. They were cop eyes or war eyes.

Haunted.

His voice was soft. "You are staring at me."

Val blushed and looked away. How mortifying. Although… how could she not stare? Dark jeans that fit very well, and an army-green T-shirt that clung to his arms obscenely.

"I am…surprised," she said and laughed nervously.

"I am glad to find you," he said.

"Should I call security?" she said half-joking. Maybe he was a stalker, but if he was, the cops would make an exception. They'd say 'lady, count your blessings and ride this one out.' She was suddenly distracted by the idea of riding it out.

Then she realized he'd said something. "Uh, what?"*Nice.*

"Why would you call for security? Are you in danger?" He had turned so he could watch the door as if something might come barging in.

"Because of you! I would call security because you are here… stalking me?"*That probably shouldn't have ended as a question.*

He flinched. "You said you did not know me."

"I don't." And now she was confused.

"But you would call security. You are afraid of me?" he asked and crossed his arms, one large hand covering his mouth, as though he wanted to protect himself from her answer, or what she might say. He had beautiful fingers. Tanned, the nails trimmed, but the tops of his hands were laced with scars.

She knew she was staring, but couldn't stop looking at the white tracery of scars. He looked familiar. But that was ridiculous. She wouldn't forget him. No one could forget this guy.

"I'm not afraid of you. Seeing you makes me feel…ignore that. So, really, why are you here?" she said, having no idea what she might have said. Seeing him made her feel a million different things, and she wasn't sure she could describe any of them accurately.

"I am here to see you," he said, and leaned back against one of the desks. He crossed his legs at the ankles as he reclined there, and she looked away from him, shuffling papers around on her desk.

"Yes, but I don't know *you,* and you don't know *me,* and so it's as if you're following me, and that makes you—" What if she said a weirdo, and he was? What if she said a weirdo, and he wasn't? What was the etiquette here? Val shrugged, having no idea how to finish the sentence.

He made her feel uncomfortable. A little bit scared, very unsure of herself and…hurt. Something about him made her feel sad. And there was a part of her that wished she had never seen him, had been able to forget.

Her hands started to tremble, and she thought she might puke. "I need air," she said and stood abruptly, almost stumbling to the door. He put an arm around her, pulling her into him as he supported her and led her out of the building. A bench was just outside, and he sat her down, kneeling in front of her. He looked up into her face, so close she could see every eyelash, see the flecks of brown and gold in his pale blue eyes.

"I am sorry," he said with such feeling that it was almost comical.

She chuckled. "It's not your fault. I'm sure you have this effect on all the ladies."

He looked down. "I am only interested in your reaction to me. Please…give me a chance to—" he broke off mid sentence and looked around as if there was a cue card somewhere, and he'd forgotten the lines. His hand lifted as if he would touch her face, and then he frowned.

"Do you believe in second chances?" he asked quietly.

The change in conversation threw her.

A little brown bird was hopping along the ground, picking up potato chips some kid had dropped. Lucas spoke before she could answer. "There are many things in life we cannot choose, many things that get decided for us or…decisions that are poor, and I want every decision that I make with you to be the right one. So, if I have disturbed you and upset you by showing up like this, then…" He shook his head, brow furrowed. "Then, I will leave. I suppose I will just leave." He sounded very uncertain of himself.

He looked at her face, studying it for a long moment as if he were memorizing her. "I will leave you here. To the life you always wanted. I want you to be happy, Valerie." For some reason, his words brought tears to her eyes. He seemed so sincere and so far from threatening that she didn't know why she'd had such an odd reaction to him. He wasn't scary or worrying. Wasn't mean or even a stalker. He was…vulnerable.

But it didn't explain what he was doing here, why he talked to her as if he knew her, or even the odd conversation they were having. And they weren't in the same league. They were playing different sports, really. He was too handsome, and Val conceded that she could bump up a few rungs to quite pretty with the right bra and make-up, but…he was not for her.

She couldn't help but look down at herself. A cute top, a boring sweater, black dressy pants and flats. It wasn't the sort of outfit that made men ask women out.

"Did you really come here to ask me out?"

"Yes."

"And you're not a crazy person?" she asked. *Cause he'll confess, genius.*

He looked confused. "No. I have a lot of experience with crazy individuals, and I can assure you that I am at least sane."

She felt her stomach drop to the floor as she said, "Then, all right."

He stood up straight, and she had to look up at him since she was still sitting on the bench. His gaze narrowed as though he were waiting for the axe to fall. "All right *what?*"

"All right, I will go out with you."*Because I feel as if I've known you my entire life. I feel as if there are unfinished things between us.* And in a way, even though he made her feel so many emotions from happiness to rage, from loss to desire, there was something about him that was more real than anything she'd felt in her whole life.

He moved his hair back from his face, and she thought his hand trembled a little. "All right. Good. Well then. Let us go," he said, and he extended his hand as if they might walk off into the sunset.

"Now?" she asked. He gave her a slightly boyish smile. The smile transformed him. It should be illegal. It would cause women to crash their cars, was a menace to society. "Oh, geez."

He looked at her quizzically.

"Nothin'. I...uh...let me go shut down the computer and lock up."

He followed her back to her classroom, and she knew he was absorbing everything. As if he were trying to learn about her by studying her things. His gaze lingered on a Disneyland snow globe she used as a paperweight.

"Are you a Disney hater or something?" she joked.

He looked startled. "What is a Disney?"

She squinted at him and pursed her lips. He was joking, wasn't he? "Disneyland. Or movies. You were staring at Mickey Mouse like you wanted to kill him."

"I was? No, I was thinking how very little I know of...this place."

"Where are you from? I noticed the accent," she said and closed down her Excel spreadsheet. Boy was Miss Stewart going to be unhappy when she learned she'd have to repeat tenth grade history. But that was a problem for Monday. Tonight, she was going on a date. Her stomach fluttered, and she wanted to giggle inanely.

"Europe."

"That narrows it down to a continent," she said with a smile.

He took a deep breath and paused for a moment. "I was born in Austria...but it has been a very long time since I have returned to that place. I have a home near Prague I am quite fond of. Have you been to Prague? Or Italy?" he asked, and Valerie felt as if it were a loaded question.

She met his intense scrutiny. "Yeah. I went backpacking after high school. I love the history of it all. You know, you go to these places, and it's like...maybe it sounds stupid, but it's like the energy of all these people who have lived before us is still there. I wonder what things must have been like back then."

"When, specifically?" he asked her. As if he could tell her the differences in minute detail if she narrowed the time frame down.

"Are you into history?" she asked.

"I feel like I have lived it," he said voice deadpan.

She stood up, put her bag on her shoulder and looked around, making sure she hadn't left anything behind. On her desk was a mug, her favorite, and it said, 'Be the kind of woman that when your feet hit the floor in the morning, the devil says, "Crap, she's up."'

It appealed to her in an odd way, not just because it was amusing, but because it meant a determination to get stuff done and raise a little hell. *Yes, Valerie, because teaching, the gym and a future of cat-hood really raises the roof.*

He held out his hand and gestured towards her bag. "Shall I carry that for you?"

She was startled by the chivalrous gesture. "Oh, no, it's okay. It's just papers and a few books." She patted the bag that hung near her waist and looked towards the door. "Shall we go?"

He nodded.

"Um...*where* should we go?" she asked. She had to look away from him because she was blushing. It was just so strange that a guy like him wanted to go out with a gal like her. But that also kind of depressed her. Every girl has the fantasy of the hotguy falling for them when they're just a plain Jane. But it doesn't happen in real life. The Brad Pitt's of the world always traded up.

"You have a home?" he asked, the picture of innocence.

She jerked back a little. "What? I'm not taking you to my place! I don't even know you."

He looked uncertain. "I meant...*oh*, I see." He blushed, which was charming. "No, I did not mean that. Where I come from, it was customary for the woman to cook a meal for the man, and I assumed you would do that. I was not trying to invite myself into your home for...other things." He looked back at her with a small grim smile as if he were waiting for something. Some sort of recognition.

"So you weren't trying to get me into bed, you just wanted a free meal? Do you like Lean Cuisine?" Valerie asked, trying to turn it into a joke.

"What? No! I apologize. It has been a very long time since I courted a woman."

"Courted?" she said, laughing at his odd word choice. "Since when—1950?"

He shrugged awkwardly. "1950, 1750, the point is that it was a long time ago. Perhaps you can choose, and then for our next… outing…I will do some research into modern dating practices…" He gave her a pained expression and cleared his throat.

Modern dating practices? It was kind of funny. Who talks like this, she wondered. Maybe that was why he was single. He was a social disaster.

"Are you a scientist or something?"

"No. I have always found science fascinating, be it alchemy or even psychology, but…" He didn't finish the sentence that would give her any more information about what he did for a living.

"Oh." She really didn't know what else to say. Speaking to him was confusing. There seemed to be an undercurrent to everything he said, and she felt as if she had to puzzle out his every sentence. *Maybe you just sleep with him for his body and don't let him talk.* "How about mini-golf?" she said brightly, trying to get her mind out of the gutter. "Call me crazy, but I suspect you have yet to be introduced to the joys of mini-golf."

He frowned sternly. "No, I know nothing of that. But if it is something you enjoy, then I will be happy to mini-golf," he said it like he was were spelling the words out in his head. They walked to the parking lot, and she couldn't help but ask, "Do you have mini-golf in Austria? I didn't see it, but I wasn't looking. I just assumed it was one of those things they had everywhere. Like McDonald's."

His response was enthusiastic. "I have eaten at McDonald's. It is a fascinating production process. Truly revolutionary."

Okay. "Let me guess, you're a quarter pounder kind of guy," she said. He squinted at her, and she wondered if she was just as confusing to him as he was to her. Maybe it didn't matter. If he wanted to keep talking to her even though every conversation was like two ships passing in the night, she'd let him.

"That's me. The car over there. Blue Highlander." He searched the parking lot, looking at the cars, and his gaze seemed to settle on a blue truck two rows over.

"A car," he murmured under his breath.

She laughed. "I know you've been in a car before. Europe is not that backward. Here we go." The door beeped as she unlocked it, and she thought he jumped a little.

He shot her an odd look. "Europe is very civilized. And of course, it would be very odd if I had never been in a car before."

She could feel his eyes on her as she opened the back door and put her bag inside, almost as if he were memorizing how to open it. Which was ridiculous. She reached for her door, and he jerked into motion, grabbing the handle and pulling lightly, then harder, so the door opened and she could get in.

She sat down and looked back at him curiously. "You can shut the door now," she said, trying to soften the command with a smile. He grimaced and closed the door gently before walking to the other side and getting into the passenger seat. He leaned forward, peering out of the dash. "Only a sheet of glass separates you from the world," he murmured.

"I suppose that's one way to look at it." He ignored her, still staring straight ahead. "Are you going to put on your seatbelt?" she asked. She didn't want to order him to do it, but she wouldn't go anywhere until he did. A friend of hers from high school had died because she hadn't worn her seat belt.

He looked confused. Val patted her chest, pulling the strap away from her chest, so he could see it. His eyebrows rose, and he tried to turn in his seat, looking for the seat belt and where it started, rather than just reaching over his shoulder like a normal person would have done.

He was too large in her car, his knees blocking the glove compartment. He was slumped just a little so that he didn't hit his head on the roof. He clicked the seat belt into place and smiled at her.

"All right. You may make it go now," he said, sounding ridiculously pleased with himself. She couldn't help but smile. He was charming in a hapless sort of way.

She started the car and he took in a deep breath, pressing his back deep into the seat. She looked behind her, putting the car in reverse and backing up. As she turned back to face the front, she noticed his eyes were closed. And he didn't look peaceful. "Are you all right?"

His eyes popped open and he turned towards her, his eyes dark and very blue. "Of course. This is nothing. People ride in cars every day. I am sure it is not particularly dangerous." And then he laughed and shook his head.

"What's funny?" she asked, pulling out of the parking lot.

His laughter stopped, and he was white-knuckling it; his hands braced against his thighs as he watched the streets go by. "It is...*odd* to be concerned about my longevity."

"Hey! I am a very good driver."

"I am certain you are," he said sincerely.

"You don't drive, do you? You must be one of those people who grew up with good public transportation so you never had to learn."

He nodded slowly. "I must, mustn't I? And a small village deep in the countryside. It was very backward and slow to modernize," he said, as though it were very important.

"Okay. So, if you don't get stuff I shouldn't be surprised, is that what you're telling me?"

He cleared his throat. "I suppose I am."

She had to bite her lip to stop from laughing. He was just so... weird. But cute. "What brings you to California?" she asked, and the thought made her sad. Sure she didn't know him, and having a conversation with him was like wading through Jell-O, but she liked him. Not that he was the sort of guy one settled down with, but still.

When he didn't respond instantly, she said, "Business or pleasure? Like vacation?" Just in case he didn't know what pleasure was. Now *that* would be sad.

"It feels like a vacation. But I suppose I am...following a dream," he said seriously.

"Are you an actor?"

His brows slashed down. "No. Why would you say that?" He sounded offended.

"Um, well, you've got presence, like stage presence, and you're so...you know." Oh God, it wasn't a big deal to say he was handsome. It was obvious. But, it *was* a big deal to be so flustered by his beauty that she couldn't even comment on it. She blurted it out, knowing that the words were far from casual. "Because you're so good-looking."

Now he did smile at her. A truly radiant and happy smile, his teeth white and even. "It is nice of you to say so, my Valkyrie."

After that, Val wasn't sure what to say, and so they drove in silence for a bit. She pulled into the mini-golf parking lot and instantly knew she'd made a huge mistake.

"So this is it," she said as they got out of the car. Lucas was staring up at the faux-castle with its plastic flags on the pretend battlements with an inscrutable expression. Probably trying to come up with a way of saying 'this is really immature and beneath me' without being offensive. It really was a pathetic attempt at a castle. A castle, arcade and mini-golf center in one.

He was so out of place in this environment that she felt like an idiot for bringing him here. "You know what, this might not have been a great idea. In fact, now that we're here, I'm quite confident this was a terrible decision. This must seem so lame and childish. I have no idea what my thought process was."

"I have made far worse," he said and put his hand out to her, wanting her to hold his hand. She did it automatically, and it was only when he gripped her hand, then laced their fingers together as they crossed the parking lot, that she realized how odd it was. Holding his hand? He was a stranger!

"I feel as if we should have gone to a nice restaurant or a museum instead."

He looked down at her, his height a little imposing. He was standing close to her, and a sudden breeze meant that she could smell him, that undefinable scent of male and cologne. He closed his eyes for a moment, as though he enjoyed the breeze and turned his face to the sun. It made her stomach flutter in a pathetic and girly sort of way. His voice was soft and affectionate. "I do not care where I am, so long as I am with you."

Wow. That's quite the line. She suspected that chicks with stronger panties than her had fallen into bed with him on that one. At the counter, she told the teenage clerk she wanted mini-golf for two. She reached into her purse to pay.

"Wait. I believe I have a wallet," he said and reached into his back pocket. He smiled triumphantly when he pulled it out, and she couldn't help but smile back; his grin was infectious.

"Did you think you'd left home without it?"

"In a manner of speaking," he said.

She shrugged and let him pay. "I'll get dinner."

He looked at her arrogantly. "No. You will not," he said, tone brooking no dissent.

"Why do I feel like I have just seen the real you?"

He blinked owlishly, and she knew by the press of his lips he was waiting for her to explain.

"You seem like someone who gets what they want, no matter the cost." They walked out to the golf course, and the sound of rushing water greeted them. There were noisy fountains and golf-ball-eating-ponds, which competed with the noise from the freeway. Lucas peered at a tiny windmill, walking around it as though it were a work of art. "This is a very small windmill," he murmured, sounding perplexed.

"Yes, and *there* is a very small saloon," Val said, pointing at it with her golf club. *What the hell was I thinking?*

"So I use the club to hit the ball into the small doors?"

"Yes, through the small doors. Where the little people live," Val said, struggling to keep a straight face.

"Now you are mocking me," he said, voice sexily low.

Val bit back a smile. "I might be."

He held out his hand for a ball. There was a blue one and a pink one. She gave him the pink one to see what he'd say, but he didn't seem to care.

"This is the first hole?" he asked, and walked up to the small strip of green AstroTurf and put his ball down on top of the divot to keep it from rolling away. Valerie watched Lucas as he squatted down, ogling his thigh muscles and the curve of his buttock. She realized she was staring, and that he was watching her out of the corner of his eye. "Some things do not change."

"Huh?" Val asked, and felt herself flush. Was he referring to how she ogled him?

"The children and their squabbles," he said, glancing over to apair of boys with anger management issues who were chasing each other, clubs raised.

"Do you have siblings?"

His mouth opened for a moment, as though he was going to say something and then stopped himself. "No. I do not."

"Oh. Me either. I think that's why I've always wanted a large family. Because it was just me, you know?"

"So you want many children?"

Whoops. Way to scare him off, Dearborn. But what was she going to do, lie? She did want kids. If he didn't, best to know now. "Yeah, I do. What about you?"

"I do not think of it overmuch. It has never been a possibility for me," he said absently.

Was he infertile or something? "Oh," Val said, not knowing what else to say.

His attention came back to her. "Oh, I see. No, I did not mean I was *incapable*." He rubbed the back of his neck as though the subject was awkward.

And it was.

He seemed to be searching for the right words. "Let me say… historically, I suppose… it was never something I would consider. There were other obligations."

"What? Like work or family?"

"Work," he said flatly.

"So what do you do?" She lined up the ball and gave it a smack, watching as it just missed the ramp up into the barn and a hole-in-one.

He rubbed his temple as if he had a headache, and she wished she hadn't asked. She was trying to think of something to change the subject to when he answered. "I have had many jobs. But none of them were particularly fulfilling."

They walked closer to one of the fountains, having to pass it to get to the next hole, and she missed the end of his sentence. "Did you say you help families?"

"No I said it was a family business…of sorts. But no longer." He bit his lip, and she could tell he was thinking about something. "My previous employment was not satisfying. But now that I am here…I suppose that here I have the luxury of doing what I want. Or not working at all. Although that seems particularly self-indulgent." His blue eyes fixed on hers. "I have a history of making poor choices. Ones that cannot be fixed or erased, and truly, I doubt I could start anew even if I wished it."

Val wrote down the score for the last hole. So far, he was winning. What was it with men and sports? He'd never played before, seemed distracted by the windmills, and yet he was still winning.

"Well, what would you like to do?"

His head tilted to the side, and he nodded very slowly. "I… had not gotten that far. I do not believe that I could help enough people to balance the scales, but I suppose I could try. I have a lot of money," he said, as if it were just barely relevant.

She decided to focus on the mistake part of that statement, rather than the money part. "Everyone has regrets. You just have to try not to make them again."

She felt his hand graze her cheek, "I would like very much to make sure that I never make them again. If there was a way that I could do that, I would." Tears filled her eyes. His tone was so laced with grief and regret, that she wondered what he wanted to make amends for. A small part of her wondered at the oddness of his confession. The way he talked, one would think he was a murderer or something. But he was a good man; she knew it.

Inexplicably, she wanted to reassure him. He wasn't evil. She just knew it. It was a certainty deep inside of her, like the difference between right and left. Once you knew, you always knew. "You are not a bad man, Lucas."

"You do not know that." He gave her a gentle smile, almost thankful, and said, "Do you have regrets, my Valkyrie?" his tone slightly hoarse, as though he were just as emotional as she was.

The weight of his attention was warm, his nearness comforting and almost hypnotizing. She found herself answering seriously, and didn't look too closely at the reasons. Here they were, a sunny day, kids screaming all around them, and she felt as if they were talking about life and death. She was close enough to touch him, and the idea of reaching out and touching his solid chest or his muscled arm was tempting. She felt as if it were her right to touch him, which didn't make any sense. She could seek comfort in him, and be honest with him, in a way that she didn't even like to admit to herself. Her next words slipped out of her mouth before she could think them through. "I'm a coward," she said. "And

I wish I wasn't. Sometimes it seems like all I do is make decisions that are safe and boring."

"That is not cowardice. Neither is it permanent. You simply decide to behave differently, to do the right thing, and you are instantly brave. But what have you had to be brave about, Valerie Dearborn? What could you have failed in this place?" He looked around them as if where they were might suddenly change. "You misjudge yourself. Underestimate your abilities. You know how to fight; you are smart and capable. You can save yourself, Valerie Dearborn. You have just forgotten how strong you are."

Or maybe I've never had anything I needed to be strong for. She turned away, her gaze stopping on two teenagers trying to swallow each other's tongues. "Good point. I don't know…it's just this sense, I guess, that I'm not really living. I'm existing, or doing something wrong."

He nodded, expression severe and grave. "You *are* doing something wrong. You are losing this game of small golf."

"I can't believe I'm losing to a guy who doesn't even know what it's called," she said, laughing and stepped up to the next hole, determined to keep the rest of the date lighthearted.

CHAPTER

$\mathcal{M}$ ini-golf ended, and they walked across the street to a brightly-lit restaurant with a menu several pages long.

For Lucas, it was a peculiar experience. Firstly, he wasn't sure he knew this Valerie. In some ways, she was relaxed. She would joke and laugh and seemed comfortable in her own skin, but he knew she was uneasy around him, and that was something he didn't know how to fix.

He wondered what she saw when she looked at him. It was clear she did not remember him. No matter what he said—or tried not to say—he had no sense of recognition from her. It was truly as though he were meeting her for the first time. He wanted her to remember him. At least, he thought he did. Valerie had never looked at him in quite this way...as though he were a man. Just a man who wanted to court her. Even though he could tell she didn't quite understand why he was interested in her, which he also found unfathomable. If anyone knew the true value of an exterior, it was him.

Valerie was not just beautiful on the inside; she was beautiful on the outside as well, as if it radiated out of her, her goodness and positivity. He feared his inside was as black as his soul, and that if she remembered him—truly remembered him—she wouldn't look at him in this new way ever again.

And of course, the other question was, why were they here? She had built up this life, made it for herself; this was a refuge from Virginia and in it she was…common. Was this actually her fairy tale? To have a job where she taught students and dated? To drive her car and pay bills?

He did not fit in a world like this. He knew bloodshed and death, not games with tiny replicas of buildings and plans for the future. He did not understand driving in a car to get somewhere… and frankly, it was terrifying to be so vulnerable. And yet, hadn't he felt engaged in a way he'd never done before?

In a sense, what they were doing, these simple things like playing mini-golf and talking about him and his feelings and life were exhausting. Because they *involved* him.

Lucas did not involve himself with life. Not anymore. He was like a spider—he sat and waited for something to catch his interest. And in the meantime he thought of nothing, wanted nothing.

Until she came along and made my world colorful again.

He was as emotionally dead as he was physically dead. But here he wasn't. And in order to have her, he couldn't be. He would have to discard who he had been for hundreds of years and become someone else.

A frightening prospect, to say the least.

This was her life now. Maybe all she would ever know about the world, for she might never come out of this state. And where did that leave him? Hadn't he done this to her? Meddled in her life for decades and brought her to this point?

At least, until Virginia or Cerdewellyn killed him. Or, until he became too weak to see her again. How long might that be? Tonight? Tomorrow? A year from now? Or more. What if he had a life here with her? He took in a shaky breath. A life. Time with her, where he was someone else.

The last thing in the world I deserve.

He wouldn't leave her here. As long as she wanted him to stay, he would. As long as he could keep Virginia unaware of Valerie's existence he would do so. Maybe she would remember, maybe in time the memories would come to her, and they wouldn't harm her. Until something happened, he had no choice but play along with her fantasy. And didn't he owe her that, after all he'd done?

And isn't that convenient, he thought snidely. He wanted her, and she wanted him. Even though she didn't know him, she wanted him. And he wanted her in a way that was beyond description. His desire for her wasn't magical, didn't revolve around blood and plotting. There was no power struggle and manipulation. It was pure—his wanting a beautiful and desirable woman. In a way, this was a gift. To feel the sun on his face, to play mini-golf and eat real food. Life for him had been like watching a movie; he had seen it but not experienced it, and now he was.

There were no vampires. No one wanted anything from him. Except for her. She wanted him as a lover, or a boyfriend. He'd taken everything from her, and this was all she wanted from him. To pretend that he could be…just a man.

Lucas closed his eyes, felt like laughing hysterically. How was he to be a man? What did it entail? She didn't want him to kill anyone for her. Or to buy her anything. She did not want things he understood. She wanted him as he could never be.

The thought was terrifying, and he knew why, but didn't want to look too closely at it. Since he had drunk her blood, he spent his days shrouded in shame and regret. Grief for the devil he had become. She wanted him to discard that and be happy.

But he didn't deserve it. That was the rub. He did not deserve to play at happiness and at being a man.

"Penny for your thoughts," Val said. Lucas looked up, meeting her gaze and smiled. It struck her as sad somehow, but she wasn't sure why.

"So why do you teach history?" Lucas asked.

"I like history," Val said, while they waited for their cheese-cake. He seemed unconvinced by the concept of a cake made with cheese, but she knew that once he tasted it, he'd change his mind. "It's just so relatable."

"I do not understand," he said and his attention drifted away from her, scanning the restaurant before returning. He reminded her of a cop, the way he continuously looked around, checking their surroundings as if he were always on the lookout for danger.

Valerie shrugged, and she hoped that when she started talking, she didn't sound like a moron. "History is made up of ex-tremes. We don't know anything about normal stuff. Only when things combine to screw up on a level like they hadn't before. Like the Donner Party. There were so many decisions that were made, and so many points where if they had just done something a lit-tle differently, they would have been all right. All those people wouldn't have died. But they made bad decisions, even impossible ones, and then they got stuck in the worst winter in hundreds of years. Roanoke was the same," she said, and thanked the waiter as he put the cheesecake, with two forks, between them.

Lucas stilled, ignoring the cake, watching her intently. "I am afraid I do not know that period of time well. What about Roanoke?"

Val blinked. For some reason, she thought he was lying to her, but that didn't make any sense. "Well, it was just a number of errors, one after the other. They didn't get along with the natives, so they had no one to help them. It was the worst drought in hundreds of years, so they had no food. England couldn't send ships because they were worried about being invaded by the Spanish. And when they did get a ship to check on the settlers over a year later, they were forced to go back because of the weather. If any of those things had been different, the colony might have survived. And then we never would have heard about them."

"We only know the failures," he said.

She nodded. "Yes, but..." Val didn't know how to make him understand how it moved her. Not just as a student, or someone who liked history, but on a personal level. "I always wonder if they knew. If they were able to look back at a certain point, and pinpoint the moment they chose wrong. Did you know the Donner Party missed the summit by a day? If they had gotten there one day earlier, they would have been over the Sierras and home free. But they thought the first winter storm was a few weeks away, and so they took a break, let the kids play, let the men rest, gave the animals a chance to eat and prepare for the last push, and all that time the weather was changing. Those hours where they thought they were safe were the fatal ones."

"You feel they should have seen the danger. That they were foolish for lingering."

Valerie felt defensive, and she couldn't say why. She picked up her fork and poked at the cake a bit, speaking without looking at him. "No, I don't think they were foolish. I think they didn't *know*. And I couldn't imagine living with that mistake. Watching the snow come down, everyone going hungry, and knowing that it was my fault."

He covered her hand with his, the warmth of him seeping into her. His touch was electric, stole her breath and distracted her from her dark thoughts. He lifted her chin, so he could see her clearly, and she blinked rapidly, hoping he would pretend not to notice her pathetic sadness.

"You grieve for people long gone. For impossible situations and tragedies that had nothing to do with you. Everyone makes mistakes, Valkyrie. It is just that usually they do not have dire consequences. You cannot look at history from that way—as a series of mistakes. You must see it as a sequence of reactions. Of attempts to fix things and make the best decisions at that time. We know where they went wrong, but they did not, and could not see it the way we do."

Her words were a whisper, "Do you think they felt guilty? That the enormity of their mistakes, the cost of lives was something they knew and regretted? Do you think people blamed them? Did they make peace with the death that was coming for them?"

His smile was tragic, his words low and almost inaudible. "Maybe they did not know they were going to die. Maybe they had hope to the very end."

"You don't believe that," she said. For some reason, that pissed her off. As if he was placating her.

"It does not matter what I believe. The past is done. Hope is irrelevant. We measure success and failure in history with a cost of lives. Penicillin saved people, and the world wars exterminated them. Success and failure. Feelings, regrets, the point where they knew they made mistakes...it is interesting but unfortunately, irrelevant. Did they go to their death and grieve for what they did? Did the makers of the atomic bomb grieve for the destruction they dedicated their lives towards creating? Who cares? They did it. Whether they knew what they were creating, or whether they talked themselves into believing it was for the best, the glory of history is being able to view it in black-and-white." His voice was cold. "However honorable one's initial intention, a villain will always be a villain."

"So you don't believe in redemption?"

He leaned closer to her, words a whisper, intense and cold. "Why would you ask me such a thing?"

She swallowed. He was too close, too intimate, the way he watched her making her feel like there was no escape and that he would lay her soul bare. "Because I want to know you," she said.

He smiled grimly. "And questions of redemption and mistakes will tell you of me? Do you see me for my villainous nature? Heroes are not born; they make the correct choice. No matter what. They choose what is best for all and not for themselves."

"Your villainous nature? No!" she said, aware that he was shutting down. She didn't want him to become distant or polite; she wanted to talk to him, really understand him. "I think of it because I wonder what I would have done. If I would have been brave, or if I would have been weak. No one sets out to be a hero, Lucas. They find themselves in a situation they cannot get out of, and all they can do is act. If they act correctly, we call them a hero. If they freeze or let fear overcome them, then they aren't."

Lucas took a sip of water, setting it back down carefully, as if he were buying himself time to think. "But those people do not deserve forgiveness. They do not deserve to...have a life or be happy."

She reached over and held his hand, her touch electric. "We don't get what we deserve, Lucas. We get what we bargain for. If there is no justice, then all one can do is go forward. And if sometimes, someone gets a second chance, then they just move on. They fix what they can, and they should never look back." Valerie let go of him, tried to make a joke. "So, what about you Lucas, would you be a hero?"

He didn't smile. He didn't make a joke of how brave he would be, or how he would always save the day. The moment lengthened as her comment fell flat and died between them. He shook his head, and a flush spread up his cheeks.

"I'm sorry," she blurted out.

"Never apologize to me, Valkyrie."

Hot tears filled with eyes. "Oh my God! What is wrong with me? I'm a hormonal mess. It's like my Coffee mate has been switched with estrogen." Valerie was beyond mortified—getting sad about people long dead, feeling guilty for making a joke about Lucas being a hero. She didn't know why, but she felt it all personally. It was as if there were undercurrents to every conversation, and she was just trying to stay above water. To...keep him. To convince him to stay.

"Thank you," he said quietly as she drove them back to the school.

"For what?"

"For...the day. For seeing things as you do."

She shot him a look. "I don't know what you saw. A slightly lowbrow date?"

"Do not do that," he commanded. "Do not belittle yourself and who you are. I am grateful to spend time with you. To see you in a place where you thrive. I thank you for that."

Val's hands clenched on the wheel, and she didn't know what to say. It was the end of the date. She was supposed to let him go now. Not be a slut and take him home with her. But he felt like... hers. The idea of him leaving scared her. As if he wouldn't come back once he was gone.

He's mine; she decided. She wouldn't let him go. Ever. Confidence and hope bloomed inside of her, and she knew she was making the right choice. He was hers, and she would keep him. She turned to look at him, to see what he would say to coming home with her...and realized that they were standing in her kitchen.

Lucas blinked, looking around in shock as the setting changed. They had been in a car; the evening had been over, and now it was morning. The clock showed it to be 9am. But the kitchen was destroyed. The cupboards were open and bare. A sliding glass door that led outside was open.

"Oh my God," Valerie said, looking at him with shock. "It wasn't like this. I cleaned this. I'm sorry. This is so...embarrassing."

"Was your home broken into?" he asked.

She crossed her arms. "Um, no. This isn't right. I didn't leave it like this. This was before you found me. I don't want to live like this anymore," she said, voice rising, close to hysterical.

Lucas came towards her, wrapping his arms around her and holding her tight to his chest. "Then we will clean it up," he said, as if it were perfectly reasonable for her house to be such a mess.

Thirty minutes later, the kitchen was put back to rights. Lucas had taken all of her broken dishes to the trash, and she had swept up all the shards of glass that littered the floor. Lucas came back in and leaned against the kitchen counter, his expression carefully neutral as he studied her.

"What will you do now?" he asked her.

Val grimaced, and busied herself by making them a pot of coffee. They still had three mugs, which was good. At least, she'd been sane enough not to break all of her coffee cups. Didn't that mean there was hope for her not spending her life in the insane asylum?

"I don't know. I don't have any plans for the day really. Some papers to grade, some plants I should put in the garden. What about you?"

She glanced at him over her shoulder, and he jerked his gaze up to hers. If she didn't know better she'd think he was looking at her ass. "I'm going to spend my day with you," he said and looked away from her.

"Oh," she said faintly, and felt her stomach flip-flop. She wanted to spend her day in bed with him. She took a shaky breath and stepped closer to him. His brows rose in inquiry, and the muscles in his arms bunched as if he were suddenly filled with tension, but he didn't move closer to her. She stopped in front of him, reaching out her hands and putting them on his forearms. She slid her palms along his skin, her fingers disappearing under the sleeves of his shirt as she touched his arms.

He moved, his own hands settling on her shoulders and sliding down to her wrists. He tugged gently, indicating that he wanted her to let him go. Very subtly he shook his head no. "What do you want to do today?"

Valerie was pretty sure she'd made it clear what she wanted to do today. She wanted to tell him that she loved him, and that she needed him to take her upstairs to prove how much he cared about her too. To block out the rest of the world, and lose herself in his touch and his taste, his smell and the sounds that he would make, the press of his body against hers.

"In my time, when a man was serious about a woman, he courted her. Please let me do that," he said, as if he were confiding a secret to her. "You have always been different. I have always wanted you, but what I never had was the chance to know you, not like Ja—" he cut himself off, "not like he did."

Valerie was confused, and her head started to pound. "He who?"

He let go of her hands and closed his eyes, pinching the bridge of his nose, as though he were trying to get his thoughts in order or unravel a complex mystery. "I apologize. This should not be so...difficult," he said with irritation in his voice.

She took a step back, feeling like a fool. "No, I get it. We can do something else. I could take you home if you want. Nobody said you have to go out with me." Embarrassment washed over her. She couldn't believe she was trying to hit on the hunk, and he wanted nothing to do with her. What sort of moron was she? The kitchen sink became blurry as tears filled her eyes.

She heard him swear from behind her, and then she was suddenly in his arms, his mouth on hers as he kissed her hungrily. She wrapped her arms around his neck, and he walked her backward a few steps and then lifted her, his strong hands around her waist, settling her on the counter. He pulled her closer, so that she could feel just how much he wanted her. As their bodies pressed together, he moaned. He kissed her jaw at the back of her neck, and then down the long column of her throat where he paused and then froze altogether. "You have a very beautiful neck," he mumbled, his head on her shoulder as she tried to catch her breath.

"Umm, thanks."

"I do not know that I've ever really looked at it."

"Oh. You're a big…neck connoisseur, huh?" Val said, arms still around his neck, the ridge of his erection against her hot core. He kissed her neck again lightly, and she shivered.

"I would hope never to hear myself described in such terms as being a neck connoisseur."

She laughed. "Yeah, it does make you sound like a bit of a pervert."

He kissed her collarbone and then the pulse on her neck. "I can assure you that I am utterly depraved."

"Not from the footage I've seen."

"You should be flattered that I do not want to take you upstairs and fuck you," he said crudely.

She pushed at his shoulders wanting him to give her space. She hadn't thought about it like that, didn't see it as something as dirty as he made it sound.

He cupped her face with his hands, making her look at him. "I want you. You know exactly how much I want you," he said, shifting closer so his erection brushed against her. She blushed in response, biting her lip a little nervously at his close scrutiny. "I have this chance to be with you, and see you as just a woman. I have spent a lot of time looking at you, but I have not really seen you."

"Are we back to the neck thing?" she asked, trying to make a joke.

He scowled. "I am trying to declare my intentions to you, and tell you that I value you in a way that goes beyond a mere coupling.

Please, let me have this chance to be with you like...like a gentleman. Like I would have treated you had we met long ago."

She thought she fell in love with him right then and there. "All right, but if I die of frustration it will be your own fault," she said.

He grinned at her. "Things will not get that desperate." He pulled her off the counter and set her on her feet. "Now, tell me what we should do as a dating couple," he said enthusiastically.

Val poured him a cup of coffee, catching him in the act of adjusting himself as she turned back around. She wasn't sure what the etiquette was for that. Should she ignore it? He took the coffee from her, and swooped in to give her a kiss on the lips. "I said it was a good idea, I didn't say it was easy."

She tried to keep her mouth shut. But gave up. "You mean it's hard?"

He took a sip of his drink, frowning into the cup. "This is coffee?" he asked.

"This is it. Welcome to the world of tomorrow."

"Hmm," he said skeptically. She took a sip of her own coffee and almost choked when he said, "Yes, it's going to be very, very hard."

CHAPTER

21

Valerie and Lucas spent time doing 'normal things' as she thought of them. They went to a bookstore and browsed around, then went to lunch. They watched TV, curling up on the couch next to each other, Lucas' arm around her shoulders making her feel safe and cherished. Their life here was wonderful, perfect.

But, every once in a while though the question would come to her, like where was he sleeping at night? Or how come he never went to his house, but always stayed with her? But almost as quickly as she thought them, they slipped from her mind. She didn't have any more episodes of thinking she was going insane, or of the Lucas-like figure who was being tortured in the dungeon. And that was a relief. Maybe he kept her sane.

There were also times when being with him felt like déjà vu. Like when they went to the bookstore and talked about Malcolm Glad well's *The Tipping Point*. She'd instantly known that he'd already read it, and she wasn't sure why she knew that. He'd never told her, had he?

Lucas had watched her and waited, his expression and body language neutral, as if he were just there to observe her reactions. As if his goal in that moment was to say nothing of how he actually thought or felt.

Her life was here. And his life was here with her. It had only taken hours of being with him before her mind had adjusted to his presence being here with her. They were together now, and they always would be; she thought.

~

Lucas walked over to the sliding glass door that led into the backyard, wearing a pair of blue pajama bottoms and no shirt. It was the partial nudity that really tied the outfit together, Val thought. "It's raining. What are you doing?" she asked. Her toes were cold, and she went to stand on the little rug next to him. He looked at her with an unreadable expression on his face.

"What do you do with this space outside?" he asked.

She bit the inside of her lip, wanting to laugh. But it would be *at* him, and so she tried not to. Managed to make it just a smile. "You mean the backyard? That big puddle of water is called a swimming pool."

He frowned at her.

"Well, what are you asking me then? It's a backyard. It's got grass and plants, cement even."

"Very edifying. But…is there someone who takes care of it? Do you have a gardener or someone who tends to it?" he asked, curiously.

"Yeah. Her name is Valerie. You probably met her. Cute. Stacked."

He looked at her quizzically. "Sarcastic? Slightly abrasive?"

"See? You have met her." She chucked and said waspishly, "Abrasive. I'm not sharing my coffee with you now. And we are out of Coffee mate so it's your loss."

He stood up straight. Turned to look at her, giving her his full attention, as though he were a king and she a lowly subject. He stared down into her coffee cup. "I like the Coffee mate. I do not understand what it is. But it is a modern miracle. You have to share."

"You think everything is a modern miracle," Val said and took a drink.

"I know miraculous things when I see them," he said, looking down at her with an expression that made her think he was talking about her. It was cheesy, but her estrogeny-self liked it anyway. She let out a sigh.

"Now tell me about the yard."

"What exactly do you want to know?"

"Do you have a spring planting schedule?" he asked her seriously.

Val adjusted her grip on the mug so it would warm her hands.

"You have no fruit or vegetables. There are no trees for shade. It is...grass, a fence and a pool. It is out there like a mirage in the desert," he said, pointing out to the yard. She could hear the disgust in his voice. "And I think the grass is too short. And the color...surely it should be greener," he said, the statement half-question and half-accusation.

"Maybe it should," Val said and took another sip of coffee. His eyes narrowed as he watched her drink.

"The yard is unacceptable. I have heard of a store that you will take me to."

This was gonna be good. "Is it Victoria's Secret?"

"Who?" he looked perplexed.

"Nothing. I was amusing myself. Go on."

"It is called The Home Depot. We will go there and get things to fix the yard." He turned away from her and looked outside. "We will need to buy a lawn mower," he said the words slowly.

"Okay. I'll bite. How did you hear about The Home Depot?"

"It was on the television. I also notice that there is no barbeque."

Valerie scowled. "I don't know how to barbeque."

One eyebrow raised. It was a look so condescending that she took a big sip of the coffee. She was going to finish it, and he wouldn't get a single drop.

"I will barbeque. It will go over there." He pointed to a corner of the yard that was filled with dirt chips.

"I don't know. I think you want to put it on cement, right?"

He crossed his arms. "Put what on cement? That is not a good idea. It is very hard to break."

This was confusing. "Wait. What the hell is it you want to do with the barbeque?"

He sighed in exasperation, as though she was the one who was confusing. "It is a pit. It goes into the ground. I see no need to take out the cement to do it when you have that open space—"

"You want to put in a barbeque pit? What's wrong with a normal barbeque that we can wheel around?"

His head jerked back as if she'd slapped him. "What do you mean?"

"Fine. I'll take you to Home Depot, and you can ogle the manly stuff. And you can do whatever you want to with the barbeque. Let me take a shower first. And just to avoid any future conflicts, let it go on the record now that I don't skin anything, and I don't camp."

She drained the last of the coffee and shoved the mug towards him. He took it in his hands and looked at the empty bottom with a frown. "That is just rude."

"I'll take you to Star bucks."

"Excuse me?" he said, and took a step after her, as though he hadn't heard her. Or what she had said was obscene.

"Oh, for crying out loud. What the heck was your life like before me? I can just imagine it now; you sitting around, in this bizarre isolation."

He blinked.

"You know what it's like? It's like you're an alien or something. A really yummy alien, but still," Val said, heading towards the stairs.

"Or perhaps a vampire," he suggested.

Val paused on the third step and looked back at him with a frown. "Now that's just ridiculous."

CHAPTER

22

Val wondered if there was any way to get him to reconsider his no-sex-request. Because it was a request, right? A guideline, rather than an unbreakable rule. Maybe if she hit him over the head and dragged him up the stairs like a cave woman would, he would sleep with her. Or maybe if he came inside, and she took off her clothes and attacked him; she could make it happen before he could protest.

"It is as though I can hear you thinking," he said.

"Oh yeah? Are you blushing?"

He sighed heavily.

"I'm just saying, life is short, and who knows what could happen tomorrow, you know?"

He didn't say anything. She pulled into her driveway and turned the car off. It didn't occur to her that he might want to go home, or have anywhere else to go. She just assumed that he was coming with her. They got to the front door, Lucas trailing behind her slowly as she went in and turned on the lights.

"You do understand that my restraint is a sign of my respect for you."

"You can respect me in the morning," Val said flippantly as she took off her shoes.

"I am attempting to treat you as an equal...No, more than that—as something precious."

"You're not a virgin, right?"

He looked around wildly. "No. But that is irrele—"

"So you'll sleep with other women, but not me?"

He lost his temper, almost shouting the words at her, "You are not other women! You are it! I love you. I will die for you!"

She shot him a disbelieving look and rolled her eyes.

"Fine," he growled, and then he took two steps closer to her, giving her a bruising kiss as he let her see just how much he wanted her.

"Up," he commanded, and she broke the kiss long enough to twine her arms around his neck and jump so that she could wrap her legs around his waist. He held her close, one hand on her back, and the other on her ass, as he effortlessly went to the stairs and carried her up them. She kissed him hungrily, and he bumped her bedroom door open with his shoulder, toppling them both to the bed rather gracelessly. "Oooff," she said as his weight landed on her. His hands were everywhere: her side, her thigh, sliding up to the side of her breast and back down again, every touch setting her on fire.

He pulled back, eyes dilated, both of them panting as he stared into her eyes. "Do you want to stop?" he asked.

"Are you nuts?" she asked incredulously, and pushed at his shoulder, urging him to roll over so that she was lying on top of him. He complied, his arms around her waist, taking her with him as he went to his back.

He chuckled at her comment, his hands spearing into her hair, as though he wanted to force her to see him. His grip was gentle, and as she looked at him, he smiled, the expression transforming his face, making him even more attractive than he usually was.

Her heart melted. His smile also had quite the effect on her libido. She sat up, straddling his waist and dragging his shirt up his chest, enjoying the revealing of his muscled chest and abdomen. He crunched upwards, his shoulders lifting off the bed so she could remove his shirt, and she watched the play of muscles beneath his skin and whipped off her own shirt.

She had the strangest feeling of déjà vu. As if this were not the first time they'd been together. Valerie closed her eyes, and the image in her mind was still there. The location was different; the bedroom filled with antiques that she intuitively knew were his.

Lucas's hands shaped her breasts, pulling her back to reality.

Valerie leaned down and kissed his neck, felt his groan vibrate through his chest as she worked her way downwards, tasting his skin and flicking her tongue over one flat nipple.

"In my time, it was customary for a man to prove his—"

"Virility?" Val suggested unhelpfully, as she reached the fine line of hair that ran below the waist of his jeans. She looked up at him playfully as she unbuttoned his jeans. He subtly arched up into her touch, his erection grazing her palm.

"No, that will not be a concern," he murmured. Val unzipped his jeans, parting the fabric and taking in the hard shape of him beneath his black boxer briefs. She kissed the head of his shaft through his briefs, and his hand tightened on her shoulder.

He looked down at her, "Come here," he said, and she looked at him questioningly. He reached down, pulling her up to him and rolling over again so that he was on top of her.

"This is not about you pleasing me. This is about us being together, despite the obstacles." He undid her clothing slowly, peeling it off her in between lengthy kisses, forcing her to slow down. He caressed her body with his hands, his lips following the path that he made until she was so wet with desire, she thought that one touch would make her come.

He settled over her, the expression on his face a curious mixture of intensity and near pain. He drew her leg up, anchoring it to his hip with his arm as he pressed the head of his cock against her. "If we stay here, I want to do it right. Have it all and be with you, do you understand? I wanted to wait because you deserve a man better than me."

Her chest felt tight with emotion as she tried to digest his words through a haze of lust. "I cannot change my past. I can only go forward and try to make you happy, treat you well and…marry you."

"You really are old-fashioned," she said, when what she actually wanted to say was 'yes', and 'I love you, too.' That no matter what he'd done, or the monster he used to be, he was perfect for her.

He eased his way inside of her, his hips rocking gently as he sank inside. He was big, hard, and careful with her, as though his movements were a representation of his promise that he would never hurt her.

"I love you," he said, as he thrust inside of her. "For now, for tomorrow, and forever. You must remember that I love you, Valerie Dearborn."

∽

Pain woke him in the night. He could hear Virginia's voice like a whisper on the wind, calling to him. Demanding he wake up and come back to her. He grunted as more pain speared him, clutching his side and looked down, surprised not to see blood pouring from him.

"What's wrong? Are you all right?" Valerie said, her voice husky from sleep. She touched his face, her hands hot on his skin.

"You can't go! Do you understand me? I love you."

She thought he was going to speak, going to tell her something, maybe that he loved her too or even that he wouldn't go, but he didn't.

And between one breath and the next, he was gone.

CHAPTER

"Time to wake up, my slaughterer. I think you have had enough rest. Your time has come to an end, Lucas." Virginia said, and a dagger appeared in her hand. She touched it to his stomach, smiling when he flinched. He blinked rapidly and tried to settle himself, focus on what was to come. She liked it more if he lost it. If he could do nothing but scream, she was happy.

"There you are," she murmured, as though he were a baby just waking up. She smiled, and he clenched his jaw, tried to brace himself for the pain as she shoved the blade deep inside of his stomach. He gasped, and blood instantly spilled out of his mouth.

"Oh, drat! I did it wrong." She took a step back, hands on her hips as she stared at him unhappily. She reached out, yanking the dagger out of him with a sharp twist and making it vanish out of sight. "That didn't hurt you enough." And then she smiled at him, humming softly as she began to carve him up.

CHAPTER

24

achel came back into the room. Trying to keep the impatience from her voice, she said, "It's not here. You look," she thrust the box at Marion. She smiled up at her woodenly. "Perhaps it's at the castle. Check our apartments in Prague. Or perhaps New York? Oh piffle, just bring me all the jewelry boxes, and I'll find it."

Rachel's lips thinned. "You don't want to go with me."

Marion laughed weakly, "I'm so tired, my love."

After a moment, Rachel nodded. "All right, I'll be back as soon as I can. And remember, if you hurt Jack in any way, Lucas will be furious."

Marion smiled sweetly, but her eyes were bright with intent, "But my sweet, you are bound to him. If I hurt him, I would hurt you too."

Rachel leaned in, giving her a small peck on the cheek, and vanished.

Marion peered into the jewelry box, silently fuming. Did they think she was stupid? The faithless bitch. To look her in the eye, demand the gem, and for what? If Lucas had wanted that stone, he would have come to get it himself. What could Rachel hope to accomplish? Her witchcraft was useless…unless she had found the book. She froze; the idea so seductive that for a moment, she couldn't even breathe.

Was that it? Had the book been found? If that was the case, there was only one person to ask. Pawing through her jewelry, she found one of Annika's tokens. If she were alive, it would act as a summons, inviting her to come here. Marion stood, going to the fire and tossing the coin into it. What would she say to the woman after all this time?

The coin ignited with a purple flame, the scent of burned honey filling the room. A form appeared in the flame, and Marion stepped back, watching as the fire flicked higher, someone materializing within. Cerdewellyn stepped out, solidifying before her.

She pasted a smile onto her face. He was not who she expected. And lord knew he probably had no interest in seeing her either. Cuckolding tended to do that to a man. "Cerdewellyn! How charming."

"Marion," he said, giving her an incline of his head. "I am surprised to see you. But perhaps I should not be. I cannot imagine that too many of Annika's tokens remain in the world."

"And how is she?" Marion asked, making polite talk.

"Gone. Dead," he said, tone conveying that he could care less. He was looking around the room, as though he found it interesting. When he saw the television, he frowned. It didn't surprise her that he would be a book-loving snob.

Annika was dead. Marion nodded. That sounded about right. Now they could move on to business. "I want to bargain, Cerdewellyn."

He had the nerve to laugh, the condescending prig. His pitch-black chuckle filled the room. "Continue."

"I assume you are looking for the Sard?"

He crossed his arms and said softly, "I am."

"I will give you the gem if you restore my daughter. It is all I have ever wanted. I should have negotiated with you directly. Let my indiscretions with Annika remain in the past. I have no hatred for The Fey. Let your grievance with Lucas stay with him. I will not attack you, even if he commands it."

Cerdewellyn's dark eyes fairly twinkled. "He will not command it."

She clutched at her heart. "What…has happened?" Was he dead? Was such a thing possible?

"Lucas is mine. His reign is over, and he is near to broken. He is close to telling me where the Sard is. I suppose that this is the answer I will get from him, is it? That the stone is with you?"

She nodded. "I come to you freely. Lucas threw me away after I challenged him, and it is only now that I have escaped. I mean you no ill-will, Cerdewellyn. Help me. Give me Margaret, and you can do what you will with the world."

He watched her carefully, seeking signs of deception.

"I have been betrayed, Cerdewellyn. By everyone around me. Lucas. Rachel. All of them. *Always* betrayal." She smiled wanly. "You understand. We can help each other."

"Where is the jewel?" he asked.

She rolled her eyes. "Agree first."

"I agree," Cerdewellyn said with a smile and a shrug. There was something boyish about it, and she found herself blushing. She did love a handsome man. Maybe it was time for a change. She wished she'd looked in the mirror before she contacted him.

She smiled shyly in return. "It's in my Margaret's crypt."

He held out an arm.

She took it, stroking his hard bicep and stepping close, as he took them away from the flat and to Margaret's tomb.

CHAPTER

Valerie was alone in her kitchen, sitting on the floor, and she had no idea why. Inexplicably, there were tears on her cheeks. She was sad, felt as if she'd been grieving and that all joy had been wrung from her. But that made no sense. She needed to get up off the floor and turn on the lights.

She stood, legs shaky and then ran to the sink, throwing up her dinner, her body heaving with spasms for several minutes. She was tired. She should go to bed. Start again tomorrow. Another day at school. Another day of thinking she was crazy.

Another day alone.

But she shouldn't be alone.

Her nose started to bleed, and her vision swam. This was bullshit. And it was so dark in here that it was making her nuts. She ignored the blood, let it run down her face, and looked at the curtains with hatred. She wanted to open them, see what was outside. Val reached for them and started to gag, her head pounding, feeling as if it were being split open, and as if someone were scooping out her brains.

She had to know what was out there. She couldn't stay here for a moment longer. He needed her. *Who?* She froze, listened intently as if the answer might suddenly be whispered in her ear.

She was here, and things were happening without her. He was dying.

Pain flashed through her, as though she'd been struck by lightning. "Who?" she asked her empty room. The answer was silence, her heart beating so loud in her ears that she wondered if she were dying. Valerie began to sweat, saw blood come out of her pores, as she gripped the curtain and held on tight. It took all of her strength to pull the curtain back. And outside was… the ocean. A barren gray landscape. A forgotten sea untouched by man.

What the fuck?

Her hand trembled as she flipped the latch, and she had to use all of her strength to pull it open. She opened the window with shaking hands and pulled herself up onto the counter, climbing out the window, handprints stark contrast to the white window frame. Cold air hit her as she fell down to the rocky ground.

The wind howled a name on the breeze: Lucas.

She hurt, felt like she couldn't breathe. The sound of the waves. A shadow loomed over her. She blinked up at Virginia, saw her wearing another long dress. White and beautiful, as if it were her wedding day. Except that there was blood on the front of it. Black and heavy, saturating it so one side of the hem dragged on the ground, painting the steps behind her.

Everything came back to her in a rush, as if the dam of her memories had been opened. This was real. This bitch had taken her over. The young woman's face was pale and pinched in anger. *Virginia Dare.*

"That's Lucas' blood," Val said, knowing it in her heart.

"It is justice."

"No." Valerie said and felt fury, let it rise within her and grow, imagined it turning into a storm, something that crunched and swallowed, leaving only pieces behind it. The wind picked up and debris flew around them, branches, dust; even droplets of water from the sea. All the elements whirled around them, agitated and ready.

Virginia didn't take her gaze from Valerie. "It is too late, Valerie Dearborn. Much too late for you," she said. "You couldn't win before, and you can't win now. I tried to be nice to you. I *gave* you a life. Gave you a chance to have what you always wanted, and you couldn't take it. Couldn't enjoy what you had. Maybe you do not know how to be happy."

Virginia had one hand behind her back, and now she brought it forward, showing Valerie a bloody knife. "He is dead. You are dead. This is over. I am the Queen of the Fey and have my king. Stay down, Valerie, and it won't hurt so much."

Valerie knew what she wanted. Lucas. Her life back. Even if that did mean monsters and danger. It was hers, and she'd live it. She rolled to the left and stood, standing on the balls of her feet, ready to move away if Virginia lunged at her.

"I will kill you unless you let my body go."

Virginia shook her head slowly, a wicked grin on her lips. "You are not a killer. I know you better than you know yourself. You are a coward. In love with the devil. Indecisive and weak, unable to make a destiny."

"Oh my God. You and your rambling about a destiny. Everything isn't about *you*," Val said, angrily. Virginia didn't know her. And if it took violence to prove that to her, then so be it.

"He screamed. Your monster. At the end, I looked like you, and he screamed. He called me Valerie." She laughed and charged forward, slashing outwards with the knife.

She let Virginia rush her, shifting at the last minute, dropping to the ground and sweeping her feet out from under her, taking her to the ground. Virginia stared up at Valerie in shock as she tried to draw air into her lungs. This was her moment. She kicked Virginia hard in the stomach, heard her gasp out in pain as she rolled to her side, clutching her stomach.

Kill her. You have to kill her.

Virginia wasn't a fighter. No one had taught her, and so now she was hurt, and she just lay there, tears running down her cheeks;unable to move.

She grabbed the knife from Virginia, having to wrangle it from her, elbowing her in the face before Virginia let go. As their hands made contact, Virginia showed her the past.

The last time she had been in this situation was when the queen had killed her. Her pure love for Cerdewellyn washed over her, and Valerie knew the enormity of what she was doing. Killing a young woman in love.

Virginia made a weak effort to punch Valerie, then kicked at her, but her legs were trapped under the weight of her skirts, and the kick was nothing. Pathetic.

She put the blade to Virginia's throat. Virginia's hands gripped hers, nails biting deep as she used all of her strength to try to keep the blade away from her neck. Valerie shoved down instead, the blade slamming into Virginia's chest, piercing her in the heart and ending it all.

It was intimate and terrible, feeling Virginia's body underneath her, fighting to survive. Hearing her gasping breath, watching her bulging eyes plead with Valerie for mercy.

It took forever. It was over in a moment.

Valerie stumbled backward, off Virginia's body, afraid that she would still be alive somehow, that she'd have to kill her again. But the body began to shrink, pulling in on itself like the corpses at Cerdewellyn's table when he'd taken its power back into himself.

You did it for Lucas. He would do it for you.

Lucas would kill to protect her in a heartbeat. He would add that layer of sin to himself, even if he felt like he was so coated with evil that he was suffocating.

With a blink, Valerie was herself again, standing in a dungeon, her body limp but standing, supported by a strong chest. She knew that chest, would know him anywhere. She straightened and looked up, but he was pale and unmoving, his body covered with bloody wounds that showed no signs of healing. But he was a vampire. Surely, if he were dead, he'd disintegrate, wouldn't he? She grabbed his head, tilting it backward so that the blood ran into his mouth.

"Release," she commanded, and the buckles came undone; dropping his lifeless weight on her as he came down from the wall. She fell backward, and his dead weight pinned her to the ground. She pushed and shoved, trying to get out from under him. She turned him over and tried again, putting her wrist to his mouth, filling it with blood, and then she forced him to swallow, massaging his throat, looking for any sign of life.

She reached out to him with their connection, but it was as if he weren't there. There was nothing to connect with. *No! Please, no!* She pushed harder, willing her life-force into him, trying to force her way into his veins. Through his non-beating heart and into his mind.

She caught a flash, like a light bulb blowing out, illuminating his mind for a brief moment. She pushed again, sending her will into him…and Cerdewellyn's too. The vines that were growing inside of her, twisting through her organs and making her like *him*; she used them too.

Suddenly, she could see Cerdewellyn, almost like a super-imposed image over her view of Lucas, as he stopped speaking and looked up at her, a frown on his face. He was somewhere dark, with someone, but she didn't know who. He was looking back at her curiously, wondering at the drain of power, but he didn't fight her. She took as much as she needed, using herself as a conduit, giving Lucas strength. The strength to live.

Another flash. Then a spark. His heart beat once, a loud echo in her own body. Then it beat again.

It was as if he restarted, as if he had to remember everything he was and had been, to return to the present. And so his life went by her; a deck of cards flipped over one at a time: A boy in the snow, his horror when his father made him kill a pig, the joy of meeting his wife, the deep peace he had felt as a father. Then his grief and change to vampire, his wish for death…and then centuries of upheaval as he lost his purpose for revenge, then found it again…centuries of pain and anger, fleeting moments of sinful pleasure and the horror of his crimes. And then a barren wasteland of numbness, of disinterest, as though the true expanse of his soul was a desert.

To love Lucas was to know his past and what he was capable of. To see the horrors of his soul, and know that he could be more. To mourn the man he had been and wish it back. *I love him*. Clear as a bell, the knowledge rang through her.

As if the devil were listening, she saw herself next. The moment he met her, his pleasure at the taste of her blood, his uncertainty of what he would do with her. His lust and longing. His surprise that she was so different from the women he'd known.

She saw his actions through his eyes and didn't flinch away. Not this time. When she opened her eyes, he was watching her. His body was healed, and he was looking at her as though expecting judgment.

"It's me."

His voice was hoarse. "You returned." He did not touch her.

"I'm sorry. Sorry I was almost too late," she said, not wanting to move away from him. The walls came up, a barrier in his mind that he used to shut her out, and keep himself apart. But in that second it took for him to lock his mind away, she'd seen the truth.

He wasn't sorry that she was almost too late. He wished she had been a moment longer, so he would have died and left her to a life without him. She shook her head, touched his face, even bent down to kiss his cold, dry lips. "I love you," she said, and saw a tear fall onto his cheek.

"No." He grabbed her wrist, pulling it from his cheek. "This is not a fantasy. Your dream is over."

She shook her head in denial, brushing her fingers across his lips, so she didn't have to hear the words. She sounded desperate to her own ears. "I know the man you were, too. And that is who I love. We can find a way to make it work. You drink my blood; you stay…emotional," she said, wishing for a better word, "And you'll be fine."

He hauled in a breath and closed his eyes, blocking her out. "I know you are not this naïve. We both understand what has to be done. If you…" A flash of agony spread across his face, and then his cerulean eyes returned to her, and her heart broke. "If you love me, then you will let me protect you."

What was he telling her, that he wanted to die? He was willing to give up and leave her alone in order to protect her? If he died, her life wouldn't be worth living. It was that simple. Valerie started to cry, dropping her head down to his chest. She begged him to stay with her, and knew he could feel her thoughts.

"Please," he whispered. He let her into his mind so she could see what he wanted to say. *Please don't cry. Please let me go. Please give me a chance not to hurt you.* "I would rather die than risk harming you."

"I need you," she said and squeezed him tight. It felt as if they lay there forever. A quiet duel between them. He made a rough sound and kissed her forehead. "Then you must bind me to you so tightly that I can never stray. Never commit an evil deed, even if I wished it. And when you die, I will die with you," he said, voice low with commitment.

She thought about what he was asking. "That would make you...a slave. No free will of your own." She looked down into his eyes and his somber expression. Her lower lip trembled, and she bit it, trying not to cry. She didn't want some puppet version of him.

"You know my heart more intimately than anyone ever has. Simply because you do not flinch away from darkness, doesn't mean that I don't. I know what I am capable of, the monster I will become without emotions. If you love me, you will not let me become that again. You would respect my wishes. I will not die. I will stay with you, but then...." *We will die together.* "I do not want to lose the courage for death."

That was stupid. How could he ask that of her? "I'm not going to make you my slave! What if I just send you out to get me donuts all day long, and make you rub my feet? You can be good."

A tear slipped down his cheek. "Try to leave enough of me so that I bring you a croissant instead."

She laughed and it turned into a sob. "That is the most feeble joke I have ever heard. I want you as you are. You can do good, Lucas." Valerie felt his denial and determination radiating from him, turning hard and unbreakable.

"Swear it. Swear that you will bind me and we will speak no more of it for now. We must find Cerdewellyn, and after that, if you make me yours, then we will live out our days together. Unless you change your mind," he said, gently.

"I won't. Why would I?"

He closed his eyes. Already things were so serious, so heavy, and so far away from what they had been. The dream of their fantasy life fading away. He laughed mirthlessly. "Children, a life in the sun, a man who can love you. If I were stronger, I would let you go. Let you have the life you want. But I do not want to let you go, either."

Had she won? It sure didn't feel like it. He framed her face with his palms, and urged her down to his lips, kissing her hungrily. She kissed him back, letting him into her mouth, wanting him to be with her, inside of her, to stay with her forever. He drew back. "We must find Cerdewellyn, and stop him from getting the Sard. I do love you, Valerie. Your safety is the only thing I want."

He urged her up and stood with graceful ease. He took her hand in his, squeezing her fingers gently.

"What?" she asked, afraid of whatever he might say. "What am I missing?"

"If I can get the Sard and make you safe with a wish, I will."

She knew she was still missing something. "What is the wish exactly?" she asked, head reeling, feeling like all of her plans were going up in smoke.

"I would wish for magic to disappear." He tried to pull her into his arms. She took a step back, not wanting him to comfort her. She wanted to see his face for this. "I am a vampire. If I wish for magic to disappear, that includes myself. The magic that animates me would be no more. I am dead, Valerie. And I would return to that state."

"So you'll be good enough for me to love, some self-sacrificing knight, but dead?"

He looked angry. "It is not easy, Valerie. I do not want to leave you, or give up my free will. But death...death is something that I am ready for. Making amends is something I must—"

"Fine. Then bind yourself to me. Do it now if you're going to," she snapped, not wanting to hear anything else.

He looked at her for a long while. "You cannot keep me from doing this. Think to control me, so that I do not avenge my family and protect you."

Damn him. "What if it's too late?"

He sighed. "Then it is. Then I can do nothing but begin to kill the vampires. All of them that I can. Either way, I will rid the world of monsters. Now come, we need to get to Cerdewellyn."

She didn't know if she wanted to cry or scream in rage. Maybe both. Talk about getting the fuzzy end of the lollipop. As long as he continued to drink her empathic blood, he would want to do what was right, even if it meant spending the next few decades killing every vampire he could. It was almost funny that this relationship had come full circle, and either she would wind up in a world with no monsters, but Lucas would be dead. Or there would be monsters, and she'd be with yet another guy determined to kill every vampire in existence.

Lucas was looking at her expectantly, ready to move on and fight the good fight. She tried to get her wits in order. If

Cerdewellyn unlocked the Sard and tapped into all that magic, he would be unstoppable. And one of the first things he would do would be to kill Lucas, create even more monsters and threats to humanity. They had to stop him, and Valerie had to find a way to keep Lucas from martyring himself in the process. "He was talking to someone. I saw him when I was healing you. It was somewhere dark."

"Can you go to him?"

She blinked in surprise. "I don't know. Can I?"

"You can try," he said, shrugging his shoulders.

"How do I do that?"

"Think about him, about wanting to be there. Focus your will, and then see what happens."

That sounded too easy. "Can I fuck it up? Like, wind up in the middle of the ocean or something."

"No."

"How come?"

"Because that would be foolish. You are not foolish," he said and gave her a slight smile.

That wasn't a very good answer. "Wait. We need weapons first," he said. And he walked over to Virginia's torture table, picking up his own sword and then handing Valerie a dagger.

"I need a gun," she said. "Knives suck. And I know just where to go to get one." And then she did it: focused her will, made them disappear and took them to Jack.

CHAPTER

Valerie and Lucas materialized in an apartment. She'd never seen it before, but a life-size portrait of Marion was in the corner of the room. "This is Marion's Paris home," Lucas said, answering her unasked question. Rachel stood next to the dining room table, an assortment of jewelry boxes and heaps of jewels on the table before her. Silver and gold necklaces, and rings of every kind, shape and size. It was like a small treasure trove.

Rachel looked up at her slowly, eyebrows lifting up in silent inquiry, as if Valerie appearing didn't even rate a verbal question. *Of course not.* That was the last damned straw. Valerie's blood started to pound, coursing through her veins in fury. Rachel had never seen her as a threat. Rachel had threatened her, harmed her, almost killed her, and then she had taken Jack. That bitch was going to die. And if she'd hurt Jack, she would make it slow.

"Where is Jack? What did you do to him?" Rachel probably thought it was amusing to bring Jack to her and Marion's love nest. But she didn't see him, and it made her scared. Was he dead?

Valerie wasn't helpless anymore. Fey and empathic power coursed through her veins, making her physically strong and finally giving her an advantage. "Now you're gonna tell me," Valerie said, and let the magic rise within her, felt it unfurling from a dark place inside of her, ready to strike. The magic woke instantly, as if it were boiling inside of her, just waiting for someone to take off the lid. But it wasn't just empathic magic; it was Fey. Virginia had taken her over, had become Cerdewellyn's queen in truth, and that magic was there too, waiting to do her bidding.

Small shoots of green vines rose from the ground, twining around Rachel's ankles, morphing and growing thorns, which scraped across her, sinking into Rachel's flesh as they tightened, filling Valerie with a malevolent pleasure.

"Jack is coming back!" she shouted at Valerie. "I get that you finally grew a pair—*ouch*, but we don't have time for this. Get your fucking plants off me." Valerie lunged forward, slamming into Rachel and taking her to the ground, her fist raised in fury. She punched her, using her supernatural strength to make the blows count. After two punches, she was being dragged off Rachel, the familiar unyielding hardness of Lucas's body at her back as he hauled her away from the witch.

The door slammed as Jack came into the apartment and ran to Rachel, dropping to his knees beside her. He reached for the vines, ripping them off her, his hands instantly becoming bloody. "Don't touch them. I'll make them go away," Valerie gasped, and dispersed the magic, the vines decaying and turning to dirt in a matter of seconds.

Jack threw her a wide-eyed look. "Are you fucking crazy?" he said in disbelief.

Her fist hurt, and she shook it, then shrugged her shoulders angrily, telling Lucas with a gesture that she wanted him to let her go. "Me? You're the jackass that chose her! Do you know where you are? What the fuck, Jack?" And some of the rage left her, as if vocalizing her fury had stolen its power.

He got to his feet slowly, looking at the blood on his hands distractedly. The bleeding stopped, the small wounds healing between one sentence and the next. "At least there are some benefits," he said ruefully and flexed his unblemished hands. "I don't remember it, Valerie. Truly, I don't. I can't imagine what I was thinking…But it's done. She could have given me to Marion, but she didn't."

"That's your criteria for whether or not it turned out okay? She didn't give you to Marion? That's bullshit!"

Jack's jaw clenched. "What do you want me to say? That I'm sorry? I am. That I wish I had chosen you?" But he didn't answer that part. Valerie waited, expecting the comment to come.

Lucas was at the table, looking over the jewels. His deep and unnaturally calm voice interrupted them. "Where is Marion?"

"I don't know. She just vanished," Rachel said. "The crafty old bitch sent us each out on a wild-goose chase, and when I got back she was gone."

Lucas turned the full weight of his attention to Rachel. Then he leaned back against the table, his fingers drumming lightly as he waited for her to answer. He'd never been so animated before. Even that small gesture, those tiny movements, were different. He was different. "What did you tell her?" Lucas asked, staying on track.

Rachel rubbed her forehead as if she had a headache. Val hoped she'd caused it. "I told her you wanted the Sard. I don't think she believed me. She became suspicious and sent me on a wild-goose chase, hence all the tat." Rachel gestured at the jewelry. "And when I came back, she was gone."

"Could she have put in a safety deposit box or something?" Jack asked.

Lucas slanted him a look that Valerie took to mean that he thought Jack was an idiot. "No."

That pissed Jack off. "If you're so fucking smart, where the hell is she then? Where would she keep it?"

After a pause Lucas said, "She did not have it on her person, and it was not in any of her homes. There is only one place she values as sacred. Only one person she would dare to leave it with. That would be Margaret."

Valerie met Jack's gaze, as they both stood there, trying to figure out what Lucas meant. "You mean it's buried with her? That's the creepiest fucking thing I've ever heard," Jack muttered.

"Ditto to what he said," Valerie mumbled with a grimace. "Now would be my opportunity to make some cutting comment about you choosing the chick who loved her, and how it makes you an imbecile, but I won't."

"Let's go," Jack said, and patted himself down, checking to make sure he had all his weapons.

"Do not be so hasty," Lucas said. "We cannot simply appear and engage them without a plan."

Jack snorted. "My plan is to shoot first and ask questions later. Sounds simple to me."

"You would risk underestimating your enemies? A small amount of patience is all that is required from you. Cerdewellyn will have wasted no time in beginning the spell. My concern is for what we will do if we are too late. The gem is a source of power, and once he is restored, he will be very powerful and dangerous indeed."

"Then let's go. Why are we wasting time?" Valerie said. Jack gave her a who-the-hell-are-you-and-what-have-you-done-with-Valerie look.

"I will engage Cerdewellyn, and take the gem. Hopefully, I will have time to change the Sard's purpose."

"Oh? And what the hell are you going to wish for?" Jack asked suspiciously.

Lucas blinked slowly as if striving for patience. "I wish to undo magic. Take it all away, no more vampires, no more Others of any kind. We undo it, so that the magic is taken from us." He looked to Rachel, saw the hard set of her jaw.

"It is what you want for Molly," Lucas said.

Rachel nodded jerkily then stood up straight. "Yeah. I had a good run of it. Almost a century of being young and hot..." her voice trailed off, and she swallowed hard.

Jack grabbed Rachel by the arm, before she could turn away, forcing her to look at him. "Why are you sad? What am I missing?" He moved his body close to her as if he could shield her from Lucas, the world, maybe even the truth. And that was when Valerie realized that Jack actually cared for Rachel. Somehow, some wacky way, and despite her massive list of monster-related detriments, Jack cared for her.

Rachel gave him a trembling smile. "No magic means no vampires. If I'm not a vampire, then I'm just a corpse."

Jack shook his head in denial.

Rachel blinked quickly, her voice wavering. "I want what is best for Molly. For her to have the chance not to be a witch is more than I ever could have hoped for. Even if it isn't what is best for me. Besides, she probably would've hated me anyway."

"Then let us go," Lucas said. His arm snaked around Valerie's waist, pulling her close to him. He kissed her fiercely, trying to say so many things with just his lips and the press of his body: *I'm sorry. I do love you. I could have loved you for all time.*

She couldn't stand the injustice of it all. She had finally found the person that she belonged with, and soon he'd be gone. He was a dream, a figment of her imagination. And he wouldn't fight it, would do nothing to try to stay with her. Even though she loved him, and even though he loved her, he was willing to die. For the first time in her life, she actually had power, and she still couldn't do anything to save the one she loved. Part of her had always thought that if only she were stronger, more powerful; that she'd have everything she'd ever wanted.

"Wait," Valerie said and Lucas frowned at her. "Cerdewellyn still thinks that I'm Virginia. I can get close enough to him to kill him. Then you guys can show up and do the rest."

"No," Lucas said flatly.

How rude! She put her hands on her hips. "And why the hell not?"

"Because you have had no success in attacking him in the past."

"At first glance, you have a good argument. But he'll think I'm Virginia, and won't expect an attack. And he will be so distracted trying to get his power back, that he won't suspect a thing. I can do this."

"I preferred it when you hid behind me," Lucas grumbled and crossed his arms unhappily.

"That's Women's Lib for you. I don't do dishes, and I stab Feykings. We're connected now. If things start going wrong, I'll send you a telepathic text."

Lucas nodded unhappily, and Valerie closed her eyes, focusing on Cerdewellyn with her Fey magic. Concentrating on getting to him. Her body tingled, and she knew she'd disappeared; was travelling through time and space and on her way to Cer, Marion, and the end.

The clarity of the moment filled her with peace. The sense of rightness and conviction giving her strength. She didn't care what anybody else wanted, be it Lucas, Jack or Cerdewellyn. Valerie was putting on her game face and taking names. She didn't have a destiny or fate, dang it. Nothing was decided yet. If she wanted a life with Lucas, she'd have to fight for it.

Valerie materialized in a crypt, the smell a mixture of dust, dirt and wet stone. The crypt was large and underground. No windows, and carved out of the earth centuries ago. Creepy. A single coffin was in the middle of the room, and the lid was pushed back, shoved to the side, which had to be a bad sign.

Valerie scanned the room, her instincts demanding she search for the corpse as if it had climbed out on its own and would attack her. Marion and Cerdewellyn stood in the corner, next to a table with a single kerosene lamp.

Cerdwellyn looked up from the book, and Valerie saw a myriad of emotions flicker across his face, as fast as ripples across the surface of a pond. Perhaps he was surprised to see her. Happy and then…something. She suddenly feared that he knew Virginia was gone. Perhaps he could see through her magic, or she had done it wrong.

Marion hissed and said, "That is Lucas' whore. Whatever she has told you is a lie."

"No, Lucas'…" Cer hesitated, as though he found saying the word whore distasteful, "female is gone." He looked down at the gem in his hand, studying it. "My true love inhabits that body. My queen. The only reason I have left to do any of this." He looked up, and she had the impression that he was thinking, calculating. Again, she was faced with the fear that he knew she wasn't Virginia.

"You must not touch her, or else I will kill you and grind your child's bones to dust." Marion made a small harrumphing noise and crossed her arms petulantly.

"It is not safe for you," Cerdewellyn said. "And what of Lucas? You were to stay in Fey."

She thought quickly. "The witch and the wolf returned, seeking to free Lucas and Valerie. I had no choice but to flee. Lucas is dead." Her voice trembled.

Marion was eyeing her, looking her over from head to toe. "After all the things that Lucas has done to your king, the *least* you could have done was let Cer finish him off. Take it from me, my dear, relationships are about *compromise*." Marion batted her eyelashes at Cerdewellyn. The idea of Marion hitting on Cerdewellyn was wrong on so many levels.

Cerdewellyn frowned and took a step away from Marion, clasping the gem in his hand. "No, it is all right. I promised I would not kill him. Besides…I would give my Virginia anything to see her happy."

Marion slanted a longing look towards Cer, her gaze fixating on his full lips. "You are a lucky girl," she said on a sigh.

Val knew how jealous Virginia had been. She would not have put up with Marion's flirtatious overtures. Valerie stalked forward, trying to do what Virginia would have done so that he didn't become suspicious.

Cerdewellyn frowned at her as she advanced and took a step closer to her, blocking Valerie's path so that she could not get close to Marion. She had the distinct impression that he was used to women being jealous over his attentions.

He looked down into her eyes, as though he could see into her soul, as though he were looking for something.

"We are ready," he said, and he walked her over to the table. She didn't like being this close to Marion. Close enough to touch. Her weapons didn't feel close enough, and she didn't trust her newfound powers. "All the power lost will be set free and returned to me. We will put an end to the vampires and reclaim the world."

Valerie nodded in agreement, even managed a smile of encouragement and hoped that was convincing enough.

"And Margaret," Marion reminded him sharply.

"Of course," Cer agreed. His hand hovered above the stone, and then he said to Valerie, "She must be there. Within you. A small part. Yes or no?"

Taken by surprise, she didn't know what to say. "What do you mean?"

He turned to face her head-on, the full brunt of his personality and attention making her want to flinch away. She was lying to him, and she felt like such a terrible liar that he would be able to see it upon her face. And then he would destroy her.

"I have one chance. One wish. This power is not a subtle thing. It is not like a sharp blade that can carve, but a sword that can split things asunder," he said intimately, as though Marion was not even there, and it was just him and his love, Virginia. "My desire must be an all-consuming command. There is no hesitancy or changing one's mind. The stone's power must be directed with pure focus of will. So tell me, what am I to wish for? Power? Love? A new beginning?" he asked quietly.

"You ask for your power to return to you so that you may make our people strong," Valerie said. "Isn't that your greatest wish?"

He closed his eyes for a moment, and Valerie wished that her blade had been drawn, and she could have stopped this cat and mouse game. Everything he said had two interpretations, and the desire to ask him if he knew Virginia was gone was bubbling up inside her.

"I cannot betray my people for love," he said.

Valerie felt a touch on her connection with Lucas, a gentle inquiry wanting to know if he should appear;if she were ready for him. She told him no, or at least she thought she did.

Cerdewellyn moved, standing before an open book that looked tattered, and as if it had seen better days. This was the book that Lucas had talked about—the Book of Life and Death.

Marion stood on one side, looking over his shoulder almost greedily. Valerie stood on his other, watching, heart thundering. She fished the knife out of her pocket and held it close to her side and out of his view.

Cerdewellyn began to speak, reciting words in a language Valerie had never heard before, the letters on the page looking to be a combination of Cyrillic and ancient English. She couldn't have guessed the pronunciation of those words had she tried. And then he straightened, swiping a blade across his palm and letting the blood fall onto the stone.

The stone began to glow, giving off a golden light. She could hear it too, the stone making a humming sound as the light grew brighter and the power built on the inside.

He opened his mouth, and she knew that he would make the wish, set the Sard on its purpose and that she had to act now or never. Valerie lunged forward with her blade, stabbing Cerdewellyn in the stomach, shocked at how easy it was. Mentally, she called for Lucas, telling him to come now!

Cerdewellyn stared at her for an endless moment; the expression of grief on his face was something else that would haunt her at night. Marion screamed, but then Rachel and Jack were there, and she heard a gun go off. Blood bloomed on Marion's chest, and suddenly Lucas was there too. He stabbed Cerdewellyn again and shoved him to the floor, ignoring him, as though he were already dead.

Valerie reached out and touched the stone, its heavy power throbbing through her, making her teeth rattle inside her head. The stone's power was waiting, building as if it were gathering into a wave and ready to spill outwards. It just needed to be told what to do.

Lucas reached out, ready to take the stone from her, to make his own wish—the one that would kill him and leave her bereft forever…And she couldn't do it.

"Hold still. I forbid you to move," Valerie said and watched as Lucas' hand froze in midair.

Lucas made an angry sound, and said to her in a rush, "You do not know what you do. Release me *now*!" His words were furious, and she could feel him fighting against the power she held over him. Containing his movements was hard. She felt him using all of his physical and mental strength against her. But he was bound to her, and she was more than she had ever been—Fey, empathic, determined—and his strength was not enough. Between Lucas fighting her and the stone's anxious pressure, her head felt like it was splitting open from the inside out.

Valerie watched Lucas as she made her wish, using her love for him to strengthen her will and force the stone to obey her command. "I wish that there were no Others, that every vampire, werewolf, witch, empath and Fey become mortal, human and alive. I wish for magic to disappear, to unwind from one and all, and be erased utterly from this world."

She was looking into Lucas's eyes as she said it, but then his eyes went wide in shock and blood arced out of his mouth, spraying across her chest and face. "Release me," he said on a gurgle, and all she could see before her was red: The red of his blood on his skin and his clothing, as well as the sword that had pierced him from behind. Cerdewellyn had spitted him like a piece of meat.

Cerdewellyn stood behind Lucas and he shoved him forward with his foot, toppling him to the ground, Lucas' body sliding off of his sword in a wet rush. Lucas' skin turned gray, and she suspected that any other vampire would be dead already. She clutched the stone to her chest, taking a step back, wanting to draw Cerdewellyn's attention away from Lucas so that he could heal.

The enormity of what she'd done made her feel weak. If the magic did what she'd told it to, Lucas would become mortal. There was no way he could survive as a human with that wound.

No! She needed to take it back. She didn't know what to say. How to amend her wish. She stared at the stone dumbly, waiting for the words to come to her when Cerdewellyn's hands slapped over her own. He ripped the stone from her hands and said, "It's not done yet."

Cerdewellyn murmured something in the same ancient language he'd used to activate the stone, and she felt the air change. The light of the stone dimmed for one second, as if it were thinking about what Cer had said, and Val snapped back to reality.

Valerie drew her gun and gripped it with two hands, hastily sighting on Cerdewellyn before drawing the trigger, and shooting him in the chest repeatedly. Blood exploded from him, and the impact threw him backward. The stone flew from his hand, skidding along the ground, and Valerie chased it, desperately praying she wouldn't be too late.

The seconds it took her to reach the stone felt like an eternity. She felt clumsy and slow. Time was precious, the window to change the wish was closing—she could feel it. She grabbed the stone and held it tight.

"Heal Lucas!" she shouted at it. "Take away his mortal wounds."

But as she spoke, the gem lost all color, becoming inert, beyond lifeless, nothing more than a rock. Panic ripped through her. And then the stone cracked open and something like vapor rose out of it, curling upwards and then out like tentacles. The vapor twined around her, settled over her as though seeking a way inside of her, and then it swept inside, swimming through her blood and rooting deep into her cells.

The vapor picked at her like the ethereal hands undoing a knot. She could see exactly what was going to happen. That the magic would send out tendrils across the world, and untie itself from every magical creature in existence. It would take from the newest first: her, Jack, Rachel, Marion and Lucas. The ones who wanted them dead would stay powerful for the longest amount of time. Long enough to kill them all, no doubt.

That was the flaw in her plan, and why Lucas had wanted to make a different wish. But Lucas was old, the oldest vampire in existence, and who knew how long it might take for the magic to reach him, maybe he'd be healed by the time it did. He had to be. And Cerdewellyn, who was so old that he made Lucas look young, how long would it take before he became mortal?

And then the air cleared around her, the vapor gone, and she felt…human. Cerdewellyn was pulling himself to his feet slowly, painfully, his clothes coated in blood. He wrapped his arm around the middle of his body, crimson blood pulsing between his fingers. He was healing before her eyes.

Lucas lay on the ground unable to move, his right hand desperately seeking his fallen blade. Valerie didn't think about what she did, but ran over to Lucas with her gun drawn, ready to protect him to the death.

"Did you hurt her?" Cer asked Valerie, stopping several feet away. His voice settled into a low register so that his words were a scrape of sound, like death's fingernails sliding along a windowpane. This was not calm, collected Cerdewellyn—this was a desperate man.

"It was her or me," she said, not willing to tell him that she had bashed Virginia's head in with a rock. It was something that would haunt her for the rest of her life. Whether that turned out to be in the next two minutes or 60 years, she wouldn't forget what she'd done to her.

He scanned her from head to toe, as though he would be able to see Virginia like a visible manifestation laid over Valerie. He smiled at her roguishly, "I wish I could say I felt bad about this, but you deserve far worse." His hand came out of nowhere, a backhanded slap to the jaw that knocked her off her feet and slammed her head into the wall, knocking her unconscious before she could say a word.

CHAPTER

Valerie disappeared, leaving Jack with Lucas and Rachel. They stood there in what could only be described as the most painfully fucking awkward silence ever, and waited; Lucas claiming that he would know the moment they should follow her. Jack didn't like the idea of waiting for an invisible signal, some magicky mumbo-jumbo that was unproven, unreliable, and if wrong, might cost Valerie her life. The urge to go now and attack gnawed at him. He didn't know if his fear and agitation were worse now that he was a werewolf, or if it was just because he loved Valerie so damned much that the idea of her walking into danger first was almost more than he could bear.

He punched his hand into his palm. He'd spent so long being pissed that Valerie was unwilling to fight the good fight, and yet now that she was; it scared the shit out of him.

Waiting. He could feel Rachel's presence standing next to him, as though she were warm all along his body. As though she were fire, and he was some hapless beggar struggling in from the cold, wet darkness seeking shelter in her warmth.

Which just showed what an idiot he was; because she didn't have a warm bone in her body. Part of him wanted to ask her yet again if she meant it when she said that she would let him kill Marion. *Let him.* What did that mean? Would she stop him? Compel him not to harm Marion? Was that what he was asking? No, it was more. He was asking her to choose him. To set aside 90 years of connubial bliss or whatever the fuck they had, and be with him.

To give him peace.

The truth settled around him like a warm blanket. She could not control him. Not in this. Not when it came down to the final battle. Killing Marion was his destiny. It was what he'd dedicated his life to. And there was no way Rachel would be able to stop him. Once the fight started, he'd be damned if he'd ask her for anything. It would be Marion and him; like two lovers ready for the last dance before the end of the world.

Just him, just her, and one of them would die.

He'd use his weapons, his strength and cunning, and if he had to use his newfound werewolf abilities, had to transform into an animal to kill her—he'd do that too.

"Now," Lucas said, and Jack knew that the time for thinking was done. Rachel put her arm around him, transporting them to Margaret's crypt in the blink of an eye. Marion was facing Valerie, and something in the set of her posture, told him that she was about to attack.

Fear crashed over him, trying to drag him under, his legs feeling weak and the gun in his hand the only friend that would ever matter. He must've called her name, because she turned and looked at him; that black soulless gaze settling on him.

Making him feel like a helpless child.

And then something that Nate had once said came back to him: never think about why you are doing something, just act. For in that space of time that one agonizes with oneself, lives could be lost.

Marion hissed at him, the deranged sound more monstrous than human. She stepped close to him, her head tilted to the side like a broken doll.

"I should have finished with you long ago. Such a small boy you were. So petulant and complaining."

Marion rushed him, emitting an eerie bloody scream as she slammed into him, the full length of her hard body jerking him off his feet. His shoulders crashed into the wall, a sudden agony that made his arms go numb. Her fingers, pale, cold and with those claw-like nails, sank into his face, shredding his skin. Sinking so deep that it felt as if she scraped bone.

Marion was suddenly yanked backward, dragged off him by Rachel. Marion spun out of her grasp, using her superior strength to evade her grip.

"How dare you?" Marion said, voice filled with rage. "You are mine, and I am yours! You would turn on me for *him*? For this pathetic abomination?"

Marion's words alone bruised Rachel. She stopped, as if momentarily frozen, her body swaying gently as though she weren't sure if she should be going forward or backward. Her eyes filled with tears, which seemed to give Marion strength. Marion stood proudly, suddenly a confident and beautiful woman. She took two steps closer to Rachel, murmuring to her in a gentle voice. "He's nothing to us. A bump in the road. A trial that we can overcome. What we had…" she let her voice trail off as she moved in for the kill, touching Rachel's face gently with her hand—establishing a connection with her. Reminding her of the years they'd spent together.

"Can you hurt him, my heart?" Marion's voice was a dirty whisper, her lower body arching forward like a harlot peddling her wares. "He would never let you do the things you like. The things we do in the dark, when you won't even let me turn on the lights. Will you forgo that? Will you become just a woman, just an ordinary boring girl who will hide behind her man, let him protect her, and at the end of the night give in to him? We both know that is a lie." She leaned in and kissed Rachel gently on the lips. Still Rachel stood frozen, standing at the crossroads, and unable in this final moment to do what was right.

"Let me take care of this, and then we will be a family. Me, you and Margaret." Marion moved away and turned towards Jack, a terrifying smile on her face. Pain ripped through him in a flash, stealing his breath. He locked his knees so he didn't fall down, and tried to keep his hold on the gun in his hand. The pain made no sense. Marion was still watching him, still gloating that Rachel wanted her more than him. Just as abruptly as the pain came it left, taking all of his newfound energy with it.

That sense of wrongness, of Otherness, and the beast lying just below the surface vanished. In a way, it was funny. Morbid humor like winning the lottery the day after committing suicide. He'd finally been strong enough to deal with Marion, strong enough to win with his own bare hands, and just as quickly that was gone.

He was mortal. Valerie and Lucas had done it.

His arm trembled as he lifted it, weighted down by both weakness and destiny. Jack sighted on Marion, and her response was a pout. As if he'd said he wouldn't take her to the opera instead of standing here threatening her life.

"Little Italian boy," Marion cooed. This was his moment.

Marion rushed him and he shot her in the chest, one bullet slamming into her cheek, the side of her head exploding outwards. Marion was on him then, taking them both to the ground. The gaping holes in her face started filling in, blood and muscle crawling over re-forming bone as she healed while she lay on top of him.

She pinned him with her weight, held his shoulders flush to the ground with her arms, and bent down, mouth impossibly wide to rip his throat out.

"No!" Rachel shouted, slamming the stake towards Marion's exposed back, ready to protect him from Marion as she'd promised. And which, it pained him to admit, was a little surprising.

Marion rolled off him, evading Rachel's strike and resting on her haunches, as she waited for one of them to make the next move.

Yellow vapor settled over Rachel, and she froze, her body swaying gently as though she were no longer the one in control of it. Rachel took in a huge breath, sucking magic deep into her lungs, confusion, fear and weakness scrolling across her features in turns.

Her skin changed, lost that hard luster, becoming pink and alive.

Fuck.

Rachel was human. He was human. But Marion…she was still a six hundred-year-old vampire.

Marion laughed and grabbed for Rachel, wrapping her hand around Rachel's throat and squeezing, choking the life out of her. Jack lunged forward, knocking into Marion so that she had to release the newly human Rachel. Rachel was gasping, clutching her neck where Marion had choked her.

Jack raised his own stake, having one on his belt, ready to stab her, ready to end it all when the yellow vapor returned, settling over Marion like fog.

Marion's eyes were wide open in fear, and as her humanity returned to her, Jack felt an overwhelming moment of grief, and he had no idea why.

The part of his soul that was dedicated to revenge screamed in fury, knowing the answer before he did. Jack wasn't even aware of the question yet. All he knew was that this was his moment to kill Marion and that he was hesitating. That somehow the game had changed, and he didn't understand why.

He stood there with his stake, ready to stab her through the heart and turn her to dust. Ready to avenge every person she'd ever killed, every family she'd ever torn apart.

But when he did it, she wouldn't turn to dust. When he killed her with the stake, she would bleed to death. A strange and barbaric way for a mortal woman to die. Should he shoot her?

Then Marion realized her transformation. She raised her hands in front of her, looking at them as if they belonged to somebody else. They were chapped and work-worn. The hands of a seamstress perhaps.

Fuck.

His heart thudded loudly in his ears as Marion turned and looked at him, confused as a baby doe. And just as innocent. That animal part of him that wasn't a werewolf—was nothing so magical, but was simply the feral wounded boy he'd always been on the inside—howled in rage.

Tears slid down her cheeks. "My baby is gone," she said brokenly, and Jack didn't know what to do. He couldn't let her go. There was no way he'd be able to let her walk out of here alive. His hand opened, and he heard the stake clatter to the floor. But he didn't let her go.

His hand was fisted into the neck of her dress; the satin fabric clenched tight, her skin warm and alive against his knuckles. The scarred part of him that ruled him, that had spent his adult life killing monsters, grabbed his gun, holding it to her temple and demanded he give her justice.

One clean shot to the temple and she would be dead. Her heart would stop beating. Her blood and brains would ooze out of her, and that would be it. It was the only thing he'd ever wanted in his whole life.

She didn't try to pull away from him, didn't do anything to defend herself. Just asked for her baby, over and over again.

Rachel approached him softly, her voice calm and soothing. She didn't touch him, but he could see her out of the corner of his eye. The gun, weeping Marion, and Rachel. Voice of reason. He laughed harshly.

"What's the plan, Jack?"

He felt blind, as if he couldn't see the world around them. He needed help. His vision blurred. His words were broken. "I don't know what to do."

And Marion, fucking Marion, just lay there like a calf waiting to be slaughtered. Making no protest, uncaring that he pointed a gun at her head and faced an existential crisis.

He shook his head, felt as if he were moving in cement. "Is she…evil?" he asked. Begging for the answer to be yes.

Rachel was silent for a long moment. "I don't know," she whispered.

Marion was sniffling, her face blotchy and sad. If he were walking down the street, and she asked him for help—a crying woman out by herself—he'd help her. Because she was helpless. Broken. He didn't hurt defenseless women.

She turned her face away from him, and he saw a gray hair mixed in with the auburn.

"She's human," he said again, dully, as if a part of him needed to hear it aloud. "If I kill her now...Is it in cold blood?" If she'd fight him, or do something to prove that she was a monster still, he could do it. But this crying pathetic creature?

It would give him peace at night when he thought back to this moment. His soul was already tainted, stained black by the mistakes he'd made. Remorse. It was looking back at that instant of his youth when his parents died, and thinking of all the things he could've done differently, and that would have been right. If he killed Marion now, was it right? Or would it just be another stain upon his soul? Perhaps the final one that he would never recover from. Was he killing an innocent woman?

"She still did terrible things. She's still crazy. Isn't it justice to make her pay for her mistakes? Maybe she will want more children." A stricken laugh. "Maybe she will even have them. Her own flesh and blood. Can you imagine that, Jack?"

"So she's evil?" he asked, needing confirmation.

"You can't ask me that," Rachel said, voice thick with tears. His attention shifted to her, to the desolation on her own face. "What about you? Are you evil?" Her lower lip trembled as she squeezed her eyes shut.

And that was when he thought of his parents. Of his mother, who would spend all day in the kitchen making Jack's favorite meal. Of his father, who had been sturdy and wise and filled with happiness. Their memory was the ultimate judge. What would they think if they if they could see him now?

Jack swallowed hard, felt his grip on Marion loosen infinitesimally "Should I kill you too? For your past? Are you telling me you're a bad person? And that you won't change now that you're human?"

He could watch her. Make sure Marion didn't do anything to hurt anyone. If it took months or years of following her and making sure she didn't hurt a soul, he could do that. And if she stepped out of line...he'd kill her. Decision made, Jack released Marion and stepped back, stumbling away from all of it.

There was a roaring in his ears and a fuzziness before his eyes. The emotional toll of the moment becoming a physical reaction. From very far away, he heard Marion speaking to Rachel. The words were weak. Almost tinny. "You promised. You told me you'd set me free."

And then he heard a sound that he couldn't mistake. A whimper, followed by a gurgle of terrible sound.

He had to see. Had to know what was happening. He turned around and saw Marion on the floor, Rachel next to her, Marion's head in Rachel's lap as Rachel held her close. Blood was everywhere. Marion was gripping Rachel's arm hard, eyes wide and desperate as blood spilled from her neck, soaking into Rachel's trousers and the floor around them.

Tears dropped down Rachel's cheeks, her lower lip beginning to tremble, moments away from sobbing in grief.

Marion was breathing shallowly; eyes glazed and unfocussed. "No," he said like an idiot, and he dropped down to his knees, trying to think of some way to stop Marion from dying; even though he didn't want to touch her. He didn't know if he could bring himself to touch her. And then it was done. He saw the exact moment Marion died. The sudden stillness. The glassiness in her eyes as they went dim.

His soul filled with silence.

Jack turned to Rachel, could hardly get the words out. "You killed her," he said, agenius statement for the ages.

"It's done." She stood slowly, picking her steps carefully to get away from the blood and not slip in the wide, heavy puddle. "It should have been me, anyway."

"I don't understand."

She turned away from him, walking towards the door. Her posture low, almost stooped. As though the last few minutes had aged her beyond reckoning. "Of course you don't. Because you're the good guy, Jack." Her eyes sparked with anger, the words flung at him like daggers. "You couldn't possibly understand the sort of relationship we had. As a sign of my love, I promised to kill her. We'd lie in bed at night after sex, and I'd tell her all the ways I'd kill her. Someday. When I didn't need her anymore for my witchcraft. And I don't need her anymore, do I?"

$\sim$

Valerie came to slowly, her mouth filled with blood from biting the inside of her cheek when Cerdewellyn hit her. The jerk. He was gone. A quick look around confirmed that the stone was gone too. Lucas was looking at her from several feet away; his face glazed with pain, a sword sticking out of his chest.

She crawled along the floor to him, too dizzy to stand. She pulled the sword from his chest, watching his black blood gush between her fingers. Black vampire blood coating her hand, as she pressed against the wound. He wasn't human yet.

Valerie couldn't have been out for more than a minute or two, she realized. Fear coursed through her. How much longer did

Lucas have before he became human? He reached up to her with a blood-coated hand, wanting to touch her face. But he was weak, and his arm fell back to his chest. "You're okay," she said. "You'll heal before you become human. You will."

He gave her a sad smile—one without promise. As if they both knew that she was lying, and he wanted to keep it that way. His eyes closed and opened again slowly, as if even blinking was hard. Lucas' blood was under her, around her. So slick and cool that it seemed impossible for more to be in his body. How could he heal himself when he'd lost so much blood? She put her wrist to his mouth, his lips cool. "Drink, dammit!" Valerie begged him.

Lucas frowned and met her gaze, staring at her tear-stricken face as though it were amazing. And then he bit down hard on her wrist, his fangs piercing into her flesh, the pain sharp, white-hot. He swallowed repeatedly, as her blood poured into his mouth. He released her, lying back down on the ground with his eyes closed.

"It is all right, my Valkyrie," he said.

He sure as hell didn't look all right! His face was pinched with pain, his breath rattling, and Val couldn't stop the tears from flowing. She had lost her mother and her father, and she didn't know how she would still live if she lost him too. Knowing she was going to lose him. She bent down and kissed him. "I love you," she said. "Please, please don't leave me."

He licked his lips and coughed, blood appearing at the corner of his mouth. Why wasn't he healing? He blinked, focusing on her. "I love you, Valerie. I would spend my life with you given the chance. For your kindness and intelligence, your beauty and grace."

She wiped her nose on her sleeve. "Oh shit, you are *not* going to die on me. I don't *have* grace! Don't say that like this is some crappy goodbye where you tell me stuff that isn't true." Valerie cried and kissed him again, begging him to stay with her mouth, and the press of her lips.

She pulled back from him, stroking her hand down his face, memorizing it. "I would not lie to you. That is why I left out your cooking." He coughed again. "And your colorful language. Both of which are truly atrocious."

"If you really loved me, you would stay. Heal faster!" she demanded.

A wisp of golden smoke snaked up his body, circling his neck and head. Another small tendril appeared, the magic hovering above him, as if it were figuring him out before striking. It was too soon. He wouldn't survive getting out of here and making it to the hospital.

"Hospital!" Val said as the idea came to her. "Take yourself to the hospital while you still can!" His brow furrowed as he closed his eyes, more of the mist settling over him.

Very slowly, as if every movement were painful, he said something to her, but it sounded like the word Royal and that didn't make any sense. And then he vanished. Valerie patted the ground stupidly as if he were still there, but invisible.

Someone grabbed her, pulling her out of the pool of blood and to her feet. Dumbly, she turned, surprised to see that it was Jack standing next to her. He pulled her into a hug, and she stayed limply in his arms.

"We have to get out of here. Where is Lucas?" Rachel asked, coming up behind them. She was out of breath.

"I don't know," Jack answered for her.

"Well, he sure as hell didn't dance out of here, so where is he?"

Valerie's voice was tinny, "He was injured as a vampire, then the magic came, and he just vanished. I told him to go to the hospital, but he was so weak that I don't know if he made it or where he would have gone or...." Her words turned into a sob.

She could hear the frown in Rachel's voice. "Well, he didn't die as a vampire or else his blood would be gone too. Human bodies don't go poof. What hospital did you tell him to go to, maybe he's there?"

Her body was numb, but she felt a glimmer of hope trying to unfurl inside of her. Valerie squashed it down, wanting to focus on the here and now. Both of her parents were dead, the man she loved had been a vampire, was now human, and probably dead too. Valerie didn't have good enough luck for her to get her hopes up.

"I didn't. I didn't say which one," she whispered, and felt tears spill over her eyes. It hadn't occurred to her to tell Lucas the hospital. "Where are we?" Valerie asked.

"Outskirts of London," Rachel said.

What if he *had* said Royal? Could he have tried to take himself to the Royal London Hospital?

"The Royal London Hospital. We have to go check!" Valerie demanded.

Rachel and Jack exchanged a look, but Valerie didn't have the emotional energy to think about what it might mean.

"There should be two cars outside with keys in them." Rachel held up a hand, to stop them asking the inevitable question. "I'm a planner. I figured there was at least a five-percent chance we might make it out of here alive, and need some way to get around. You can thank me later. Don't scratch the paint."

"Aren't you coming with us?" Jack asked.

Rachel nodded shallowly and looked at the ground, her voice lacking conviction. "I have to get things settled here," she said, "The bodies and stuff."

"We need to talk," Jack said to Rachel.

"Take Valerie to find Lucas. We'll talk later. I promise." Rachel didn't meet Jack's gaze.

Valerie mumbled a thank you and went towards the stairs, ready to get the hell out of that crypt.

They found the car parked outside of the crypt, complete with a navigation system that told them how to get to the Royal London Hospital. The drive had taken an hour, and Valerie and Jack had barely spoken to each other the whole time. Each of them lost to their own private thoughts.

"Do you think she'll come to the hospital?" Jack asked, startling Val out of her morbid thoughts.

"She said she would. She promised."

"I thought you didn't trust her."

"I don't. Leave me the hell out of it." Val felt bad for her unsympathetic response. "But she clearly has feelings for you, and if there is anyone she won't lie to, it's gonna be you, right?"

Jack made no response, and the rest of the drive had passed in agonizing slowness.

∾

"Do you want another sandwich?" Jack asked. Lines of fatigue were etched into his face, and Valerie knew she didn't look any better.

"Sure. I guess. But no pickle, that was disgusting."

Lucas had made it to the hospital, appearing out of nowhere in the entryway and scaring everyone half to death, apparently. He was in surgery for hours. When the doctor finally came out, he looked grim, and asked a lot of questions about what could possibly have caused such strange wounds.

The doctor told her it looked as if he had been run through with a sword from the front and the back, but somehow missed the heart. She couldn't tell the doctor that his heart must have healed before he became mortal, but that he hadn't had enough time to repair the less vital skin and muscles around the wound.

"Is he going to live?" Jack asked bluntly.

The doctor sighed heavily and stared down at his clipboard, as though he'd written it down somewhere. "He lost a lot of blood and was seriously injured. It's going to be hard, but he looks as if he knows his way around a fight."

That was almost 24 hours ago, and as Valerie sat by Lucas's bedside, waiting for him to wake up, all she kept thinking was that he was a fighter. He was willing to fight for her, to die for her. Now she just had to hope that he was willing to live for her too.

EPILOGUE

Two years later

*M*olly watched the house from under the camouflage of a nearby tree. And thank God for that because it was fucking hot, and she'd been waiting around forever. Lucas was outside with his brat, pushing her in a red plastic swing that hung from a tree branch.

The child was fair, with golden hair and pink cheeks, as well as the fattest legs Molly had ever seen. Every time the little girl came down towards him, he tickled her feet. The kid loved it, and she could hear the thing squealing like a pig from across the street.

It was fucking disgusting.

Molly didn't want to see him. Despite his appearance as the doting father, she knew what he'd been. Ruthless. Now he was a philanthropist, and spent his days giving money to children in need. How barf-worthy. The idea that he was happy no longer being a vampire, but procreating and living a boring life in suburbia, was just stupid. But no surprise since her damned Aunt Rachel felt the same way. Happy to be powerless. Ready to die like a normal person.

Well, I'm not.

In what seemed like an eternity later, the door opened, and Valerie peered out. She said that it was dinner time, and Lucas took the little girl out of the swing and held her close;the baby's chubby arms wrapped tight around his neck. Her name was Kate. She was cute if one liked that sort of thing. Molly thought Rachel had told her the kid had just turned one, but she couldn't remember. Rachel was always blathering on about something. Molly just had to tune her out.

Lucas went inside and Valerie came out, walking towards the mailbox. Molly grabbed her backpack and jogged across the street, intercepting her just as she pulled down the lid.

"You're Valerie Dearborn, right?"

"Um, yeah," Val said, smiling cautiously. Valerie's brown eyes were scanning her from head to toe, curiously, head tilted to the side while she waited to hear what Molly wanted.

"I'm Molly."

The polite smile froze, and Valerie looked around the street, perhaps wondering if she were alone, or if Rachel was around.

"Hi, Molly," she said, smiling. "I've heard a lot about you. Do you want to come in?"

"No. I want to know what happened to Cerdewellyn," she said, and studied Valerie for the minutest change in expression. After all, whatever she said was probably going to be a lie. Everybody lied about everything unless somehow it was more valuable to tell the truth.

Valerie recoiled as if Molly had asked her what her favorite sexual position was. "What do you mean?"

Great. She was going to play stupid. "All I've heard is that he was there. That you undid magic, stripping us of *everything* that made us who we were. But what no one tells me is what happened to *him*."

Valerie's face paled, and she licked her lips. "He's dead, prob- ably. Or human."

"So you didn't see what effect the spell had on him?"

"Well, no. But it was his magic."

Molly raised her eyebrows in disbelief. "Okay, sure." She blew out a sigh. "So you haven't seen him?"

"No. Come inside. Let me call your aunt. I'm sure she's look- ing for you."

"She's always looking for me," Molly said.

Valerie nodded, reached out a hand and put it on Molly's arm. That pissed her off. She didn't tell Valerie she could touch her.

"Why don't you come in, just for a minute," she said coaxingly.

Molly chuckled and stepped back, just managing not to rip her arm free from Valerie's grip. "No, I don't belong in there. Not with you and your little family. Congratulations, Valerie Dearborn, I guess you got what you wanted. Be damned to the rest of us." She couldn't keep the bitterness out of her voice.

Molly turned and walked away, ignoring Valerie's pleading calls. She had things to do and people to find.

Dear Reader,

If you enjoyed Love is Mortal, please consider leaving a review. If you do decide to leave a review, please email me and I will send you a copy of an exclusive scene from Love is Mortal that didn't make it into the final version.

Although the main portion of this series is concluded with Love is Mortal, there are still a lot of characters whose stories are not finished. That book, set in the Valerie Dearborn world, will most likely be out in 2014 and will feature Jack, Rachel, Cer and undoubtedly Val and Lucas who will hopefully be living in connubial bliss.

If you would like to be added to my email list which will tell you about upcoming books, as well as contests, please go to http://eepurl.com/v7VxT or email me at CHcarolinehanson@gmail.com.

P.S.-Yes! I know you want me to write a continuation of Bewitching the Werewolf and I must say, I've been thinking about it. A lot. My blog and Facebook page will hear about it first. The links are below.

P.P.S.-Thank you so much for not only reading this series, but for liking Val (and Lucas) just as much as I do. You guys are the best!

Big hug,

Caroline Hanson

Made in the USA
Middletown, DE
14 August 2015